*The Dog Sitter Detective's
Christmas Tail*

By Antony Johnston

The Dog Sitter Detective
The Dog Sitter Detective Takes the Lead
The Dog Sitter Detective Plays Dead
The Dog Sitter Detective's Christmas Tail

The Dog Sitter Detective's Christmas Tail

ANTONY JOHNSTON

Allison & Busby Ltd
11 Wardour Mews
London W1F 8AN
allisonandbusby.com

First published in Great Britain by Allison & Busby in 2025.

A CIP catalogue record for this book is available from
the British Library.

First Edition

ISBN 978-0-7490-3191-6

Typeset in 11.5/16.5 pt Sabon LT Pro by
Allison and Busby Ltd.

By choosing this product, you help take care of the world's forests.
Learn more: www.fsc.org.

Printed and bound in Great Britain by Clays Ltd. Elcograf S.p.A

EU GPSR Authorised Representative
LOGOS EUROPE, 9 rue Nicolas Poussin, 17000, LA ROCHELLE, France
E-mail: Contact@logoseurope.eu

For all the fake reindeer, dashing through the snow

CHAPTER ONE

I stopped suddenly at a market stall, breath misting in the cold winter air. Pretending to browse, I hoped he hadn't seen me.

My quarry stood barely ten yards away, scanning the packed crowd of shoppers and tourists who jostled and weaved through the Covent Garden Christmas market. Trying to blend in, I stole a glance in his direction. He continued to look around, as if searching for something . . . or someone. But he showed no sign of recognition. He hadn't seen me.

With a shrug of his broad shoulders he resumed walking, moving easily among the crowd despite his size. I followed, weaving through the always-changing stream of slow-paced walkers, past people browsing and haggling. My lack of height was both a blessing and a curse; it made me difficult to see amongst all these people, but restricted my own field of vision. He was tall enough to stand out, but if I didn't keep him in sight I might lose him altogether. That was unacceptable.

It was sheer chance I'd spotted him to begin with, browsing the market stalls. Wondering why he was here, I'd debated whether or not to shadow him. It wasn't why I'd come. But I couldn't let the chance slip away.

He stopped again, this time taking out his phone. Had someone called him? No, he was making a call. I slipped past two tourist families, hoping to get closer, maybe catch a word or two of his conversation—

My own phone buzzed in my pocket. I removed it, finger already descending towards the Decline button, when I saw who was calling.

It was him.

Should I answer? This could ruin everything . . . or give me the information I sought. I backed away so he couldn't hear me above the crowd and tapped Accept.

'Hello, Birch.'

'Morning! Wanted to say, um, "break a leg" today. You know, good luck. With the audition.'

My heart melted a little. I wasn't short of auditions these days, to be honest. My agent was putting me forward for lots of things in order to re-establish my name with casting directors and remind them I was reviving my career, following a ten-year hiatus. Precious few of these auditions led to booking a role, but DCI Alan Birch, retired, called me before each one to wish me luck. Since we'd officially become a couple, he'd opened up a little and become more visibly affectionate.

Nevertheless, we normally made video calls. Not today.

'Thank you, Birch,' I said, then asked innocently, 'it sounds quite noisy where you are, what's going on?'

Leaning through a gap in the market stalls, I spied him looking at the surrounding crowd, trying to think up an excuse.

'Oh, yes. I'm in . . . Trafalgar Square. Thought I'd come and see the lights. How about you? Sounds lively.'

'Carnaby Street,' I lied. 'But I'm about to head home.' I'd actually come here to look for a Christmas gift for Birch, and him fibbing about his whereabouts made me suspect he was doing the same for me. Not that either of us would admit it.

Suddenly the market's seasonal carol singers began belting out 'Good King Wenceslas', their voices travelling up from the basement shopping area and down the phone line.

'Carol singers at Trafalgar Square,' Birch blurted, unprompted. 'Carol singers.'

'So I can hear.' I tried not to laugh. 'I bet they're freezing.'

'Bit of a weird echo, actually. Like I can hear them twice . . .'

'Oh, um, must be a bad line,' I said hastily. 'I should be going. I'll call you later.'

I ended the call and stayed at the gap, watching him.

'Can I help you, madam? 'Cos if you're not buying anything, sling your hook and make way for someone who will.'

The stallholder glared at me, his arms folded. I

hadn't really taken in where I was, and now I realised I was blocking anyone else perusing his stall. I looked down and saw shelves of colourful handmade Christmas gifts: Santa ornaments and woodcut reindeer to hang from a tree, felt candy canes, door wreaths made of fabric. It wasn't my sort of thing, and more importantly it wasn't Birch's. What do you get the widowed former Met detective who has everything?

Then I spotted a section of pet gifts and, feeling rather guilty about blocking the man's stall on a busy morning, picked up a set of fake red antlers made from plastic and felt. I quickly paid the stallholder – rather too much, if you ask me, but that's Covent Garden for you – then checked through the gap again. Birch was gone.

I pushed through the crowd to the end of the aisle, but it was too late. Wherever my boyfriend (and I was still getting used to thinking of Birch in that context) had moved to next, it was beyond my sight.

Whatever he was getting me would have to remain a surprise. And whatever I was getting him would have to wait for another day; I'd run out of time. I hurried back to the Tube station.

It was quicker to get the Piccadilly Line straight through to South Kensington and walk than change trains twice to reach Sloane Square. Regardless, I speed-marched all the way home to Smithfield Terrace and fell in the door. Well, after opening it with a well-placed kick. It had started sticking a few weeks ago, when winter had begun to properly set in. I'd have to get that fixed in the new year.

I'd only just leant back against the door to catch my breath when someone knocked on it, startling me. I didn't need to look to guess who it would be: the Dowager Lady Ragley, my black-clad next-door neighbour and vigilant defender of the street's honour. I really didn't have time for an extended discourse about the ongoing repairs to my house. Could I pretend to be out? No, she must have seen me come in the door to be knocking so quickly afterwards. If I didn't answer she'd know I was snubbing her.

Still wearing my coat and panting for breath, I opened the door. It stuck six inches in, so I peeked out through the gap.

'Guinevere, my dear,' said the dowager with what passed for a smile on her sharp-featured face. 'Are you well?'

'Very well, my lady,' I replied. She'd been a dowager several times longer than her late husband had been a baron, but insisted on being properly addressed. 'It's lovely to see you, but I'm in a hurry. I have an audition—'

'I shan't keep you,' she said, with a brief, disapproving glance over my shoulder. 'You evidently have much work to do.'

Harsh but fair, I supposed. The hallway was no longer filled with my late father's stacks of old *Financial Times* newspapers, after I'd finally got most of them to the recycling, but in their place were new stacks of other

11

papers, files and magazines that I'd begun to clear out. The house contained decades of my family's history, and sorting it all out while trying to also have a life of my own was a slow process.

'Merry Christmas,' the dowager added, thrusting an envelope at me.

I stared at it, dumbfounded. By the time I found my voice and replied, 'Um, Merry Christmas . . . ?' she'd already turned on her heel and gone back inside her own house. The dowager had an uncanny talent for doing so without a sound.

After closing the door with a shove, I finally removed my coat and scarf, dropped the bag with the fake antlers in the kitchen, then carried the envelope through to my lounge. I couldn't even remember the last time my neighbour had sent a Christmas card. I'd have to write one for her in return, but had no time to think about it right now. I hadn't even put up any decorations yet. The tree, and its accompanying boxes of tinsel and ornaments, remained in an upstairs room where they'd been since last year. That had been the last Christmas for which my father had been alive, and I'd put the tree up just to make him smile. Without him here, what was the point?

Daydreaming in the middle of the lounge wasn't getting me anywhere. I left the white envelope unopened on the mantelpiece, knowing that seeing it again later would remind me, and hurried upstairs.

Twenty minutes until the audition; enough time to shower, then set up. It was to be a video call, conducted not in a rehearsal space or even a director's office but 'remotely' from my own living room, through the medium of my phone's camera. I'd grumbled to my agent about this, doubting that anyone would ask Judi Dench to audition via her iPhone, to which he'd replied that Dame Judi wouldn't be auditioning for a second-tier role with a third-tier director in the first place. *Touché*.

Frankly, I wasn't sure I even wanted this role. The director in question was Colin Prendergast, a man with whom I had history, as they say, dating back to when I was a stripling actress in my twenties and he was a rising star. We'd had an altercation which resulted in me being replaced. I'd never worked with him again, and he hadn't asked me to, for the rest of my career.

That career had ended a little more than ten years ago when I'd retired at the age of fifty to care for my father, after my mother passed away. When he finally joined her a decade later, I discovered he'd left me nothing more than a few grand and this tumbledown old house. So I'd had no choice but to restart my career, which was something of an uphill battle. Good roles for grey-haired sixty-something women were already as rare as hen's teeth in this world of glamour and bright young things, let alone for someone who'd been out of the spotlight for a decade.

To make ends meet I did a spot of dog sitting on the side, but as much as I loved that, it didn't bring in anywhere near enough money to repair the house and bring it up to a sellable condition. Not that I had any such dog sitting jobs on the calendar at the moment anyway.

All of which meant that if Colin Prendergast was willing to consider me for a role in his new play, *A Teardrop of Life*, I was willing to bury the hatchet and audition for it. I've worked with plenty of similarly belligerent directors, both in TV and on the stage, and work is work.

Fifteen minutes. I had to stop daydreaming and get ready.

Showered and dried, with five minutes to go I prioritised only what they'd be able to see, from the waist up. I tugged a brush through my hair, then threw on a pullover and light scarf to hide my pyjama top. The bottoms, with their pattern of grinning cartoon dog heads, I left uncovered because they'd be out of frame.

Then I took my phone into the lounge, where I spent another minute deciding which background to adopt. I opted for the bookshelves, rather than the front curtains or TV, assuming that would appeal more to a playwright. Finally, I made sure my current half-completed jigsaw was out of sight, opened the curtains for some light, and propped the phone on a pile of books so it was level with my head and shoulders.

I'd already installed the app, and held a practice session with Birch to get to grips with it. If I needed to do anything more than turn on my camera I might be in trouble, but after a couple of taps I was faced with a big blue Join button. My finger hovered over it, ready to tap, when I suddenly realised I'd forgotten my sides, which are generally considered handy when auditioning. *Silly old Gwinny, where's your mind these days . . .*

I found the script on the kitchen table, ran back into the lounge, repositioned myself and joined the call. In the three seconds it took to connect I exhaled, reset my expression, and was all smiles when the casting director appeared on screen. Acting!

'Gwinny, how lovely to see you. I'm Verity, the casting director. I must say, I was surprised when Bostin Jim put you forward. I thought you'd retired years ago.'

'Bostin' Jim Austin was my agent, a born-and-bred Brummie (the nickname was apparently local slang). He was a good strategist, landing me small roles and helping me get back up to speed. I quickly re-read my handwritten notes in the top corner of the script, made when Bostin Jim explained the situation to me. An actress had left the play for personal reasons so they needed a swift replacement for the role of Tabitha, a scheming old spinster. Jim said I was perfect for it. 'How charming,' I'd replied, but I knew what he meant.

'I took a short break,' I said to Verity, keeping up the smile. 'Now I'm here again. Shall we wait for Colin?'

'He's tied up and sends his apologies. But don't worry, we're recording all auditions so he can watch them back.'

If he really did 'send his apologies', he was a different man from the director I'd known thirty-odd years ago. I'd hoped to get the measure of him during this meeting, but it would have to wait.

Verity continued, 'Let's start with act two, scene three. From the top, please . . .'

We ran through the scene, one of the more involved for Tabitha, with Verity reading the other parts. Surprisingly, I was rather nervous. I put it down to doing this online. Prior to my first retirement I'd spent thirty years auditioning everywhere from rehearsal spaces to dressing rooms to basement offices, but always with other people present. The idea of doing it over a computer connection would have struck everyone as absurd. Now, though, the world was quite different. So here I was performing to a propped-up phone in my own front room, and the nerves made me edgy. I knew I was rushing through the lines.

To calm myself I imagined that this was a play within a play, with 'Gwinny' just another role I'd already landed, as she now auditioned for a part in the metafictional play. I managed not to daydream myself to pieces, and I think it worked. Besides, a certain amount of nerves is expected and allowed for with any audition. That's what I told myself.

'That was wonderful, Gwinny, thank you so much,' Verity gushed when we finished. She'd have said that even if I stank, of course.

'Thank you, Verity. I look forward to hearing from you.' Why I'd suddenly decided to sign off like I was writing a letter to the bank, I didn't know. Something about the odd nature of being on-screen, perhaps.

Besides, whether I booked this role or not they'd call Bostin Jim, not me directly. What on earth was I thinking?

Verity gave me an odd look and I panicked. Flustered, I hastily said goodbye and grabbed my phone to end the call, but as I leant forward I knocked the pile of books on which it was propped. The phone promptly fell into my lap, giving Verity an unexpected close-up of my dog pyjamas. When I finally got a grip and turned the screen upright, the last thing I saw was her amused face as she ended the call.

I stared at the black screen, wanting the earth to swallow me up.

CHAPTER TWO

To distract myself from the audition's disastrous end (and procrastinate the matter of calling Bostin Jim to tell him how it went), I marched upstairs to continue tackling my father's filing cabinets.

The house's top floors were mostly used for storage: my parents' clothes, old dog beds, storage boxes . . . if it wasn't regularly used, it had been shoved up here. One small room was effectively an archive of my father's records. Not an office per se, as there was no desk or chair, but it was filled with filing cabinets, boxes and piles of papers. He had never been the world's tidiest man, preferring to simply stack new things on top of old things, and I'd put off going through these records for some time. While he was alive there hadn't been time, as I was too busy caring for him; after he'd gone there seemed little point in rushing, especially as the hallway downstairs had been filled with all those copies of the *Financial Times*. But I'd finally made a dent in those with trips to the recycling centre, and if I was ever going to get this house repaired and sold I'd have to deal with all these too.

I probably shouldn't have been surprised how far back the files went. Henry Tuffel had worked in the City for most of his adult life, after emigrating to England with his family before the outbreak of World War II, and it really did seem like he'd kept every file and record since. The oldest I'd found so far was a tax return from 1962, though there were many more files and papers from the 1970s onwards. Nobody could see this house without knowing my father was a hoarder, but until now I hadn't quite realised how deeply ingrained the habit had been.

I'd spent the past week tackling the top three drawers of the cabinet nearest the door, and most of their contents had now joined the piles in the hallway, so now I pulled out its final bottom drawer to begin rifling through it. The drawer made an odd sound while sliding, as if it was catching on something. I closed and re-opened it, hearing the same sound again. I couldn't see the cause, but it was consistent and seemed to be coming from the back. I pulled all the hanging folders towards the front and peered past the drawer.

There lay a manila folder, curling up from the base to the rear wall, with edges crumpled by the drawer's movement and paper sheets poking out from inside. The noise I'd heard was the folder being dragged back and forth along the metal runners. It must have fallen out of a higher drawer at some point and become trapped.

That my father hadn't noticed or retrieved it suggested how infrequently he'd actually needed these old files.

I stretched beyond the drawer at full reach, took hold of the folder with my fingertips and attempted to pull it out. It resisted, with a bottom corner still wedged in a runner, but after a minute of waggling it finally came free. I flipped the folder open, expecting to find another old financial record ready to toss in the recycling.

But it was much more than that.

I had no idea at the time, but finding this file would begin a cascading series of events that led to murder, exposed secrets and one of the strangest episodes in my life.

The first thing that made the file obviously different from the others was the photograph: a black-and-white picture of a man I didn't recognise, sitting outdoors at a café. There was no indication of when it had been taken, but his clothes, not to mention the style of the people around him, suggested it was from decades ago. The photo was attached to two sheets of typewritten paper with a clip, so I removed it and flipped it over to check the back. In pencil, someone had written the name 'Dieter Gerber'.

The name meant nothing to me, and I didn't recall my father mentioning it. Had he been a business associate of some kind? Why keep a photo of him?

I scanned the typewritten pages, hoping they could furnish an explanation, but came up short. They listed Gerber's name and vital details – date and place of birth, next of kin and so on – followed by a short biography. He'd been born in Munich, then after the war had trained as an engineer in Berlin during its reconstruction. Later he returned to Munich and started an electronics business, Radio Gerber GmbH, which manufactured radio and communications equipment.

None of which my father had ever shown any interest in. How strange.

The file went on to describe Gerber as unmarried and possibly a 'confirmed bachelor', an old-fashioned euphemism for gay men, though that wasn't certain.

Even more strangely, the second page of this odd biography listed places Gerber was known to frequent: his favourite restaurants, commonly visited bars, even the golf club where he was a member.

And there it ended. Or it would have except for two handwritten notes, both in my father's handwriting. First, in blue ink:

Partial success – contact & interest

Then, in red ink:

COVER-UP!

C1972

20-31-3

319-23-4

359-14-6, 154-3-10 187-22-7, 404-3-4, 42-18-7 288-12-5 105-24-10

7-16-3 228-10-3?

When my father had passed away, collapsing in the lounge as he finally succumbed to illness, I was naturally distraught but considered myself lucky to have few regrets. He was, emotionally speaking, a self-sufficient man who tended to deflect questions he considered too personal. But he also enjoyed holding court, so during the decade spent as his full-time carer I'd cajoled him through many conversations I knew I'd otherwise regret not having. He was always willing to expound on his love for my mother, for example, and I certainly made sure he knew that I loved him, despite the days when I could have throttled the stubborn old sod.

But here was a subject I hadn't even known to ask about, now lost for ever. What had this man Dieter Gerber been to my father? Why had he never come up in conversation? Why was there a file on him tucked away in these filing cabinets, along with a note mentioning a cover-up and a series of random numbers?

Most importantly: were there more?

Ten minutes of quickly rifling through every other drawer in the room furnished an answer to that question. No, this mysterious file was unique.

I scanned it again, noticing something my eyes had passed over on the first read. On the first page, underneath the initial listing of Gerber's vital statistics, was a single line:

Liaison: ROY SINGLETON – *Telephone 01 9460909*

The only date on the file was the line 'C1972' in my father's pen. '01' was an old London dialling code that had been obsolete for more than thirty years, so that made sense. And here was another unknown name, someone else my father had never mentioned to me: Roy Singleton.

Was the file my father's at all? Perhaps someone else had left it here, or it had accidentally been delivered to him, before falling down the back of a cabinet to lie forgotten and undiscovered until now. But there was no doubt my father had made the handwritten notes. I'd recognise his penmanship anywhere.

The thought made me return to the back of the photo, where Dieter Gerber's name had been written in pencil . . . but *not* by my father. It was someone else's handwriting. So had the picture, and perhaps the whole file, been given to him by someone else? What did 'Partial success' and 'COVER-UP!' mean anyway? How I wished I could have asked him.

Perhaps there was someone I could ask, though.

Sitting cross-legged on the floor, surrounded by towers and cabinets of my father's archives, I took out my phone and tried dialling the 'liaison' number on the file.

'*The number you have called was not recognised,*' said the automated woman's voice from BT. '*Please check the number and try again.*'

Fair enough. I hadn't expected it would work, given the old dialling code, but I had to try.

Then I had another idea. I swapped out the old dialling code with a modern one, making the number 020 7946 0909. I still didn't think it would work, of course.

But it did.

'Central,' said a woman's voice at the other end of the line.

'I – well, goodness – sorry, I didn't think anyone would actually pick up.' Flabbergasted, I stumbled over my words. Then I checked the name in the file again. 'Is, um, Roy Singleton available?'

The line suddenly went blank – not the quiet you get when someone simply isn't speaking, with a little ambient hiss in the background, but the sort of complete silence that normally means the line isn't working. Or the call has ended.

I was about to put the phone down when the woman returned and said, 'Mr Singleton hasn't worked here for some time. Soup of the day?'

What a strange thing to ask. 'Forgive me, I'm very confused,' I said. 'Are you a restaurant?'

The woman paused momentarily – staying on the line, this time – then said, 'I believe you have the wrong number. Goodbye.'

The line went dead again, and though I waited a full minute, this time she didn't return. I took a deep breath to regain my wits and redialled, hoping I could get more sense out of her now that I wouldn't be taken by surprise. Or perhaps someone more helpful would answer.

But this time when I dialled the number, the automated BT voice informed me it was disconnected.

CHAPTER THREE

'Probably some kind of legacy number,' suggested Birch when I told him about the phone call that afternoon. 'Restaurant might not have even known they were paying for it.'

We'd met in Kensington Gardens to walk his black Labrador, Ronnie. Unlike the humans, red-nosed inside our wrappings of winter layers, the dog was oblivious to the cold. He seemed equally oblivious to the idea that other animals might not be quite so insulated, so, despite the frost, continued his usual practice of diving into every bush we passed, hoping to find squirrels wandering about in near-zero temperatures. I once heard Labs described as 'man's best friend with the brains of a gnat', and Ronnie was a fine example.

I'd described the file and my odd phone conversation to Birch as we walked the familiar paths. 'She didn't even ask me who I was, or if I wanted to book a table or place an order. What kind of restaurant gives you one chance to answer a non sequitur, before putting the phone down on you?'

Birch shrugged. 'Sounds like the sort of place the Met brass eat at. Not for the likes of you and me, so they vet cold callers. Keep the riff-raff out.'

'Are you calling me riff-raff?' I said with a smirk, nudging him.

'You be riff and I'll be raff, ma'am.' He smiled, twitching the ends of his moustache and flashing his bright blue eyes.

Birch and I get funny looks from people when he calls me 'ma'am'. It's a habit from the many years he worked under a female police superintendent, of whom I apparently reminded him when we first met. To be fair, at the time I was giving him a dressing-down for not keeping Ronnie under control. I subsequently met the superintendent in question and it's fair to say we didn't get on, but then they do say like opposes like.

'Did you look up the chap in the photo?' Birch asked.

'No, I didn't think of that, I was so surprised by the whole turn of events. I'll give it a try now.'

I took my phone from my pocket, while Birch took a ball from his to distract Ronnie from chasing phantom squirrels. As he threw it, I searched the internet for 'Dieter Gerber Radio Munich'.

Predictably, the first page was nothing but ads for radios and links to stores like Argos and Currys. But near the bottom of the second page was a link to a German blog post mentioning someone named Dieter Gerber. I tapped it and was delighted to see the same man. The article's photograph was different to the one in the file, showing a younger Gerber posing, unlike the candid snap I'd seen. But I have an actor's memory for faces, and was in no doubt it was him.

My German has always been substandard, thanks to my father's desire to anglicise as much as possible following the war, but I have enough that I could stumble through the blog post and confirm his identity: Dieter Gerber, owner of Radio Gerber GmbH, based in Munich. Reading on, though, I realised this was no simple biography. It seemed to be an account of Gerber's unexplained disappearance.

'Look at this, Birch.' He threw Ronnie's ball, then turned to my screen. 'I can't quite read everything, but this appears to say that Gerber went missing in Munich in 1988 and was never found. How mysterious.'

'The file you found was from '72, you said? So he disappeared sixteen years later.' He peered at my screen. 'Why can't you read everything? Need glasses?'

'No, Birch, because it's in German. I speak a little, but I'm not fluent.'

'Oh, easy enough. Here.' He took my phone, and for a moment I thought he was about to demonstrate a hitherto unknown multilingual ability. Instead, he tapped a few times on the screen, then handed it back. Somehow, the article had changed to English.

'Built-in translation,' he explained. 'Better than nothing.'

I wasn't entirely sure about that, reading the rather stilted grammar that resulted, but it seemed broadly accurate. Further down the page was another big surprise.

'Good heavens,' I exclaimed, 'listen to this. It seems that after Gerber disappeared, his company collapsed and rumours began to emerge that he was a Soviet spy.'

Birch threw Ronnie's ball again, then shrugged.

'Plenty around in the eighties. Munich wasn't a million miles from the Iron Curtain. This is all starting to sound like something out of le Carré,' he added with a smile.

'Don't be ridiculous,' I said, but smiled along. 'I just can't understand how any of this connects. At first I thought Gerber might have been a business associate, but my father was never involved in importing goods or manufacturing.'

'As far as you know.'

'It would be an odd secret to keep, though. I've found nothing in his files to suggest it, or anything else like the Gerber file. It's baffling.'

'Hard to see what it has to do with a restaurant, too.'

'No, I think you're right on that one. The number must have been either forwarded or reallocated years ago. The restaurant had nothing to do with it.' I paused, suddenly confused. 'Although . . . then why was it suddenly disconnected when I tried again?'

'Good question. Want me to look him up?'

'Who, Gerber? I just did.'

'Roy Singleton. See if I can find a connection.' Despite being retired for some years, Birch would always be a copper at heart and maintained contacts in the Met.

'Yes, why not? It's not the most unique name in the world, but you never know.'

Privately, I thought it would be a small miracle if he could somehow track down the mysterious file's 'liaison' based on nothing but a name and possible connection to my father. But if he did, and assuming Roy Singleton was still alive, I'd jump at the chance to speak with him.

Birch was right that this had begun to sound like a peculiar kind of spy novel. But the idea that my father, a grumpy City trader with a house full of dogs and a permanent tab at Antoine's, had been in cahoots with a Soviet spy was absurd.

Wasn't it?

I put my phone away, stood on tiptoe to thank Birch with a kiss on the cheek, then tried to put the matter out of my mind and focus on the moment. That's what they say these days, isn't it? Live in the moment. Especially for those of us with fewer moments ahead than behind, it seems like good advice. So I held tight to Birch's arm, taking in the crisp air and the sight of many others also enjoying the gardens, despite our red noses and flushed cheeks. London in winter can be a harsh place, but at Christmas it becomes quite lovely, even peaceful.

That peace was soon broken by a loud woman's voice from behind me.

'Ooh, Gwinny Tuffel? It is you, isn't it?'

I turned to see a smiling woman in her forties, wearing a red bobble hat and one of those belt contraptions with several dog leads attached to it. The leads in question held five dogs, ranging from a sombre German Shepherd to a feisty little Yorkshire Terrier.

Adopting my meet-the-public smile, I said, 'How do you do? It's always nice to—' I'd been about to say *meet a fan*, but I was saved once again by that memory for faces, which told me she was familiar. I wracked my brains trying to think where I'd met the woman before, then spied the Last Chance Dog Rescue logo embroidered on her gilet and things fell into place. '—to run into someone from the rescue again,' I said, recovering as naturally as I could. 'You're in Kensington, aren't you?'

Last Chance was one of several local dog rescues my father would help out from time to time by fostering. Sometimes they gave him dogs who needed to get used to living in a house with people, before they could hopefully find a new home. Other times they sent brand new arrivals for whom the rescue didn't have space in their kennels. And sometimes, if we happened to have a dog-free house at that moment (admittedly rare), they sent him dogs that simply didn't get on with others, so they could live in a place free of conflict.

I say 'we', but the truth is it was mostly my father. My mother was fond of dogs, but he was the real soft touch for anything with four paws, and all the local rescues knew it. The house in Chelsea had been a revolving door for all kinds of dogs while I'd been growing up.

That's why this woman's face seemed familiar. I seemed to recall she'd been younger and thinner when I last saw her, but then hadn't we all?

'I'm just getting this lot out of their kennels for a while,' she replied, indicating the motley crew attached to her waist. 'My name's Yvonne. We met before, when you came in with your father. How is he?'

'No longer with us, I'm afraid. Actually, there's a thought. Are you looking for donations? Old dog beds, that sort of thing? He left quite a few in the house.'

Yvonne smiled again. 'Yes, we can always use any spares you have, assuming this one's got enough?' She indicated Ronnie, whose ball had been completely forgotten in favour of enthusiastic mutual sniffing with Yvonne's dogs.

'Ronnie belongs to my friend Birch, here,' I said, introducing him. If he'd been wearing a hat he would have doffed it, but he settled for an inclination of the head instead. I continued, 'Sadly I can't manage a dog myself at the moment, as it's just me at home and I'm often out all day working.'

'That's right, you're an actress,' she said, remembering. 'But doesn't that mean you sometimes go a long time between jobs? We have some other actors on our roster, you know. Maybe you could foster when you're not working.'

'Um . . . well, I hadn't considered it. I've actually been dog sitting when I have the time, to keep me afloat—'

'That's no problem, we'll be sure to give you friendlies so you could do both. Fostering's wonderful, you know, I do it myself with some of the dogs who come through Last Chance, and the rescue pays for everything, while you get to bring some happiness to all these poor pooches who've got nowhere else to go, and sometimes it's only for a few days before they're adopted, although other times they can be there for months, oh, but we can always take them back off your hands if you suddenly get an acting job, and we'd have to do a home check of course, I'll pop round next week, but I'm sure you'll pass that with flying colours, it's mostly a formality to make sure you're not living in a hole, which I'm sure you're not, so there's really no reason at all not to do it, don't you agree?'

I blinked, taking all this in. A home check? Pass with flying colours? She obviously hadn't seen my house lately.

'I'm flattered to be asked, but I'm not sure it would really be a good fit at the moment,' I said. She looked crestfallen, and the tiny Yorkie suddenly yapped at me as if to say it wasn't angry, just disappointed. I relented a little. 'Let me at least think about it, OK? It's not a decision I'd want to make lightly.'

Her smile returned, and we swapped phone numbers before she resumed her multi-dog walk. Ronnie trotted alongside for a while before he realised we weren't joining them and hastily returned to Birch's side.

The former policeman fussed the Lab, then turned his blue eyes on me. Normally I'd consider myself a lucky woman, but at that moment the unspoken question within them irritated me.

'What?' I demanded.

He smirked. 'All this talk of your father. Now by

chance you meet someone he used to help out, and they offer you a dog? Feels like fate, doesn't it?'

'Since when did you become spiritual?' I replied sceptically. 'You just want me to get a dog so Ronnie has a companion.'

I hadn't mentioned it to Yvonne because I didn't want to give her any more ammunition, but the lack of dog sitting work in my calendar had been preying on my mind. It had dropped off with the turn to winter, as fewer and fewer people went away and thus needed a sitter.

As if summoned by those fickle Fates, at that moment my phone rang with a call from Bostin Jim.

'Jim, hi,' I said, before he had a chance to admonish me. 'Listen, I'm sorry I haven't called yet, but as soon as the audition was over I got caught up in, um, domestic matters. I promise I was going to call soon.' I put a finger to my lips, cautioning Birch to be quiet.

'No problem,' said Jim, voice booming with his thick Birmingham accent. 'Verity told me all about how it went.'

My heart sank, imagining the casting director's retelling of events, but I tried to remain upbeat. 'Yes, I'm sure she did. Luckily there's always another audition.'

'Eh?' he said, confused. 'She thought it went very well, despite the technical difficulties.'

Technical difficulties was certainly a generous euphemism for the morning's wardrobe disaster, but if Verity had said no more, then I wouldn't elaborate for Jim's benefit.

'Oh. Well, I suppose it's fingers crossed, then,' I said. 'Assuming Colin wants me.'

'Don't see any reason why not. He needs an actor, and you'd suit the role. What more is there to it?'

Bostin Jim Austin was enough of an industry stalwart to know this was nonsense. Show business runs on networking and personalities, and if the director decided for any reason that he didn't want me, my audition would go straight in the bin regardless of quality. But I appreciated that Jim was trying to keep me thinking positively. We said our goodbyes and ended the call.

'Heard both sides,' Birch said. 'Hard not to. You got the part, then?'

'Don't count your chickens. There's a long way to go from first audition to landing a role.'

'Still, every step counts. I'll be there on opening night to cheer you on.'

That was the last thing I wanted. Opening night is often the worst performance of any production, an edgy mixture of nerves, bravado and unfamiliarity. But I couldn't tell him that. Instead I said, 'That's very sweet of you, but how? You can't leave Ronnie alone all evening.'

He frowned. 'I'll give him to a neighbour. Unless you know a good dog sitter I could call?'

I laughed and took his arm as we walked on through the gardens. Perhaps things were looking up after all.

34

CHAPTER FOUR

Later that week I was halfway down a step ladder, my arms filled with papers and office stationery I'd gathered from a pile on top of a cabinet, when my phone rang.

Torn between going back up and replacing everything on top of the cabinet, or continuing down and putting it all on the floor, I opted for the latter and hurried down the rungs. Which was a mistake, as, in my haste, one foot became caught in the bottom rung and I toppled backwards, dropping everything. Luckily the thick carpet prevented it (and me) from breaking.

Lying on the floor I pulled out my phone, mercifully also unbroken, and saw Birch was calling. I answered voice-only to preserve my dignity.

'Afternoon, Birch. How are you?'

'Very well, ma'am. Is everything all right? Can't see you, for some reason.'

'It's fine, I'm just in the middle of something.'

'Ah, well. Brief it is, then. Called to say we've tracked him down.'

'Sorry, who's tracked who?'

'Roy Singleton. The chap from your father's file. I called a few old colleagues yesterday, and now we've got him. At least, seems to be. Same name, same age, retired civil servant.'

'Birch, that's extraordinary. How on earth did you do that?'

'Copper's secret,' he said. 'Focusing on former government employees narrowed it down, though. Guess where he lives?'

I almost suggested 'Mars' to stop him sounding so smug, but I had to admit I'd feel pretty smug too if I'd found someone so quickly based on such scant information. 'Please just tell me.'

'Somerset, or at least that's the area code of his last known phone number. Do you want it?'

I hesitated. Of course I wanted it . . . didn't I? The chance to clear up this mystery around my father's file, and what it all meant, was why I'd tried calling the old number in the first place.

'What if he's dead?'

'Beg pardon?'

'You said his *last known* phone number. But if he was the same age as my father, he might have passed away years ago.'

'Mmm. Hadn't thought of that. Still, never know unless you ask.'

'All right,' I said. 'Give me the number. I'll call him today.'

He texted it to me, and for the next few minutes I remained on the floor, staring at my phone screen and trying to think what I would say if Roy Singleton really did answer this number.

There was no point waiting around. What good did that ever do anyone?

With my heart going nineteen to the dozen, I dialled the number and waited. After three rings a man's voice, deep and rasping, answered, 'Hello?'

'Hello. Could I speak to Roy Singleton?'

'Are you sure you have the right number? Who are you?'

My heart sank at what sounded like another dead end. But I had to try. 'My name's Tuffel, Gwinny Tuffel. My father, Henry, knew Mr Singleton. I'm not sure in what capacity, to be honest, but my father worked in the City. He passed away recently and now I'm trying to locate Mr Singleton. Can you help?'

'Gwinny, did you say? As in Guinevere?'

'Yes, that's right. Nobody calls me that, though.'

'Henry Tuffel . . . who was his favourite author?'

'I beg your pardon?'

'Answer the question.'

Caught off guard, I stammered, 'Um, he had several, I suppose. Frederick Forsyth, Clive Cussler . . . I know he enjoyed le Carré and Wilbur Smith, too. Sorry, he never really expressed a single favourite to me. Why do you—'

'His pet name for his wife?'

I almost laughed out loud. My parents had adored one another, but no matter how much self-willed anglicisation my father had engaged in, I could only imagine the scorn he'd have received from my mother if he ever tried to call her 'flower' or 'pudding'.

'Nothing at all, and nobody who truly knew my father would even ask the question. What's going on here?'

Now the other man *did* laugh, a deep rumbling that sounded like he was gargling stones, before his tone switched to something much more friendly.

'Capital! Sorry about the old cloak and dagger, but I had to be sure. As it happens, Henry always maintained to me that Forsyth was his favourite, particularly *The Day of the Jackal*. But I know he enjoyed those others as well. The pet name was a trick question, of course.'

'What do you mean, you had to be sure? I don't understand. Are you Roy Singleton?'

'Eternally single, that's me,' he said, chuckling. (I could have sworn I heard a woman's voice in the background mutter, 'Oh, for God's sake.') He continued, 'I read about your father's death, but was unable to attend the funeral. I don't get out much. Please accept my sincere condolences.'

All things considered, the funeral hadn't been that long ago, yet it had already become something of a fugue in my memory. Given I had no idea what Roy Singleton looked like, I wouldn't have registered his presence even if he'd been there.

'Thank you,' I said automatically, 'that's very kind. So, um, I was wondering – Mr Singleton, how did you know my father?'

'Roy, please. No formalities here any more. But first, tell me how you found me?'

'You're mentioned in a . . . file that turned up while I was sorting out his papers.' I decided not to mention Birch's part in tracking him down.

'Really?' Roy said, sounding impressed. 'Well, now, that's very interesting. Which file, exactly?'

The question suggested there could have been more than one, and Roy had already made a reference to 'cloak and dagger'. My mind began to race, speculating what this could all mean.

'A file from 1972, about a man named Dieter Gerber. He was a German businessman who went missing in Munich some years later.'

'Good lord,' Roy said quietly. 'Good lord. 1972, you say? Are you sure?'

'I'm not sure about anything, to be honest. I hoped that you might be able to explain why my father had this file . . . and why he hand-wrote comments on it. Something about "contact and interest", and then a cover-up?'

Roy didn't answer immediately. After a pause he said, 'Where are you, Guinevere? Still on Smithfield Terrace, in Chelsea?'

I reeled momentarily. Who was this man?

'Yes, I inherited the house. How do you know the address?'

'You won't remember, but I visited a couple of times. You were very young. Listen, I'm in Somerset these days. Why don't you come up to the quad and have a chat? We don't get many visitors, and I'd be delighted to meet you in person. I heard lots about you from your father over the years, and talking face to face would be simpler. Bring the file, would you? To jog my memory.'

After the effort Birch had gone to tracking Roy down, not to mention the revelation that he knew my father well enough to have visited our home, I was sorely tempted. I didn't have much on, besides the never-ending process of repairing the house and clearing it of my parents' possessions. But until two minutes ago I'd never even spoken to Roy Singleton, and I needed time to think.

'I'd very much like to,' I said, 'but I'm not really in a position to leave London at the moment. Perhaps sometime next year?'

'Fair enough, but make it as soon as you can. I'd hate for you to visit only to find me six feet under after all this time!' He laughed again, but this time the gravel overtook him to become a wracking, hacking cough. When he finally brought it under control, Roy wheezed, 'Call us when you're coming and I'll give you the address. We're near Nempnett Thrubwell.'

'*Gesundheit.*'

'Yes, I know. We're actually in the middle of nowhere, but that's the official postal address. Don't worry, I'll supply directions.'

Roy kept switching between singular and plural

pronouns when talking about the house. Presumably, the long-suffering woman in the background was his wife.

He continued, 'In the meantime, perhaps you'd send me a copy of the Gerber file? I can give you the full address.'

'Why don't I take photos and text them to you, instead? Just give me your mobile number.'

He snorted. 'No signal around here, old girl, only this landline. We do have internet, though. How about email?'

'Yes, I can do that. Give me your address and I'll send photos.' He did, and we said our goodbyes.

Directly I found the Dieter Gerber file in my father's office and took photos, including my father's enigmatic notes. I then emailed the pictures to Roy, hoping they'd jog his memory.

They do say to be careful what you wish for.

CHAPTER FIVE

The remainder of that week was occupied with two more auditions, this time for small TV parts and thankfully held in town at studio offices; plus, when I wasn't doing that or walking Ronnie with Birch, more cleaning out of my father's archives. They were all much more ordinary than the mysterious Gerber file. In fact, they were downright tedious, including financial records that went back more than fifty years. Why he'd kept them for such a long time I had no idea, but he certainly didn't need them now. I began filling boxes, wondering whether they'd be safe at the recycling centre or if I should shred everything first. Not that I had a shredder, so I'd need to buy one. Another expense.

At the end of the weekend I flopped into bed and declined to set an alarm for Monday morning. I had nowhere to be and nothing to do, and frankly wanted nothing more than a day in bed, by myself, with the covers pulled over me. Maybe with a dog curled up beside me. *That would be nice*, I thought as I drifted off to sleep.

All such hope was roundly shattered when the doorbell rang at 8.30 a.m. I leapt out of bed, hastily pulled on my dressing gown, then ran downstairs while wondering who it could be. Had I forgotten about a delivery?

I pulled open the door, almost losing my balance when it stopped after six inches, then regained my composure and peered out through the gap. Yvonne from Last Chance Dog Rescue stood on the doorstep, beaming a smile that I considered unnecessarily chipper for this early on a Monday.

'Morning, Ms Tuffel. I'm here to do the home check.'

My still-half-asleep response was mostly wordless, a sort of, 'Whuuu-*uu*?' I did at least manage to make it sound like a question.

'I said I'd visit this week, and there's no time like the present. Is that all right? You're not busy, are you?'

I wanted to say no, it wasn't all right, and to come back when I was actually expecting her and felt vaguely human. But she was right; I wasn't busy, and even if I had been expecting her the house wouldn't look any different. I yanked the door fully open, stepped back, and invited her in. It was only as I followed her down the hallway, past the piles of old papers and journals, that I caught sight of myself in a mirror and groaned.

One blessing of having short hair is that it doesn't knot in bed, but the downside is that instead it sticks up at random angles, and combined with a lack of make-up I looked like the Ghost of Christmas Past . . . or maybe Scrooge himself upon seeing the ghost. I thought back to my experience on *Draculania*, the gender-swapped remake of *Dracula* I'd recently filmed, and wondered if anyone had done the same with Scrooge. Now there was a part for which I'd be 'suited', as Bostin Jim had put it.

'Ms Tuffel?' Yvonne called from the lounge doorway, breaking me out of my thoughts. I hastily pressed down my hair, adjusted my dressing gown, and followed her into the lounge.

I had a dim memory of home checks being done here many years ago, when I was a child, but my parents had always dealt with them. I had no idea what to expect, and was suddenly beset by visions of endless forms to fill out, pages of checklists to tick off, all while Yvonne peered into every room with a measuring tape in hand, tutting to herself. But it wasn't like that at all. She walked through the downstairs rooms, presumably ensuring I didn't have metal spikes embedded in the floor, then checked the garden was enclosed and secure. Finally, we sat in the kitchen and I made coffee while she asked what supplies I had, or would require them to provide, before taking in a foster dog.

'I've got pretty much everything these days,' I said, handing her a cup of hot coffee. Normally, my own first cup lasts about three gulps, but as I had company I sipped it gently. 'Since I started dog sitting,

I've replenished a lot of the supplies we used to keep around. So there's always kibble and treats in the house, plus a first aid kit, calming pills, the usual. We could never bring ourselves to get rid of the beds my father's old dogs had, so they're all still kicking around too. And I keep an "emergency dog bag" in my car,' I added, ticking off its contents on my fingers. 'Food, bowls, another first aid kit, spare collars and leads, towels, a torch, and coats in different sizes.'

Yvonne beamed. 'I do that as well. You never know when you might need it. I remember I once found a stray terrier running along the side of a road, and managed to tempt him with some treats I had in the glove box. Then I slipped a collar on him and bundled him up in a blanket to take in to the centre.'

'What happened to him?'

'Archie went to live on a farm in Cumbria with two Scotties and a Collie, if I remember right. He fitted right in, once we found the perfect family.'

'That's good, well done. So . . .' I said, making a general gesture to encompass the house, 'Do I pass?'

Yvonne frowned. 'Downstairs is fine. According to the notes I have here, it doesn't seem like much has changed since the last time your father took a dog from us.'

'Believe me, you have no idea how true that is.'

'You haven't shown me upstairs yet . . . ?'

I grimaced. 'Aside from my bedroom, upstairs is rather a mess. I'm still trying to clear out the house but it's a, um, long-term project. Whenever I have a dog here I close the other doors, though, and I never leave them alone in the house.'

'What happens if you need to work? With your acting?'

'I try to make sure nothing overlaps when I'm scheduling dog sitting work. And if anything clashes, I have a good friend who can look after them for a few hours. You met him the other day in the park. Birch. He's an ex-policeman,' I added to emphasise that he could be trusted.

'Canine unit?'

'Not at all, but he's a dog owner himself. It's how we met.' In this case I neglected to add that Birch's control over Ronnie often left something to be desired. Yvonne looked thoughtful, so I added, 'I'm sure it won't come to that. To be honest, acting work has been a bit thin on the ground lately. And this was your idea to begin with, remember. You approached me.'

Her smile returned. 'You're right, and we really do need new foster homes at the moment. Things are very busy. I'll discuss it with my colleagues and let you know. Assuming all's well, we'll then be in touch when we have a dog we think would be suitable. Does that sound all right?'

It did, although if I'd said no I'm not sure what difference it would have made. We said our goodbyes and I showed Yvonne out.

It wasn't just acting work that had been lacking recently. I hadn't found much dog sitting work either, though I was hopeful that with Christmas just around the corner things would pick up. Plenty of people jetted off somewhere warm to escape the cold and had to leave their dogs behind.

Clinging to that hope, and now fully wide awake, I climbed the stairs and prepared to face another day.

The day in question mostly consisted of a trip to John Lewis to buy a shredder, followed by lugging it home and running several sheets of old financial records through it as a test. It worked, but I quickly learnt that shredded paper takes up significantly more room than its pre-shredded form, which meant I'd have to make even more trips to the recycling. Once again, I'd made a rod for my own back.

Later that evening, feeling rather low, I microwaved dinner and ate in front of the television. Then I left it on quietly in the background while I continued working on a jigsaw I was halfway through, to try and lift my spirits. It was a winter-themed puzzle I'd bought the week before, an idyllic village green scene with snow piled on bucolic cottages, children building snowmen and having snowball fights, and wrapped-up villagers walking equally wrapped-up dogs. It was a fantasy of false nostalgia, of course. No place like this has ever truly existed in England or anywhere else. But I wouldn't let that spoil my enjoyment of imagining what it might be like to live there.

The house suddenly felt very quiet and empty. I'd become used to it, although Birch being a more regular visitor these days helped assuage the solitude. I hoped I passed the rescue's home check. At moments like these I wanted nothing more than to reach out a hand and find a warm, wet-nosed ball of fur snoozing beside me on the sofa.

Instead, I found myself reaching for my phone as it rang unexpectedly. Who on earth could be calling at this time of evening?

'Gwinny,' Bostin Jim's voice boomed down the line. 'Looks like we might be on to something. Now the director wants to meet with you.'

'Which director?' I asked, bewildered. I'd auditioned for several roles in the past few weeks, and had difficulty keeping track of them all. That was Jim's job.

'Colin Prendergast,' he said. 'For *A Teardrop of Life*. Funny title, if you ask me.'

'I've played in funnier, darling. Does he seriously want to see me?' Decades-old memories resurfaced, and suddenly I felt quite nervous about the idea of meeting the belligerent director again.

'If he wasn't serious, I doubt he'd have called me personally at this time of night,' Jim said. 'He wants to see you tomorrow, and they're already in rehearsals so you'll need to book a train soon as.'

'A train? What for? I live in Chelsea, remember.'

'Exactly. You're not going to walk to Bath from there, are you?'

'Bath?!' I almost dropped the phone. 'You didn't tell me it was in Bath. I thought it was a West End role.'

I could almost hear Jim shrug over the line. 'I

definitely told you. It's at the Theatre Royal.'

In truth he might have and I'd simply forgotten. I pride myself on still having a good memory but actors audition so much, for so many different roles, that the details often go in one ear and out the other until we actually book something.

It wasn't important. What mattered was that I'd got a callback. If I was cast, it would mean spending a month or more in Bath – but so what? I wasn't doing much of anything in London at the moment, and I needed the work. All I had to do was be willing to work with Colin again.

'Tomorrow? That's rather short notice.'

'You've got to walk through the door before it closes, Gwinny, especially these days.'

I couldn't argue with that. 'All right. I'll drive, though, rather than take the train. It'll save me having to fork out for a hotel room.'

'That's up to you. I'll tell him to expect you tomorrow after lunch.'

As he ended the call I felt a nervous tension in my stomach, a combination of excitement and anxiety. My 'history' with Colin was almost forty years old. Was it really all water under the bridge?

I texted Birch with the (potentially) good news, then spent the rest of the evening trying to tamp down my nerves, without much success. I barely placed more than twenty new pieces in the jigsaw, then finally dragged myself upstairs to bed, where I set an early alarm before trying in vain to find sleep.

At two in the morning, I suddenly remembered the home check and Last Chance Dog rescue. Much as I'd been pining for a dog earlier, I'd have to go without for a while yet. I resolved to call Yvonne in the morning and tell her to hold off until I knew what was happening with the play in Bath.

CHAPTER SIX

Following a mostly sleepless night, I woke bright and early, ready for a long drive and determined to put my best foot forward with Colin, the director. I took heart that despite our history, and even after what I'd thought was a very mediocre audition, he still wanted to see me.

I was going through this thought process, looking for the positive to put myself in a good frame of mind, while on my second breakfast coffee. My plan was to set off after finishing it; with rush hour now over I should reach Bath around noon, giving me time to spare before Colin expected me.

Things didn't quite go to plan.

It started with a ring at the doorbell, which I assumed was the postman, though I didn't recall having ordered anything that wouldn't fit through the letterbox.

So imagine my surprise when I opened the door to

see Yvonne from Last Chance Dog Rescue holding a lead, at the other end of which was a liver-and-white Spaniel energetically wagging its tail.

'Good morning,' Yvonne said, smiling from ear to ear. 'This is Spiggy. Spiggy the Spaniel. He's two years old, so still a bit unruly, but very affectionate.' She reached out her hand, passing the lead to me. 'Just take that and I'll carry the food inside.'

'But I told you, I already have food,' I said, bewildered.

'Can't hurt to have more,' she said, turning around to pick up a large tote bag printed with the rescue's logo. She hefted it with both hands, shuffling forward through my doorway. I shuffled back to give her space and Spiggy the Spaniel naturally followed, hopping over the threshold. Yvonne dropped the bag right inside the front door, and the act of placing it inside my house seemed to clear the daze that had been forming in my head.

'Wait, wait,' I protested. 'You can't dump a dog on me like this. You haven't even told me if I passed the home check yet. Besides, I'm going to Bath today. I was going to call you.'

'Oh, you passed the home check,' Yvonne said, still smiling. 'And Spiggy really does need a foster quickly.'

'But I have an audition— Hang on, *why* does he need a foster quickly?'

Yvonne shrugged. 'I told you we're at capacity. I mean, it feels like we're always at capacity, but we're *really* at capacity this week. We tried placing him with another rescue, but everyone's full at the moment. I dread what it's going to be like after Christmas, to be honest. New Year is always a nightmare. But Spiggy's perfectly healthy, nothing wrong with him, we've given him worming tablets and sprayed him for fleas. He just needs some care until we can find a new forever home. I promise he won't be any trouble, he's just a typical working Cocker.'

I looked down at Spiggy, who was currently weaving around in the hallway with his nose down and shaggy ears flapping. From his patchy liver-and-white colouring I'd assumed he was a Springer Spaniel. I tried to recall if we'd ever looked after a Cocker before, but came up empty.

'We had a Springer Spaniel once, I think. What's different about a Cocker?'

'A bit smaller, a bit smarter, a bit more sociable. Honestly, he won't be any trouble.'

Something about her forced cheeriness convinced me there was something she wasn't saying.

'Yvonne, if Spiggy's so wonderful and perfect, why is he in a rescue home to begin with?'

Her smile dropped for a moment. 'He was abandoned, found tied to a fence post in Chiswick. We think he was probably kept outside.' The smile returned. 'But now you can help make him ready to live in a house for someone. It's so good of you to volunteer, you know. I'm sure it won't be for long; Spaniels are very popular.'

I tried to wrestle back control of the conversation. 'Wait. It's not that I don't want to help. Of course I do. But I'm driving to Bath today for an audition. The timing couldn't be worse.'

'I know,' she said, and for a split-second I thought she was genuinely sympathetic. Then she continued, 'But the warden was going to put him down first thing this morning, so we had to take him today, even though, as I said, we're at capacity. The timing really *couldn't* be worse.'

I scowled at her. 'Are you seriously telling me that if I don't take him in today, he'll be put to sleep? That's emotional blackmail.'

Once again, for just a moment her smile was replaced by a serious expression. 'You're right,' she said, 'but it's true.'

Spiggy was still sniffing the carpet, and my feet, as if they were the most fascinating things he'd ever come across. Perhaps they were. Had he even been inside a house before? For the millionth time, I wished dogs could talk and tell us their stories.

'OK, fine,' I said at last. 'But in future you really must give me more notice.'

'Of course, of course,' Yvonne said breezily, turning to go. 'I've got your number, so I'll be in touch. Bye, Spiggy. Be a good boy for Ms Tuffel!'

She hurried away to a bright red minivan parked a few spaces down the road. Spiggy barely registered that she'd gone, until I closed the front door and he looked from it to me. Was he waiting to follow my lead (no pun intended)? I decided to keep him clipped on for the moment, while taking him around the house to familiarise him with the sights and smells.

First stop was the kitchen. I retrieved my phone from the table where I'd been enjoying coffee, and promptly video-called Birch.

'Morning,' he answered. From the background I could see he was in his own kitchen. 'Setting off soon?'

'I was planning to, but then the local rescue threw something of a spanner in the works.' I angled my phone down to show him Spiggy, who was occupied sniffing the base of my cupboards and apparently oblivious to everything else in the world. Not so different to Springers, then.

'Looks lively enough,' Birch said. 'Assume you want me to look after him while you go to Bath?'

'Actually, I thought perhaps I might take him with me . . . along with two more, if you're not doing anything?'

'No can do, ma'am. Tomorrow is the old coppers' do at the Dog & Duck, remember. Christmas lunch.'

Every so often Birch and his former Met colleagues got together to drink and tell stories from the old days. He wouldn't want to miss it, especially not the Christmas bash.

'I'm not staying overnight,' I reassured him. 'A quick drive down, meet the director, then drive back. You won't miss anything. We could even have a bit of a day out in Bath, if you like.'

He considered it, then smiled. 'In that case, why not? Ronnie will love it, I'm sure. We could pop round and see that old friend of your father's, too.'

Roy Singleton! I'd forgotten all about him. He'd said he lived in Somerset. Combining the two trips into one was perfectly feasible.

'Do you know, that's not a bad idea. I'll call him now, then I'll pick you up on the way. Be ready in twenty minutes.'

'Right you are.'

We signed off, then I scrabbled to find Roy Singleton's number again and called him. After three rings, the phone was answered.

'Hello?'

'Roy, it's Gwinny Tuffel. Henry's daughter. It just so happens I'm going to be in Bath today with a friend, so I wondered if perhaps you'd be open to us popping by later this afternoon.'

Silence from the other end of the line. For a moment I wondered if he could hear me. Then: 'Sorry, did you want to speak with Roy?'

It was only now I realised that this was a different voice to the one I'd heard before – stronger and more resonant, the accent a little less Home Counties and a little more West Ham.

'I'm sorry, I assumed you were Roy. Is he there?'

The man didn't reply, but I heard the phone receiver being placed on a surface, followed by a door opening and closing. A minute later, the same sound preceded footsteps and the phone being picked up again.

'Roy Singleton speaking.' I recognised the voice right away, with that coarse, phlegmy cough lurking beneath its surface. I said hello and repeated the offer of visiting, to which he replied, 'Absolutely capital, old girl. Yes, that would be wonderful. I need to thank you again for sending over those photos. Brought back many memories, let me tell you.'

'I'm glad. Can you give me your address?' I asked, scrabbling for a pen while trying not to tread on Spiggy, who zigzagged back and forth around my feet with his nose to the floor. That brought another thought to mind. 'And by the way, do you have pets? A dog, or cat?' If they did, I might have to leave Birch and the dogs outside while I saw Roy alone.

But he replied, 'Not a one. Don't think any of us is really cut out for it.' Then he read me his address, spelling out the village name and their postcode, adding a warning: 'Our postcode covers the entire road, so your GPS will only bring you so far. After that, there's nothing for it but to drive up Stone Lane until you find the quad. Don't worry, though, we're the only house. You can't miss the building when you see it.'

'Thank you. Who answered your phone just now, by the way?'

He chuckled. 'That was Arthur. I'll introduce you when you get here. See you soon.'

He ended the call before I could ask who Arthur was. A relative? His son, perhaps? There was no point trying to work it out. I'd meet him in just a few hours' time.

I checked the clock. All that spare time I thought I'd have to make it to the theatre was quickly disappearing, but it was worth it. Now I could have all my cakes and eat them. Spiggy would be looked after while I saw the director, I'd finally meet the mysterious Roy Singleton, and I'd get a day out with Birch into the bargain.

Things were definitely looking up.

CHAPTER SEVEN

Before setting off I gave Spiggy a quick look-over. His coat was a bit rough, but I didn't see any bald patches anywhere, and his ears were clean. His claws could do with a clip at some point, but not urgently. His teeth weren't great, especially for such a young dog; some were broken and chipped, all needed a good clean, and his warm breath was a bit, well, doggy. Given he'd been found tied up and abandoned, I wondered what sort of life Spiggy had endured before the rescue took him in. Evidently not one with a dental plan, but his spirit remained lively and cheerful. His nose was cold and wet, as it should be, and he showered me with licks once the inspection was over.

I knew travelling in the back of my old Volvo wouldn't be Spiggy's first time in a vehicle, as Yvonne had brought him to me in a minivan, but several hours each way on the M4 might test him. So I added an extra duvet and pillow to the boot, toileted him in the garden for safety, then set off to Shepherd's Bush to pick up Birch and Ronnie.

Like many Labs, Ronnie is the friendliest dog you could hope to meet, so when I arrived we gave him and Spiggy five minutes to circle and sniff one another, despite the cold. Birch also put himself in the Cocker's good books by revealing a packet of cooked sliced ham from his coat pocket. He tore off several strips for both dogs, which Spiggy and Ronnie gladly inhaled. Greetings over and acquaintances made, we finally put them in the boot and settled in for the drive ahead.

Birch leant over and kissed me on the cheek. 'Exciting day,' he said. 'You'll be great.' An unfailing belief in my acting talent has always been one of his more endearing traits.

'I wish I felt that confident,' I said, as we made our way through Hammersmith and Chiswick to the M4. 'Colin Prendergast and I have a history, you know.'

'Oh?' His eyes narrowed. 'Like what?'

'I didn't sleep with him, if that's what you're asking.'

He sniffed. 'None of my business if you did.' Which was true, but he was obviously relieved all the same.

'It was much more prosaic. Many years ago, when we were both very early in our careers, I was in one of Colin's plays. He had a few notable shows under his belt, and a reputation for shouting and screaming. Lots of directors did back then. Anyway, one day a few weeks into rehearsal he was in a particularly foul mood and I couldn't seem to do anything the way he wanted, no matter what I tried. We got into a shouting match, which I regret, because I called him a jumped-up moon-faced megaphone who wouldn't know a good line reading if it slapped him in the face.'

Birch snorted and coughed, trying not to laugh. 'Sorry,' he said. 'Yes, very naughty of you. Do go on.'

'Well, more fool me for phrasing it that way, because in response he slapped *me* in the face.'

Birch's grin vanished instantly. 'He what?'

'Yes, I know,' I sighed. 'It was the eighties. We still romanticised the yelling director, the artiste's passionate anger. And Colin was very, very angry with everyone and everything. Looking back, that probably included himself. I doubt he was a happy man.'

'Still,' he grumbled. 'Inexcusable.'

'Absolutely, and I said so. In fact, I walked out and told my agent I wouldn't return without a full apology and extra pay.'

Birch nodded. 'So he's been mad at you ever since, eh? How did the play go in the end?'

I gripped the steering wheel a little tighter. 'That's the problem. Colin wouldn't apologise. Instead, he fired me and cast Jessica Fulman.'

'*The* Jessica Fulman? Wouldn't she be even more expensive than paying you extra?'

'Not back then. That play turned out to be her breakthrough. A year later she jetted off to Hollywood and never looked back.'

We both fell silent. I didn't know if Birch was wondering what might have happened if it had been me in that breakthrough role instead of Jessica, but I've wondered it myself on more than one occasion. If I'd been less bolshy, if I'd sat there and taken it, perhaps I could have been the one headed for fame and fortune in Tinseltown. But at what cost? If I hadn't faced up to Colin, could I have faced myself in the mirror every morning? Was career success worth enduring such bullying? I didn't think so at the time, and I didn't now either. I couldn't claim to have no regrets in life, but telling Colin Prendergast where to shove his play wasn't one of them.

'It was almost forty years ago,' I reminded Birch. 'We were both young and hot-headed, and there's no sense in holding a grudge for that long. Besides, it's not often I get to feel like I'm the one doing a director a favour.'

He reluctantly agreed. I changed the subject to explain what Yvonne had told me about Spiggy, and we drove on through Slough and beyond.

I hadn't been to Bath in many years, but it seemed that not much had changed. Some parts were centuries or even millennia old, so a decade or two probably didn't register much in the grand scheme of things. I drove directly to Victoria Park, where I knew there was a large car park, rather than try to find something in the city centre. Bath's 'city' moniker is deceptive, in any case; the whole place is only about twice the size of Fulham and easily walkable, so long as you don't mind hills.

After paying an outrageous sum for a few hours' parking I walked with Birch and the dogs to the Royal

Crescent lawn, then pointed him in the direction of the park proper if he wanted somewhere more expansive. Leaving them to it, I turned back towards the centre, walking via the picturesque Circus down to the Theatre Royal. As I neared the centre, seasonal decorations began to appear, with lights strung over houses and wreaths on doors. Even the theatre had a tree inside the lobby.

Bostin Jim's typically vague instructions had simply told me Colin Prendergast would be waiting for me at the theatre. As the current run was a *Puss in Boots* panto for Christmas, I assumed Colin was using afternoons to rehearse *A Teardrop of Life*. I could just imagine trying to practise heartfelt social commentary against backdrops of fairy castles and gaslit streets.

Inside the main entrance, a young man was working behind the main counter. 'Can I help you?' he asked as I entered.

'Gwinny Tuffel,' I replied. 'I have a meeting with Colin.' He looked me up and down with a sceptical eye. Given the cold weather I hadn't dressed up for the occasion, but I was hardly in my roughest dog walking gear either. I sighed and added, 'I'm an actress, and may join the production.'

He seemed no less sceptical of this notion, but came out from behind the counter and led me through into the auditorium. Three actors were running through a scene on stage, not stopping when we entered. The young man led me down the aisle to where the unmistakably mountainous form of Colin Prendergast sat at his director's desk in the stalls, script spread open under a reading lamp.

'Mr Prendergast,' the young man said quietly. 'Gwen . . . sorry, what was your name again?'

Before I could correct him, Colin saw me and roared in greeting.

'Gwinny Tuffel! How delightful to see you. Come, come!'

Despite his age the director remained loud and larger-than-life, an impression bolstered by a matching waistline. He jumped to his feet, clasped my hand in both of his, and pumped it up and down like he was drawing water.

'Big fan, big fan,' he said enthusiastically. 'Fantastic that you're available. I thought you'd retired!'

'That's a long story,' I said, smiling. I was taken aback by his warm, friendly greeting. I'd worried there would still be ice to break, but it seemed he couldn't be happier to see me.

'Let's get you a script. Lulu!' A young woman appeared by his side, seemingly from nowhere, and silently handed him a printout. Colin thumbed through it, looking for a particular page. 'Now, Tabitha, Tabitha . . . here we are, scene four. That's your entrance.' By now the actors on stage had paused their run- through. Colin turned to them and bellowed, 'Act one, scene four, so we can break Gwinny in. Chop, chop!'

With that, he handed me the script and returned to his desk.

'Sorry,' I said, flustered. 'I wasn't . . . my agent only said you wanted to meet me. I didn't know I'd be doing another audition.'

'Audition? Christ on a unicycle, we open in three weeks! You know I had to fire my previous Tabitha? Useless, a horrible little diva. I need someone with their wits about them to save me, Gwinny. How soon do you think you can get off-book?'

Until now I'd only read through the entire script once, and hadn't needed to memorise it for the audition anyway. I quickly ran through what I'd noted at the time, recalling that Tabitha had around thirty minutes of total stage time, of which she spoke for about two-thirds. 'It's hard to say exactly,' I replied, still a bit bewildered by how quickly things were moving. 'But for a part this size . . . perhaps a week? I'll definitely be ready before opening.'

'Hmmm.' Colin narrowed his eyes at me, as if assessing my trustworthiness. 'I know roles for women your age don't come along every day, Gwinny. I need to be confident you can handle it.'

'Of course I can handle it,' I said, a bit miffed. 'I'm a working actor, darling, not a charity case.'

His smile returned. 'All right. But don't let me down! You're my saviour.'

'I bet that's what you said to Jessica all those years ago, too.'

He looked puzzled. 'Jessica?'

'Jessica Fulman. When you brought her in as a last-minute replacement.'

'Oh, Christ!' he roared. 'Yes, yes. She was brilliant, you know. Saved my bacon, and did a star turn of her own. Look at her now! She replaced an awful girl, hormonal type who got hysterical at the slightest criticism. I wonder what became of her?'

'Lots of TV,' I said, forcing myself to laugh along. 'And then an enforced hiatus. Still, all's well that ends well, eh?'

'You know her?' he said, surprised. 'Who was she? Damned if I can remember the girl's name.'

My smile froze as I realised he wasn't joking.

All this time I'd been worrying about whether I should bury the hatchet to work with him, when there was nothing to bury, because Colin didn't even remember me. In my mind, I replayed the previous two minutes in a new light and saw it all fitted this revelation. He really thought this was the first time we'd be working together.

I could have taken the easy route. It would have been so simple to play along, pretend that young woman was somebody else, and not make a fuss. I knew that's what I should do. But something inside me couldn't get past the revelation that this man – who'd physically assaulted me, fired me when I complained, then replaced me with someone for whom the role became a springboard to fame and fortune – didn't even have the decency to remember it.

'It was me,' I said calmly, my smile disappearing.

'What? No, no. Can't have been. I'd remember.'

'Apparently not. But I can assure you that I do.' I stomped to the stage, mounted the steps by the footlights, and dropped my handbag by a refreshments table in the wings. 'I can give you one hour, and then I have to return to London. If that's a problem, you can take it up with my agent.'

He didn't argue, and for the next sixty minutes we ran through all of Tabitha's scenes. It didn't go well. My anger at Colin's solipsism simmered away throughout and I all but spat lines onto the stage, making the other players flinch and back away.

For all that, though, I was barely in the moment. My mind was preoccupied with how I'd been taken for granted at every step of this process. Having to do an audition online instead of in person; being summoned to Bath with less than a day's notice; being expected to immediately get on stage and rehearse before I'd even formally been offered the part; the assumption that I could give my entire afternoon to the rehearsal without warning; and the final insult, that Colin didn't even remember that the 'awful girl' he'd fired all those years ago was me. I wondered: had the previous Tabitha really been fired, as he claimed? Or had she quit because she couldn't work with him any more?

When the hour was up I thanked the other actors – none of this was their fault, after all – and took a fresh water bottle from the refreshments table. Then I climbed down the steps and walked up the aisle, tossing the script at Colin as I passed. In my peripheral vision, I saw the elusive Lulu appear from the shadows to snatch it from the air before it landed in his lap.

* * *

I called Birch immediately upon leaving the theatre, and he walked back into town with the dogs. We passed an amiable half-hour wandering around Bath centre, with Birch listening patiently and tutting in all the right places as I angrily explained what had happened, then sat outside a café with coffees. Ronnie and Spiggy both sensed my mood and nuzzled up to me, which helped calm me down.

'What are you going to tell Bostin Jim?' Birch asked, and I honestly had no idea.

I didn't have long to decide, either. As we walked back to the park my phone rang, and Bostin Jim asked how the 'meeting' had gone.

'A bit of a disaster, I'm afraid,' I replied, and related events to him.

When I'd finished he surprised me by asking, 'So do you still want the part?'

'Darling, after today, I doubt Colin would want me even for free. Short of going back there and licking his Hush Puppies, which I refuse to do.'

'Gwinny, don't try to tell me you've never argued with any other director before. It would make you a freak of nature.'

He had a point. There were plenty of people in the business I'd disliked, but worked with for the sake of a role and my career. None of them had previously fired me, however.

'All Colin remembers from forty years ago is that I was "awful". I don't think he even remembers the slap he gave me, much less that it *was* me.'

'Sounds like an opportunity to start again with a clean slate, if you ask me,' Jim said. 'Put the past behind you.'

'Well, he certainly has,' I grumbled.

Jim ended the call with a promise to follow up and get Colin's perspective on the afternoon. I was pretty sure I knew how that would go.

Birch took my hand as I replaced my phone in my handbag. 'Shall we go and see Roy Singleton? Should cheer you up, I think.'

'Will it? I'm not really sure I'm in a socialising mood any more.'

'Shame not to, after coming all this way. Besides, it'll take your mind off the play. If we go straight home now you'll brood for the entire M4.'

'I will not!'

He said nothing, but raised his eyebrows at me. The problem with ex-policemen is that sometimes they see right through you, and much as I wanted to deny it, he was right. I was still fuming about Colin Prendergast, and without a mood palate cleanser I'd continue to fume for hours.

'All right,' I relented. 'Let's go back to the car and give the dogs a quick snack. Then I'll decide.'

We returned to the car park, where I took kibble from my emergency dog bag and put a handful in each of two bowls. I didn't trust either dog not to fall on it immediately – Spiggy was likely untrained, while Ronnie was, well, a Labrador – so I sat on the lip of the car boot, holding the bowls, and told them to sit. They did, eagerly.

I made them wait five seconds, then said, 'Good dogs, *go on*,' and put a bowl on the ground in front of each. They hoovered up the lot in less than a minute, crunching happily and wagging their tails.

There was no public tap in the car park that I could see, so when they'd finished I took up both bowls and used the water bottle I'd taken from the theatre to rinse one of them out. Then I poured in the remaining water and set it down. Ronnie lapped it up, while Spiggy took a few gulps before returning to sniff the ground around the car.

Going through these mundane motions with the dogs, I felt myself relax. Perhaps Ronnie would never put on a critically acclaimed production of *The Crucible*, but he'd always show me nothing but love, and that had to be worth something.

My thoughts turned to Roy Singleton and his remote house nearby. Birch was right – we were so close that it made no sense to wait. There was snow forecast over the next week, so I wouldn't be driving back any time before the new year. And even if I was somehow cast in the play, I wouldn't have time to visit while the performance was running. Finally, as uncomfortable as it was, there was his age to consider. Roy himself had said not to leave it too late, and if this man was a contemporary of my late father, who knew how much time he had left?

'I've made up my mind,' I said to Birch while repacking the dog bag. 'Let's visit Roy, and then drive home this evening. I feel more up to it, now.'

Birch smiled. 'Glad to hear it. Sure you'd regret it if you didn't. Chance to hear stories about your father from someone who knew him.'

I agreed. But if I'd known what would happen over the next few days, I'd have run a mile and never looked back.

CHAPTER EIGHT

Roy hadn't been joking about the GPS. The moment I turned onto Stone Lane my phone loudly informed me, '*The destination is on your right.*'

Unless my destination was an overgrown hedgerow bordering a field, however, the perpetually cheery voice was mistaken. I ignored it and continued driving, going slowly and carefully while looking for the 'quad'.

Stone Lane was a winding, single-car road lined with tall hedges that meandered through the gentle hills of the Mendips, distinctly lacking in line-of-sight or passing places. If we met something coming the other way, one of us would have to reverse all the way back to the nearest junction, a prospect I didn't relish. My rusty old Volvo creaked and swayed around turns and over blind dips as I listened out of the window for other vehicles, though I could barely hear anything over my own engine noise reflecting off the hedges. Birch clung to his over-door handle with grim fatalism, and the dogs were silent.

Then, descending from a rise into a deep valley, I spied a driveway (on our left, thank you, Mr GPS) leading off the road and even further down. As we drew near, I slowed so Birch could lean out and look down. In the rear-view mirror, I saw Spiggy and Ronnie stand up, scanning the landscape in anticipation.

'Roy said his was the only building on the road,' I said. 'What does it look like?'

'Farmhouse,' Birch said simply. 'Must be it.'

I turned off the road. The driveway was steep, affording a view which looked upon the house below, and I finally understood why it was called the 'quad'.

The house was stone-built, rectangular, with two long sides and two short. It was two storeys high, with the sparse and small windows commonly found in old farmhouses. Four chimneys sprouted from its tiled roof, one at each compass point, but the house wasn't a solid block. In the centre was a large private garden, completely enclosed by the house's four sides. Presumably this was the quadrangle for which it was named, and it made the house look more like a prep school or monastery than a farm.

The grounds in which it sat were mostly open fields, broken by a flowing stream at the foot of the valley. Further on, the stream wound through a large wooded area, its branches winter-bared. On the other side of the stream were more fields and trees, all rising to another hill in the distance.

The driveway ended in a paved area to the front and one side of the house, where several cars were parked;

more than one each for Roy and his wife, plus the mysterious Arthur. I parked at the front and reached for my phone to call Roy Singleton's number, in case nobody had seen our approach. The place felt isolated enough that watching out the front window for visitors probably wasn't high on the agenda. Neither I nor Birch could get any phone signal, though, so instead I sounded the horn and got out of the car.

Spiggy and Ronnie began to whine in unison. Birch opened the boot and clipped them both on-lead before letting them jump down, then perhaps regretted it when they tried to shoot off in opposite directions: Ronnie towards the house and Spiggy, predictably for a Spaniel, towards the open grounds.

'You look like you're about to be drawn and quartered,' I said, laughing at his outstretched stance, and took Spiggy's lead from him.

'Spiggy, *heel*,' I said to the dog, who looked back over his shoulder at me in disbelief. He didn't come to heel, but he at least stopped straining at the end of the lead, which was probably the best I could hope for. The rescue trainers would have their work cut out with this one.

'Guinevere, old girl!' called a phlegmy voice. I turned to see an elderly man, at least as old as my father had been, emerge from the front door with a warm smile. Tall, thin and seemingly devoid of all hair, he wore a well-fitted pullover and slacks, with fur-lined tartan slippers on his feet. 'Roy Singleton,' he said, as if I hadn't guessed, and turned to Birch. 'Who's this?'

'DCI Alan Birch, retired.' He introduced himself and the two men shook hands, sizing one another up in that way they do. My eye was drawn to how skeletal Roy's hands and wrists were. The clothing hid it well, but he was a bag of bones. Even I could probably lift him up.

'The rozzers!' Roy exclaimed with a grin. 'I wasn't there, nobody saw me, and you can't prove a thing, m'lud.'

'If you've nothing to hide, you've nothing to fear,' Birch countered, his moustache twitching.

Roy's smile faded. 'I seem to recall the Stasi said something similar, and with about as much conviction. Anyway, come in and meet the gang. You can let the dogs off, by the way. None of us have allergies, as far as I know.'

Birch bent to unclip Ronnie, but I interrupted. 'I don't think that's a good idea, Mr Singleton.'

'Call me Roy, please. We don't stand on ceremony here.'

'Well, Roy, not only are these dogs rather boisterous, they're also completely dedicated to the pursuit of food theft.'

'Ronnie's a good boy,' Birch protested.

'A good boy who'd try to eat a house brick if you let him,' I countered. 'It won't hurt to keep them under control for a while in a strange house.'

As if to prove my point, Spiggy was currently running back and forth between me and Roy, sniffing our feet and the ground between us with typical enthusiasm.

Birch grumbled but acquiesced, and kept Ronnie on-lead as we followed Roy inside the house. The door opened into a long, stone-flagged corridor that ran directly through the house, with an internal door set in each wall and an external door at the far end which led into the quadrangle garden. Halfway down, by one of the internal doors, stood an old-fashioned telephone table beneath a memo board. The table itself held a modern walkabout-style phone, while on the board I saw several numbers scribbled with a marker. A coat rack hung next to the memo board, and underneath that were several pairs of shoes and Wellington boots, plus one pair of pink, fluffy slippers.

'We're a shoes-off house, if you don't mind,' Roy said, pointing to the slippers. 'Jane lent me her spares for you, Guinevere. Wasn't expecting a second, though, so hang on a moment.'

He exited through one of the internal doors, leaving us in the corridor as we removed our coats and shoes. I slid my feet into the pink slippers and, out of curiosity, opened the door opposite and peeked through. I saw a kitchen and dining room, with a utility room beyond.

'Seems a pleasant chap,' Birch declared as I closed the kitchen door. 'Ex-forces, is my guess. Has the bearing.'

'He does, doesn't he? I suppose it never really goes away. Perhaps that gave him connections in Whitehall, and that's how he knew my father.'

Our host returned holding a pair of large novelty slippers of brown fur, with a teddy bear's face on each toe cap.

'Arthur's spares. They'll fit you,' he said cheerily. Birch looked at them like he'd been handed a sequinned ballgown.

'How lovely,' I said quickly, before he could protest. 'That's very kind of you, Roy.'

Birch turned to me in disbelief, but took the hint and put them on. Roy watched, smiling, and I wondered if this was some kind of macho power play, perhaps an extension of rivalry between the army and police. Still, Birch could lump it. I was here to find out more about my father, and if that meant letting Roy establish his male dominance, we'd both have to live with it.

'I can see why you don't get many visitors around here,' I said, following Roy through the internal door from which he'd just come. 'On the bright side, it must be very peaceful.'

'It certainly is that,' he replied. 'Out of sight, out of mind is how we like it. Isn't that right, gang?'

The door opened into a large sitting room, with walls of exposed stone and wooden beams. A deep pile carpet lined the floor. In the fireplace a wide iron stove held blazing logs, giving the room a cosy warmth absent from the entrance corridor. Deep-set windows at the front and back afforded views of the driveway and garden quad respectively. Shelves fixed into the stone walls were crowded with books, ornaments and candles. A TV and stereo occupied one corner, and next to them stood a fake Christmas tree decorated with tinsel, baubles and lights. Strings of lights also ran around a couple of windows. It wasn't much more than a token effort, though I wondered if Roy couldn't handle doing much more.

More interesting than the room itself, though, were the three people waiting inside it. A man and two women, one of whom was in a wheelchair.

'Gosh,' I said, surprised. 'Roy, when you said "we" I assumed you meant just you and your wife.'

'Wife?' he said, smiling. 'Never had the pleasure, old girl. No, the six of us live here as a collective. Works quite well, if I do say so myself.'

The other man, who sat close to the fire, rolled his eyes. 'Yes, Roy, it was a great idea. You're a genius. As if we haven't all been saying so for the past five years.'

He was heavyset, with dark, deep-lined skin and a clutch of grey, tightly curled hair atop his head. His broken nose and meaty hands were those of a boxer, an impression bolstered by the large gold signet ring he wore on one thick finger, but his deep voice was quiet and delicate.

'I'm Arthur. I share this place with Roy, for my sins.' He peered at Birch. 'I remember you. Fresh-faced detective, you were. Eucalyptus, something like that? No, I've got it. Larch!'

'Birch,' he replied curtly. 'Apologies, you're not ringing a bell. Ex-Met?'

'No, but I knew a lot of police.' Arthur didn't elaborate further.

'I'm Gwinny,' I said, introducing myself to the room. 'The dogs are Ronnie and Spiggy. Spiggy's not actually mine, but I'm fostering him for a local rescue.'

'Springer, is he?' Roy asked.

'Cocker,' I replied. 'I made the same mistake, because of his colouring. I'm told they're a little less bouncy than Springers. Now, are there definitely no pets here we should know about? Not even a house cat?'

Roy smiled sadly. 'Even a cat would be too much responsibility for us, I fear.' He guided us to sit on a small sofa, with just enough room for Birch and me. Ronnie flopped at Birch's feet, while Spiggy strained as far as his lead would allow, sniffing. It was only then that I noticed how many chairs and sofas this room contained. More than enough to accommodate all four gathered residents, plus us as impromptu guests. Perhaps this was where they regularly gathered to socialise.

One woman stood in front of a window strung with lights, leaning against the radiator, looking like she belonged in a campervan driving around Stonehenge. She and Roy seemed about the same age, but there the similarities ended. Her features were soft, framed by a bouffant of untamed silver hair illuminated by the fairy lights, and she wore clothes as multilayered as they were multicoloured.

'I'm glad you could come, Gwinny,' she said, with a broad Essex accent. 'Roy's talked about nothing else since you phoned.'

'That's not true, Jane,' he said, settling in an armchair with his back to her.

'Yes it is,' said the second woman from her wheelchair. She was a marked contrast to Jane, with short-cropped hair dyed black and dark eyeshadow visible through glasses with thick black frames. She wore simple slacks and a T-shirt, also black. 'We don't get many guests, you see. Most of the time it's just us. I'm Zoe, by the way. I remember you from the telly.'

'Oh, how lovely. Thank you.' I don't often get recognised any more, but everyone in this room was older than me. Looking around, though, I realised that something literally didn't add up. 'Roy, you said there are six of you living here. But I only see four . . . ?'

As if in answer, the door behind us opened and a man entered. Tall, slim and upright, his hair was thin, his glasses rimless, and his clothing nondescript. The only memorable thing about him was the walking stick on which he leant, and even that was hardly remarkable given his age.

'Has anyone seen my pocket torch?' he asked brusquely.

'Your what?' said Zoe.

'Pocket torch. LED, black aluminium, about four inches long. I just spent ten minutes searching for the damn thing.'

'You'll have put it down somewhere and forgotten, Paul,' Roy said. 'Your mind's going.'

'Probably in the same place as my bloody lighter,' Jane said with a sigh.

Paul, the new arrival, turned to her with a puzzled expression. 'You don't smoke.'

'It was a gift. Normal people do that, you know. Forty years I've had it, and then last month it vanished. I did mention it at the time.'

Roy laughed. 'See? Losing your marbles. Paul, this is Guinevere and Larch.'

'Birch,' I corrected him.

'That's the one.'

Paul seemed to notice us for the first time. 'Of course. I apologise, I'm not normally late.'

He limped to a wing-backed chair in front of a low table covered by a cloth, then reached down and, to my surprise, lifted the cloth to reveal a half-completed jigsaw puzzle. My attention caught, I tried to make out the image, which was upside down from my viewpoint. Water, buildings and sky; probably a city skyline.

'How's it going?' I asked him, indicating the puzzle.

'Slow but steady,' Paul answered non-committally, lowering himself into the chair.

'This is the communal meeting space,' Roy explained. 'He keeps a puzzle on the go here for whenever he graces us with his presence.'

'OK, well, that's five of you . . .' I said.

Zoe looked apologetic. 'Willie's working in the shed. I told him to come, but it's hard to drag him out of his man cave sometimes.'

'Zoe, didn't you have something to tell us?' Arthur asked, fiddling with his signet ring.

She frowned, trying to recall. 'No, I don't think so. We're just here to meet Gwinny, aren't we?'

'Absolutely!' Roy clapped his hands. 'So let's kick things off properly. Jane, be a girl and make a pot, would you?'

I exchanged a sympathetic glance with Jane, though

given the age of everyone in the quad, I shouldn't have been surprised they'd expect a woman to wait on them. Still, I was a guest and it wasn't my place to comment.

Roy continued, 'Now, Guinevere, tell me about your father. What side of him did you see at home? What did he do when he retired?'

'More of the same, just less of it. He continued following the markets and stock trading, and—' I hesitated, wondering how much to tell these strangers. I still found it rather embarrassing that my father had managed to pull the wool over my eyes about his finances, so I stuck to the facts. 'Well, he did that until my mother died. Then he liquidated his portfolio and lived off it for the next ten years, until he passed himself.'

The truth was more complicated. He'd let me believe he was still trading following my mother's death, when I moved back in to care for him. Hence the house being stuffed full of old editions of the *Financial Times*. In fact, the whole time we'd been living off his savings – which were initially substantial, but a decade of continuing to spend as he always had reduced them to almost nothing. These people didn't need to know that.

'The "side" of him I saw wasn't much different to how he'd been before,' I said. 'Other than a great sadness at losing my mother, of course.'

Birch took my hand in sympathy.

'Did Henry continue to travel?' Paul asked. 'Trips home to Germany, for example?'

'Once or twice, early on, but his health deteriorated

to the point where he couldn't. Not that you'd have known; if you'd met him the day before he died, you'd have barely noticed any difference. He was still the same grumpy old man, just . . . a bit slower, a bit weaker.'

'I think we can all sympathise with that,' Paul said without looking up from his jigsaw. The others all murmured agreement.

I turned to Roy and smiled. 'Your turn. How did you know him? And what does it have to do with this Dieter Gerber chap?'

He shrugged a thin shoulder. 'I worked in government,' he said, choosing his words carefully. 'Overseas affairs. Being a German national, Henry was able to help us out from time to time, and let us know whenever he planned to visit the Fatherland. Natives often find it much easier to talk to one of their own, rather than a foreigner.'

'But my father wasn't "native". He moved here as a child, and became a British citizen shortly after the war.'

'Blood is thicker than passport ink. Remember, Germany was still a divided nation at that time, with Ivan looming in the East. So to have a charismatic man like Henry willing to help . . . yes, he was rather useful.'

I'd known my father did 'little favours', as he called them, for the Foreign Office from time to time. Introducing other businessmen to diplomats, mostly. 'Is that how he knew Dieter Gerber?' I asked.

'In a manner of speaking. Gerber ran a radio and broadcast manufacturing firm. In '88 we asked Henry to meet him as a potential investor and persuade him to visit London, where we could talk to him. That's why my name is in that file.'

If not for Spiggy fidgeting and grumbling contentedly at my feet, you could have heard a pin drop. Everyone was looking at me, seemingly waiting for my reaction. I tried to maintain my poker face, not wanting to voice what now seemed obvious.

'Blimey!' Birch exclaimed, unable to contain himself. 'You were right, Gwinny. Your father was a spy.' He turned to Roy. 'You were a spy!'

CHAPTER NINE

The residents all laughed in unison.

'Henry wasn't a spy,' Roy said, his laugh threatening to turn into a cough. 'He didn't go about following people, or cracking codes. He was just a businessman. From time to time we asked him to meet people and introduce them to us. As for me, all I did was sit behind a desk in Whitehall writing memos and making phone calls.'

This was all something of a revelation. Roy might claim otherwise, but I'd read enough Graham Greene and John le Carré (mostly from my father's own collection) to know that what he described was how most real-world spying actually worked.

Before I could respond, the door from the corridor opened again. This time a short, wiry man bounded into the room. His skin was weathered, criss-crossed with expression lines, and his head bore a sparse tonsure of grey stubble. He wore casual, workman-style clothes and, rather than being shod in slippers, he was barefoot.

'What's this about spies?' he said in a broad Scots accent. 'Do we need to be on our guard for Russkies?' He gave Zoe a kiss in greeting, then flopped into an empty chair next to her with his bare feet dangling over the arm. He raised a hand to me. 'Willie Mac, gardener and general dogsbody. You must be Gwinny. I see you come with an entourage.'

I introduced Birch and the dogs. Hearing his name, Ronnie lumbered to his feet and promptly sniffed around Willie's bare feet. The Scot yelped as the Lab's wet nose touched his toes and withdrew them, tucking his feet safely under his body.

'Where have you been, Willie?' Roy asked. 'You're late.'

'Aye, well, the temperature's dropping like a lead weight, and someone's got to bring in the plants overnight. Not going to be you, is it?' He shrugged.

Before Roy could respond, Jane re-entered carrying a tray of steaming mugs. She placed one each for Birch and me on nearby occasional tables, then gave a third to Arthur before leaving to fetch the remainder.

'I don't suppose you've seen my torch, Willie?' Paul asked. 'Small, black aluminium. Did you borrow it?'

The Scot shrugged. 'Not me. Probably in the same bloody Bermuda Triangle as my old gardening gloves.'

'Yes, well, never mind all that,' Roy said. 'We have guests, remember.'

I took a sip of tea. 'Don't mind me, I'm still taking this all in,' I said. 'I suppose it explains why there were politicians at my father's funeral, as well as City traders. But what happened to Gerber? The press said he was suspected of being a spy, but my father obviously disagreed. You saw his comments on that old file, Roy.'

Once again, all eyes in the room turned in a single direction, though this time it was towards the old spy.

'You must understand how the game was played in those days. The Cold War inflicted fewer casualties than fighting Hitler, but it was no less vital to the nation, and, in times of war, secrets are kept from the public. Officially, we accused the Russians of snatching Gerber and taking him behind the Iron Curtain. This caused confusion on their side because they'd done no such thing, and confusing the enemy is always useful. One Moscow source told us they thought we were covering up success, and that Gerber was now working for us. Every cloud has a silver lining.'

'But what actually happened?'

Roy sighed. 'Gerber was supposed to meet your father in Munich. He did, in fact, but before they could meet again Gerber turned up dead. Henry found him, in fact. So we covered it all up, your father came home, and it was all swept under the carpet.'

Some of the other residents gasped.

'You told me Gerber had gone to Moscow,' Paul said in a disapproving tone. 'I wondered why we never heard about him again.'

Roy shrugged. 'As I said, a useful deception. Need-to-know only. Sorry, old boy.'

Paul tutted quietly. Jane returned with another tray of

tea for the others, which occupied everyone's attention. I looked between Roy and Paul, trying to gauge their relationship; while Roy was clearly the garrulous host of this little party, the straight-backed Paul seemed more like a headmaster, keeping the others in line and passing occasional judgement.

I thought back to the comments on the file. Roy had said Gerber died before a second meeting, which presumably explained the note *Partial success – contact & interest*. But the later notes, in different ink, had presumably been made afterwards.

'So that must be what my father meant about a cover-up. What about these numbers, though? What happened in 1972?'

Roy shrugged. 'That's all Greek to me, I'm afraid. Something to do with your father's City investments, perhaps. Anyway, that was the last time we crossed paths, and the Cold War ended soon afterwards. I know Henry continued doing favours for the FO, but not in my circles.'

The room fell silent again, though whether out of respect for the dead or reluctance to continue discussing the subject I couldn't tell. Keeping Spiggy on a short lead, I stood and began browsing the tinsel-fronted shelves, in the time-honoured tradition of house guests everywhere. A collection of old vinyl records occupied the shelf by the stereo, but near it was a large bookcase, which I found much more interesting. They say you can tell a lot by the books someone reads, and nothing I saw contradicted what I'd learnt so far. Mostly thriller and espionage titles, not very different to my father's own shelves, apart from an extensive collection of newer books I wasn't familiar with.

'Max Calibre,' I said, reading the author's name repeated across some twenty-odd volumes. 'I gather someone's a fan?'

'Oh, yes, the Jack Spitfire books,' Arthur said enthusiastically from the fireplace. 'Do you read them?'

'I can't say I'm familiar.'

'I am,' Birch said, answering Arthur. 'Have you got the new one, *Target: Spitfire*? I haven't read that yet.'

Arthur hesitated, thinking. 'I suppose we must have. Is it up there?'

I read along the spines. *A Magnum for Spitfire, Red Alert: Spitfire, Spitfire's Revenge* . . . 'Yes, it's here,' I said, pulling the latest instalment from the shelf.

'B-grade potboilers if you ask me,' Roy said, grinning. 'Spitfire travels the world shooting and punching his way through the baddies, while inevitably falling for a beautiful femme fatale. Still, they pass the time of day.'

'Don't forget all the firearms statistics,' Willie added from his relaxed position. 'That's the best bit. Well, after killing Russians.'

'I'm sure Guinevere didn't come here to debate the merits of Jack Spitfire,' said Jane, with a roll of her eyes. She'd returned to the window, watching the group dynamics keenly.

'Please,' I said, 'just "Gwinny" is fine. Only my parents called me Guinevere.'

Paul turned his schoolmaster's gaze on me. 'Indeed.

An unusual name, especially for a German family, if you don't mind my saying . . . ?'

'After the war, my father wanted to anglicise as much as possible,' I explained. I decided not to add how my parents had discovered too late that 'Guinevere' was a Welsh name, not English.

'I expect that's also why he changed the family name to Tuffel, from von Tüvelsgern?'

Spiggy pulled towards Paul, keenly sniffing the would-be schoolmaster. I took the opportunity to follow and look at his jigsaw properly. It was an old London skyline, from an age when St Paul's still dominated the landscape.

'That's an old picture,' I said.

'I'm an old man,' he replied. 'This is the London I remember, and prefer to still think of. They can build all the bloody skyscrapers they like, but they can't escape the past.'

Spiggy suddenly stood on his hind legs and placed his paws on Paul's leg. 'He seems quite keen on you,' I said, smiling. Paul subtly recoiled, horrified that this furry ball of chaos might take an interest in him, so I pulled the Spaniel away.

'So much for Cockers being less bouncy than Springers, I suppose.' I returned to the sofa with Birch, keeping a good grip on Spiggy. 'Paul, you're right that my father changed our family name to get on better in England. But that's not common knowledge. Did you know him, as well?'

He demurred. 'Only by reputation.'

I suddenly felt like a fish in a bowl, as if my every statement was being carefully watched and noted by the 'gang', at least two of whom had known my father and another of whom somehow recognised Birch.

'If you don't mind me asking, how do you all know one another? Were you all at university together, or work colleagues . . . ?'

Willie roared with laughter. 'University! That'll be the day.'

Roy rolled his eyes at the Scot. 'As it happens, Arthur and I did share a college at Oxford. But the rest of us . . .' He hesitated, and Paul shot him a sharp look.

'For God's sake, there's no harm in it now,' Jane said from the window. She turned to me. 'Yes, Gwinny. A long time ago, we all worked together in some capacity or other. Then we retired, Roy found this place, and one by one we came to live here.'

'No families?' Birch asked, with characteristic bluntness.

'Well, now, that's a long story,' Roy said, smiling. 'Or rather several. Why don't you stay for dinner, and we'll regale you? I can tell you more memories of Henry, Gwinny.'

He made it sound as if my own father had been a stranger to me; someone I barely knew, rather than a fixture of my entire life and someone I'd recently spent a decade caring for twenty-four hours a day. But was Roy so wrong? My father had never once mentioned Roy Singleton, Dieter Gerber or dead bodies in Munich. It seemed there was a whole side to him I hadn't known.

Had my mother? Whenever I asked her about his 'little favours' for the Foreign Office, she'd remained tight-lipped.

Despite my natural curiosity, though, I wasn't sure how much I *wanted* to know. Plus, something about Roy and the 'quad gang' gave me pause; there was an insular dynamic at play here which felt vaguely hostile to outsiders.

'Perhaps another day,' I said. 'It's really been lovely meeting you all, but the dogs need a walk—'

'Walk them here,' said Roy. 'Everything down to the stream is ours. You're welcome to it. Then you could stay for dinner afterwards.'

'Sounds good to me,' Birch said cheerfully. 'Haven't eaten since breakfast.'

I felt rather press-ganged, but forced a smile and nodded.

'Yes, of course. Wonderful.'

CHAPTER TEN

I decided I was being silly. There was no reason not to stay for dinner, especially having come all the way from London. I put my misgivings down to the afternoon's dealings with Colin Prendergast and decided I might as well take the chance to learn more about this previously unknown side of my father.

As Birch and I let the dogs off-lead in the quad's grounds, though, I questioned how much I'd previously suspected. I'd known Henry Tuffel was a figure in the City, and that he had friends in the Foreign Office. He'd always insisted it was nothing special, and that, following the war, they took an interest in all first-generation Germans. Had I believed that? Or had I simply *let* myself believe it, because the alternative seemed absurd? The bookshelves in Chelsea were filled with my father's collection of thrillers, as well as the many I'd bought myself over the years, thanks to his influence. Good old-fashioned yarns, he called them.

My mother had never liked them. Was that because she knew her husband was a tiny part of that world? It seemed unreal.

Perhaps that was why I'd felt uneasy. Roy had been polite and friendly, but I was struggling to come to terms with this new truth about my father. Should I have left it alone to begin with? No, that was out of the question. It would have tortured me, knowing I'd missed the chance to find out what lay behind the Gerber file. I've always been a proponent of following the facts, believing that, ultimately, it's always better to know the truth, no matter how hard it may be.

I shivered, suddenly feeling cold. Birch reached out and wrapped an arm around my shoulders.

'Temperature's dropping,' he said. 'Be a frosty one tonight.'

It didn't bother the dogs. I had a couple of spare coats in the car, but Ronnie and Spiggy both had thick, luxurious fur and seemed unaffected by the chill wind blowing down from the hills. After swiftly toileting, they trotted around the fields, with Ronnie eagerly running through the bare branches of the wood while Spiggy kept his nose to the ground, sniffing in the typical zigzag fashion of Spaniels.

'Funny bunch, don't you think?' Birch said, throwing a stick for Ronnie. 'Had the distinct feeling there's something they're not telling us.'

'That's the natural suspicion of a policeman talking,' I said. 'But I do agree. Paul in particular seemed to have more to say than he did. Perhaps he'll open up at dinner.'

'It's that Arthur I want to talk to. Said he "knew a lot of police", but didn't elaborate, did he?'

'No . . . are you sure you don't remember meeting him?'

Birch shook his head. 'Don't recall coming across him before. Another "government worker", do you think? The Met often liaises with security services.'

'It's possible, isn't it? Goodness – what if they're *all* former spies? Jane said they all worked together in different capacities.'

'A house of spies,' Birch said quietly. 'Well, I never.'

Spiggy's sniffing was taking him ever closer to the stream. This was typical of Spaniels, whose love affair with water knows no limits. Never mind camels; if you're crossing the desert, do it with a Spaniel – they'll find any oasis within a hundred miles. So when Spiggy inevitably leapt into the stream, I simply thanked my own foresight for including a towel in the emergency bag.

Labs and Spaniels don't have all that much in common, but one thing they do share is large reserves of energy, so we kept both dogs running around as long as we could. Nevertheless, December twilight comes early so we soon decided to head back inside.

As we walked towards the house, though, Spiggy suddenly veered off to the right, his zigzagging scent tracking becoming straighter and more direct. He headed towards a large wooden structure, either a small barn or a large shed depending on your point of view. It stood free in the grounds, some distance from the main quad building. Presumably, something inside smelt interesting: rats, fertiliser, or even greasy cloths. I've known dogs go crazy for the pungent scents of oil and grease.

Ronnie followed Spiggy, making a beeline for the shed doors, and I rushed after them in case they tried to get inside. The last thing anyone wanted was two dogs blundering about in the dark surrounded by sharp tools.

Luckily, they were quite safe, as the doors were shut tight with a heavy-duty padlock. Even the cleverest Collie wouldn't get past that, let alone this pair.

'Get away from there!' a voice shouted from behind us.

I turned to see Willie Mac hurrying through the snow from the direction of the other 'long house', which backed onto the grounds. Its external door stood ajar.

'Don't worry, they can't get in,' I said. 'They're just sniffing around. Maybe there are rats inside?'

'Aye, but either way they've no business in there, and neither do you.' The Scot rapidly closed the distance between us. 'So call them off.'

Birch moved to block his path. 'Now then, sir, take it easy,' he said in the universal policeman's cadence. 'No harm done, and no intent for such either. What's in there, anyway?'

'It's a shed,' Willie scowled. 'What do you think's in there? Tools, a lawnmower, gas bottles. Even a Met copper should be able to work that out.'

Birch bristled at the insult. I was too busy trying to clip Spiggy back on-lead to do anything about it, so I asked innocently, 'Gas bottles?'

'Look where we are. You really think this place would be on the grid? We run on LPG, and looking after it is part of my job, so the bottles are stored in my shed—'

Still soaking wet from the stream, Spiggy chose that moment to slip out of my hands and shake himself vigorously. Birch and I were used to it, but Willie was caught by surprise and recoiled under the water bombardment.

The Scot growled. 'A shed which neither you nor your dogs have any business with. Now get lost.'

'We understand,' I said, finally clipping on Spiggy's lead. If this went on much longer, I worried Birch would punch Willie on principle. 'We should get back inside for dinner anyway.'

The mention of food did the trick, and after clipping Ronnie back on-lead, Birch and I walked back around to the front of the house. I opened my car and took the dog towel from the emergency bag before we re-entered Roy's front door.

'Jumped-up little goblin,' Birch grumbled as he removed his shoes.

I used the towel to dry Spiggy, or at least downgrade him from 'soaking wet' to 'quite damp', then removed my own shoes.

'It sounds like Willie works harder than anyone else in the quad,' I said. 'Believe me, caring for my father was hard enough. I can't imagine how much more difficult it must be with a wheelchair user, not to mention also being the house's groundskeeper, gardener, and apparently in charge of everyone's gas supply to boot. I think we can make allowances, don't you?'

Birch exhaled in frustration. 'If you say so. Wouldn't want to spoil the evening.'

I leant up and kissed his cheek. 'Besides, for all we know, Willie is also the resident cook. The last thing you want is him poisoning your dinner.'

CHAPTER ELEVEN

In fact, the resident cook was Jane. I supposed I should have expected that.

Dinner turned out to be a very informal affair, though it was clear the 'gang' had put in more effort than they normally would for an evening meal. The dining area was at the back of the kitchen, overlooking the interior quad garden. The table was quite large, but clearly intended to seat only half a dozen people, so everyone had to squeeze up to accommodate Birch and me. Still, it was friendly enough and we sat down to a table filled with pots of roast potatoes and assorted vegetables, bowls of pasta, and baskets of warm bread. Spiggy and Ronnie would have loved it but we'd already shut them in the lounge, trusting they were tired enough to sleep for a while. If need be, I'd feed them later from the emergency stores in my car.

'Not often we have guests,' Roy said by way of explanation, as I took in the table. 'We don't always eat together, but tonight's a special occasion. How's the beef, Jane?'

Jane speared the roast with a probe thermometer. 'Just about ready,' she replied, 'hold your horses.'

'This is all rather communal,' I said. 'You're almost like a family, aren't you?'

Roy smiled. 'I like to think so. At first it was just me and Paul in the quad, you see. Then the new recruits came along, one by one.'

'Recruit? You make it sound like a barracks.'

'Boys will be boys,' Jane said, placing the joint on the table and taking her seat.

'But who made dinner before Jane came along?' Birch asked. 'If it was just the two of you to begin with.'

'We ate a lot of takeaways,' Paul said, helping himself to potatoes.

'Oh, rot,' said Roy, pretending to be offended. 'I cooked a bit, didn't I?'

Paul held his gaze for a moment then repeated to me, 'We ate a lot of takeaways.'

Willie laughed and reached for a knife to carve the joint. 'They were hopeless until I came along, recruit number three. Lucky for them, I can cook a wee bit more than baked beans on toast.'

'You've had plenty of those too, though,' said Arthur, piling vegetables onto his plate.

'Aye, well, that was a long time ago.' A brief frown passed over the Scot's face, before he was all smiles again. 'Anyway, I cooked until Jane arrived. The secretary does it better than any of us, which is just as well, as there was plenty for me to be getting on with in the garden.' He placed the first slice on my plate.

'Secretary?' I said, a little offended on Jane's behalf. I asked her, 'Is that really what they call you?'

She shrugged. 'Old habits die hard.'

Once again, I looked around the table at them all – so obviously comfortable together despite being so different – and remembered what Jane had said earlier.

'So you moved here because you all worked together, is that it? Did you all know my father?'

'No, no.' Willie paused mid-carve. 'We weren't all in a squad, or anything like that. Were we, Arthur?'

Arthur rolled his eyes and said, 'No,' around a mouthful of potato.

Willie continued, 'But we were all government people, one way or another, so our paths crossed. And like Paul said earlier, Henry Tuffel had a reputation. A good one,' he added hastily. 'Your father was well liked.'

'The quad was my idea,' Roy said. 'Lots of people in our line of work never marry, or if they do it seldom lasts. So I thought: rather than spending our retirement wasting away alone and depressed in shabby Pimlico flats, why not bring some old pals together to live like a family, as you said. Paul found this place, so we put the plan into action and here we are.'

Paul looked from Roy to me. 'As I'm sure you can imagine, there were many more steps in between those two phases.'

'I'm making conversation, not writing a report,' Roy

said, laughing. 'You don't want me to give away all our secrets, do you?'

For a split-second the room fell silent. Then Roy stood up and declared, 'Time for wine.' He selected two bottles from a narrow wall rack, opened them, and returned to the table.

'No, thank you,' I said when he offered me a glass. 'I'm driving back later tonight.'

'In the pitch dark?' he said, aghast. 'No need for that. We have a guest room upstairs, why don't you stay the night?'

'That's very kind, but we don't want to impose,' I said, trying to decline politely. 'Especially with the dogs.'

Roy smiled. 'Not at all. The guest room is next to Arthur, and you couldn't wake him with a pneumatic drill.'

'We didn't bring toilet bags, or nightclothes.'

'Don't you worry about those. I always keep some in hand for guests.'

Willie snorted. 'In all the years we've been here, when have you ever had guests?'

'You never know when things like this will happen, Willie,' Roy said. 'Patience is a virtue.'

'And you'd know all about that, wouldn't you?'

'That's not what I meant, old boy. Let's not drag up the past.'

The temperature around the table seemed to drop suddenly.

'You've done nothing but drag up the past all bloody night!' Willie shot to his feet, trembling with rage. 'Oh, what a jolly jape we all had, playing the Great Game against Ivan! But you have no idea— You didn't— You weren't—' I couldn't quite tell if he was about to burst into tears, or leap across the table and throttle Roy.

'Willie, that's enough,' Paul said sternly.

'No, let him get it all out,' Roy said. 'It's been a while since—' Whatever he was going to say next was lost as he began to hack and cough, short of breath.

I thought Willie might ease off in sympathy, but the Scot was livid. He leant on the table with his fists, spitting fury at Roy. 'You never said sorry, did you? Not once! You never gave a second's bloody thought—'

'William!' Jane's voice cut through. 'Stand down. We have guests.'

That seemed to resonate with him. Willie looked around nervously, as if suddenly waking from a dream. Or a nightmare.

'Roy?' Jane said pointedly.

With one last hack, Roy cleared his throat and dabbed at his mouth with a handkerchief. 'Willie, I'm sorry. I've always been sorry, you must know that. I promise I didn't mean anything by it. Careless phrasing, that's all.'

Willie turned on his heel and walked out into the house's central corridor. Zoe wheeled herself away from the table to follow him.

'Don't worry,' she said to me. 'Nothing to do with you. He'll be OK.' She frowned at Roy, then wheeled herself to the door.

Roy turned back to me. 'I'm sorry about that, but

do say you'll stay. There's so much more to talk about regarding your father.'

I looked at Birch. 'What time is your Christmas lunch tomorrow?'

'One o'clock at the Dog & Duck. I suppose if we leave early . . .' I could tell he was reluctant, but as he said, if we set off before ten we'd be back with plenty of time before his policeman's get-together. Besides, he was the one who'd committed us to dinner in the first place. Otherwise we could have already been halfway back to London.

'All right, then,' I said, taking a glass of red. 'Why ever not? Tell me more about this unusual building, first. You said it's four houses, but it looks just like one. And how does Zoe get about?'

'The quad is a single building, but each side is a separate dwelling,' Paul explained. 'Roy and Arthur live here, while Zoe and Willie live opposite in the other long house, where she has a stairlift. Jane and I each have one of the short houses to either side.'

'Zoe and Jane's houses are new,' Roy added. 'Well, relatively. The original farmhouse was this one and Paul's next door, but we extended it by building a mirror image to form the quad and enclose the garden. Capital idea, don't you think?'

'So long as you all get along,' I joked, then realised what I'd said. 'Well, most of the time, anyway.'

'Don't worry about Willie,' Roy said. 'Water under the bridge. But yes, the reason this works so well is that we all have our own houses rather than living on top of one another. Even friends sometimes need time apart.'

'Speaking of, just how well did you know Gwinny's father?' Birch asked, bringing us back to the ostensible subject at hand. 'You said you worked with him more than once, and visited him at home.'

'I'd like to think we were friends, yes. Certainly enough that Henry often spoke of how proud he was of you, Guinevere. I recall him saying he saw a lot of his wife in you.'

That surprised me. My mother, Johanna, was a strict Teutonic woman who rarely let her hair down, even in private, and kept a tight rein on the household finances despite my father's best efforts. That had always been her main objection when I took to the stage; she didn't try to stop me, but was perpetually worried I wouldn't be able to earn a living. By contrast, I admit I'd always been rather blasé about that side of things. I knew my family had money, and while I hadn't consistently been a leading lady, I'd always worked . . . even if it had become something of a struggle once I passed the magical age of forty, becoming officially 'old' in the eyes of casting directors.

On the other hand, my mother loved dogs almost as much as my father. Perhaps that's what he was referring to.

'That's lovely to hear,' I said to Roy, not sharing my doubts. 'I'm so glad I found that file in his records, now. Where did he go on your behalf?'

'Well now, let me think. Munich, obviously. Hamburg,

once or twice. Busy port, you know. Did we send him to Vienna?' he asked Paul.

'Not on my authority,' Paul replied. He turned to me with a smirk. 'Of course, that never stopped him. You might be thinking of Strasbourg, Roy.'

Our host smiled. 'That's right. A fine job, Strasbourg. Henry bagged us a KGB sleeper, whom we later turned.'

Speechless, I took this all in. There really had been a side to my father he'd kept hidden from me, and possibly from my mother as well. I wished I'd known, and could have asked him about this when he was alive. Grief is a hole that is never truly filled, but rather diminishes over time until it becomes small enough that you can step across it without thinking. Now I felt it growing again, as if I should grieve for another man altogether – one I'd never truly known.

'It really is quite amazing,' I said. 'My father never spoke about any of this.'

'There are things about Henry Tuffel I'm sure even we never knew,' Roy said. 'He played his cards close to his chest his whole life. It's what made him useful to us.'

I drained my wine glass as the door to the corridor opened; Willie Mac and Zoe returned to their seats at the table to resume dinner. Nobody mentioned the outburst.

CHAPTER TWELVE

Over the course of the evening, I learnt that everyone here was either divorced, widowed, or had never had a family to begin with. Living at the quad seemed to be a way of avoiding the dreaded care home, with all the residents keeping one another lively and engaged. It didn't seem such a bad arrangement, assuming you could afford it of course.

Several courses and wine bottles later, we all sat back, relaxed. Jane stood up to gather plates, swaying on her feet, and once again I felt annoyed on her behalf. She hadn't even drunk that much, and the men must know she was a lightweight, but they still expected her to clean up afterwards. I was about to nudge Birch to give her a hand when Willie stepped in.

'Let me,' he said, taking the plates from Jane's hands. 'It'll do me good to be upright after stuffing myself.' He winked at us, and Jane gratefully sat down again before reaching for her wine glass.

'Willie's the one who has to stay sober,' Zoe explained. 'I can get plastered if I want, because he has to carry me regardless.'

'So is this retired life, then?' I said with a smile, feeling the need to make conversation about something that wasn't my father. 'Willie looks after Zoe, which I know from my own experience is a full-time job. Paul has his jigsaws. What about the rest of you?'

'We take it easy,' said Roy. 'Willie tends to the garden, as well. Jane does a lot of the cooking. Arthur and I are the layabouts, sitting around watching documentaries about the war.'

Arthur smiled and raised his glass in agreement.

'And you, Zoe?' Birch asked.

She shrugged. 'I fool around on computers. It's what I spent my career doing.'

A lull fell over the table. Feeling pleasantly tipsy, I leant my head against Birch's shoulder. At least, that was the plan. Somehow I missed and fell sideways, unable to catch myself before my head was on his lap. Instinctively my legs flailed, kicking the table and knocking over my wine glass. Just as well it was empty.

Birch gently took hold of my shoulders and lifted me upright. 'Dogs will need walking,' he said. 'Bit of fresh air might do us all good.'

I wasn't too drunk to know that by 'us all' he meant me. Holding on to him to steady myself, I got up and we made our way to the lounge.

Ronnie and Spiggy were curled up tail to tail on the sofa where Birch and I had sat earlier. They sprang to life when we opened the door, but I could tell it was from a state of restful sleep, and was glad they were getting along. Not every dog I'd looked after in the past saw eye to eye with Ronnie, who, despite his Labrador size and strength, was actually a soppy old doormat.

We let them out into the corridor. Birch clipped leads on them both while I took twice as long as normal to put on my shoes.

As I finished and stood up, reaching for my coat, the door to the kitchen opened again and Roy stepped out.

'I made the guest room ready before dinner,' he said. 'I've put some spare pyjamas out on the bed for you, as well. When you've walked the dogs I'll take you up.'

'Much obliged,' Birch said, handing me the dog leads while he put on his boots.

Roy took me aside. 'Before you go tomorrow we should have another chat, just the two of us. What I said earlier was a bit of a fib, actually.'

'What do you mean?'

'I deciphered your father's notes on the Gerber file. It's quite extraordinary.'

'Really? Tell me what it says.'

'No, you've had enough surprises for one evening. Get some rest, then we'll talk tomorrow morning, OK? Bright and early.'

Jane sauntered out from the kitchen, her voluminous hair falling over her eyes. She mumbled goodbye, then swayed drunkenly out the back door into the quad garden.

'Isn't that the wrong door?' I said, confused.

Roy smiled. 'All the houses open into the garden, so

we use it as a shortcut. Easier than going all around the front. In fact, why don't you walk the dogs there before you go to bed? It's fully enclosed by the houses, so you can let them wander.'

We did, stepping out through the garden door and down a short concrete ramp. While that was probably for Zoe's wheelchair, I noticed a grab-handle also mounted on the wall, for the benefit of all the quad's elderly residents.

The night was dark and bitterly cold, even with several glasses of wine inside me. There appeared to be no security lights in the garden, so I took a pocket torch from my coat and lit the way. The quad was more rectangle than square, as Paul had said, with two long and two short sides opposite each other. Stone paths weaved between high bushes and ivy-wrapped archways, punctuated by occasional wooden benches. Even in this cold season it was very pretty, and I imagined that in spring and summer the garden was beautiful. Willie Mac knew what he was doing.

The paths and junctions didn't quite form a true hedge maze, but it wasn't far off, so Birch and I stayed close together and kept the dogs on-lead. Spiggy eagerly sniffed everything in sight, then finally found a spot deemed worthy of marking and cocked his leg up a bush. Ronnie had gone the moment we stepped outside, but now went again on top of Spiggy's, using the 'reserve wee' male dogs seem to keep in store for urgent territory marking.

Willie Mac and Zoe passed us, him pushing her wheelchair, and bid us goodnight. Then we heard Paul say goodbye to Roy, followed shortly by the sound of a door closing. By this point we were shivering in the cold, but the dogs were blissfully unbothered so we continued on. Just as we reached a stone fountain in the centre of the garden, a phone rang from inside one of the houses. It seemed to bring us back to our senses, and in silent agreement (because our teeth were starting to chatter) we turned back to Roy's house, guided by the lights around the window.

The cold had sobered me up a little, but I was still tipsy enough to be startled when Birch, halfway through removing his boots, suddenly exclaimed, 'We haven't fed them!'

'Heavens, you're right. Poor dogs. Hang on.'

I walked through the corridor and out the front door, careful not to let the dogs follow. Fumbling for my car keys, I weaved around my car and opened the boot, hauling out the emergency dog bag. The night was absolutely silent, with not a sound to be heard, not even wildlife. They really were in the middle of nowhere, out here. I could see the attraction.

All I had to feed the dogs was kibble, but they fell on it as if it were caviar. After we washed and dried the bowls I dropped the emergency bag in the hallway, ready to return to the car in the morning. By the time we entered the lounge, Roy was the last man standing – or rather, sitting – reading a biography of Harold Wilson.

He led us upstairs to the first floor where he showed us our guest room and the bathroom, said goodnight, then closed the door behind him.

The guest room was small, its double bed taking up most of the space. There was no dog bed, or even much room for one, and even I didn't keep spares of those in my car.

Birch didn't see it as a problem. With a policeman's efficiency he inspected every drawer and cabinet, eventually finding a spare duvet in the top of the wardrobe. He folded it a couple of times, then placed it outside in the hallway. I knew that at home Ronnie slept in a dog bed outside Birch's room, so he'd probably be fine there. But I didn't trust Spiggy enough to let him potentially wander around while the humans slept. Besides, I enjoyed sleeping with a dog at the foot of my bed.

'We can't leave them outside, Birch, not in a stranger's home. I know Ronnie's well behaved, but Spiggy might lead him astray.'

'Where else? There's no room on the floor in here.'

'No, but there's a big double bed. They can share with us.'

Birch frowned. 'Ronnie won't like it. He's a dog of routine.'

'He'll go anywhere you do. It's just one night, you won't spoil him.'

Birch frowned, but acquiesced and replaced the duvet back in the wardrobe. Ronnie was terribly confused, as he'd already been eyeing it up for a sleeping spot, but when I invited him onto the bed, he gladly jumped up and wagged his tail. Spiggy followed without waiting to be asked.

Also on the bed, as promised, were two sets of matching pyjamas. I unfolded them to discover a repeating pattern of holly leaves and berries, although the faint musty smell that wafted into the air during their unfolding put paid to any thoughts that they might be new for the season.

'They really don't get many visitors here, do they?' I said, holding up a pyjama top. It was at this point I noticed they were both the same size; Birch noticed two minutes later when he couldn't quite button his, while mine draped over me like a raincoat.

'No good,' he said with a sigh. 'Undershirt it is, then.'

'Don't you dare,' I said, trying not to laugh. 'There's no chance we'll get cold anyway, not with the dogs on the bed.' By now Ronnie and Spiggy were both curled up back to back, perfectly comfortable despite this change to Ronnie's 'routine'.

With a resigned sigh, Birch got into bed and lay on his back. I joined him, rested my head on his bare chest, and fell asleep with a smile on my face.

CHAPTER THIRTEEN

Suddenly, I awoke.

If I'd been dreaming, I didn't remember it. I opened my eyes, thankful that the room was too dark for it to spin, and wondered if one of the dogs had jolted me awake. No; I felt them still sleeping, curled up at the foot of the bed. Birch lay on his back, quietly snoring as usual. Nobody had moved. Nothing was amiss.

So why was I awake?

Straining my ears, I heard more snoring from another room. Perhaps it was Arthur, whom Roy had said slept like a log. But it wasn't loud enough to have woken me. Then I heard the creak of a floorboard, as if someone was moving around. Still a bit unfocused thanks to the wine, I wondered if Arthur's snoring kept Roy awake. Perhaps it was him walking about, and the sound had woken me.

I shifted my position, snuggling closer to Birch.

Spiggy woofed quietly and shuffled around himself, before we both settled back down.

Drifting away, I thought I heard an odd sort of scraping sound. But it could have just been my imagination, and moments later I was sound asleep once more.

CHAPTER FOURTEEN

I was awoken the next morning by someone dropping a lead weight on my chest, followed by a blinding light. I recoiled, quickly shielding my eyes with my arms – or would have done, if they hadn't still been under the covers and now trapped by Spiggy, who lay on top of me.

The light came from the window, Birch having thrown open the curtains. As my eyes slowly adjusted (and my head throbbed from the night before) his silhouette came into focus, standing in his pyjamas and making displeased noises.

'What's the matter?' I croaked from my prone position in bed.

'Take a look for yourself,' he said without looking away from the window.

'I gladly would but I'm rather tied up, not to mention half-blind. What's up?'

'We had some snow overnight.'

I wriggled my body to tip Spiggy off my chest, which gave me enough freedom to move my arms and throw back the covers. I folded them over him so he'd return to dozing, and sat up.

That wasn't the best idea in the world, according to the anvil orchestra playing in my head, but I gritted my teeth and continued until I was upright, then took a few careful steps to the window and stood beside Birch. Ronnie was already up, pressing himself against Birch's leg and slowly wagging his tail.

I looked out upon a white world, punctuated only by occasional branches of trees and hedges poking through the thick, deep snow. Our guest room looked out over the driveway, but if I hadn't remembered where I'd parked my Volvo, I'd never have been able to tell it from the other cars. It was perfectly picturesque, with undisturbed snow as far as I could see in all directions. But it was also frustrating.

'What are the chances they grit the lane?' I wondered aloud.

'Low,' Birch replied gruffly. 'Anyway, how would we reach it? Look at that driveway.'

He was right, of course. The steep drive I'd driven down yesterday must now be mounted in the other direction, and with what looked like a full foot of snow on the ground, that simply wasn't going to happen.

'Oh, your policeman's party,' I said, suddenly remembering Birch's plans for this evening. 'If we get stuck here, you'll miss it.'

'Safe to say we're already stuck. Can't see this melting

any time soon, not with the temperatures we've been having.'

'I'm so sorry. This is my fault.' I leant my head on his shoulder, looking out at the cold expanse. My head was still ringing, and the sun reflecting off the brilliant white snow made me wince, but I kept any complaints to myself.

'Couldn't be helped,' he said quietly. 'Emotional time, talking about your father.'

He was trying to make me feel better, but I knew it wasn't a good excuse. If I hadn't begun drinking we could have returned home last night to London, where snow ploughs and gritting teams would surely be out in force to get the city moving again as fast as possible. Instead, here we were in sleepy Somerset, isolated from the world for who knew how long.

Nevertheless, life goes on and dogs care nothing for human plans. We were reminded of this when Spiggy decided that was quite enough snoozing and stood up to have a thorough shake.

'We'd better get this pair outside,' I said, reaching down for my clothes. A little too fast, as it set off the heavy-metal percussionists again, but I fought through it to quickly get dressed. Birch did likewise, and in a jiffy we were ready. We both donned our borrowed slippers, clipped the dogs on-lead, and made our way downstairs through the empty lounge into the central corridor.

The door to the other side of the house was open, so I peeked in. Arthur stood in the kitchen, wearing slippers and a dressing gown. All the drawers and cupboard doors were open as he rifled through their contents, grumbling to himself.

'Morning,' I called out, making him jump with surprise. 'Are you looking for something?'

'My ring,' he said. 'I can't find my ring.'

My gaze dipped to his hand, where I'd seen the large signet the day before. Sure enough, it was missing.

'It's always on my bedside table,' he said. 'But it's not there.'

'Did you take it off to wash, perhaps? I can't imagine why it would be in a kitchen drawer. Could you have accidentally knocked it on the floor?'

He paused, thinking. 'I don't think so. I'll take another look.'

'In the meantime, is it OK if we let the dogs into the quad?'

'Oh, yes,' Arthur replied, rummaging in one of the cupboards. 'Go ahead, the door's always unlocked.'

I supposed that made sense – any burglar would have to climb over the roof first, in order to access an internal door from the garden – but then I remembered those strange noises in the night and felt uneasy.

'What if everyone's out of the house at the same time?' Birch asked, thinking along the same lines. 'Surely you lock them then.'

Arthur paused his search and looked confused, as if the question had never occurred to him before. 'There's always someone here. Never leave the base unmanned.'

In the corridor I spied two pairs of Wellington boots under the coat rack and called out, 'Arthur, are these wellies yours and Roy's? Can we borrow them, just to walk the dogs?'

Arthur's big frame appeared in the kitchen doorway, filling it. 'But Roy's not here.'

'Well, where is he?'

'On his way down. I saw him coming out of the bathroom. He's always late for breakfast,' he added, smiling.

I was surprised Roy had managed to rise so early, with him being up and about in the middle of the night. 'I'm sure he won't mind,' I said confidently. 'We can't wait, the dogs need to go—'

Right on cue, and unable to wait any longer, Spiggy crouched in the corridor and dropped a poo on the stone floor.

'As you can see,' I said, sighing. Taking a plastic dog bag from my coat, I picked up the mess and tied it off. Spiggy had been so good up until now that I didn't have the heart to scold him. Even a fully house-trained dog can only hold it in for so long. 'Now, can we borrow these wellies?'

Arthur looked at the small stain left behind on the floor and wrinkled his nose in disgust. 'I'll fetch a mop,' he said, ducking back into the kitchen.

Birch reached into his coat for the packet of cooked ham. We took it in turns to tear off strips and keep both dogs occupied while pulling on the rubber boots. Arthur's fitted Birch very well; Roy's were comically large for me and made my feet look like a child's drawing, but they were dry, which was what mattered.

Finally, we put on our coats and opened the (unlocked, as promised) door at the far end, before walking out into the garden.

The snow in the quad was undisturbed and pristine, like on the driveway and hills. That didn't last long, as Ronnie and Spiggy both dived paws-first into the powder, barking and wagging their tails. Confronted with the dazzling white snow and sub-zero air, my head began to ring again, and I groaned. Birch didn't notice; he was too busy huffing as he laboriously dug Ronnie's business out from the bottom of a snow well. At least the Lab had waited until we were outside.

We agreed it was safe to let them off-lead and unclipped both dogs to let them wander. I had a flash of concern, imagining one of them opening a door to another house and running rampant inside, but dismissed it. Spiggy was too short to open anything, while Ronnie could be outfoxed by an open gate with a sign saying 'Please Enter', let alone a door handle.

Both dogs promptly cocked their legs up the nearest hedge, then went their separate ways. Spiggy put his nose down and began zigzagging along the ground, in the way Spaniels do when trying to pin down a scent, while Ronnie ran this way and that through the hedges, presumably hoping to find a squirrel or two. I doubted any 'little furries' would be out in this weather. I wasn't exactly keen on it myself, and could barely feel the end of my nose.

'Let's just give them a few minutes and then head back in,' I said to Birch, shivering from the cold. He murmured agreement, but I could see he was distracted. 'What's up?'

He cleared his throat. 'Nothing. Just thinking what an odd little community this is. Fancy retiring, then deciding to live next door to your old colleagues.'

I nudged him playfully. 'No plans to live in a similar arrangement with your old Met pals, then?'

'Not on your life. Solid chaps, but I wouldn't want them for neighbours.'

'It's like children. They're lovely, so long as you can hand them back.' Birch chuckled, a sound which always warmed me inside. 'I suppose the familiarity is a source of comfort. Like a retirement village on a small scale. I hope I'm still as independent as them in twenty years' time.'

'Apart from Zoe.'

'Yes, poor woman. But at least she has Willie Mac.'

Last night's confrontation came back to my mind. What had Willie meant about Roy 'never saying sorry'? Why had Roy apologised, when it was the Scot who'd flown off the handle?

We called the dogs back, which took some time with Spiggy as he evidently had no such training. By the time he came to me, he looked as if he'd been diving underwater, not just frolicking in the snow. I led him back inside, where a mop and bucket leant against the wall. Drawing closer, I saw Arthur had also left Spiggy's poo stain on the floor, and sighed. When he'd said he would fetch a mop, I assumed that meant he would also clean it up.

'Men,' I grumbled, squeezing out the mop and running it over the stain.

'What was that?' Birch asked, removing his wellies.

'Never mind.' On reflection, as it was 'my' dog who'd made the mess, it wasn't unreasonable to expect me to clean it.

Spiggy himself was still soaking, so I rubbed him all over, even though the towel from the emergency bag was still damp from the night before. I'd have to ask Roy if I could borrow a fresh towel.

'Sorry, Ronnie,' Birch said as he hung his coat on the rack. 'Looks like more kibble for you.'

'They'll live,' I said, removing my boots. 'Maybe we can cook them some fish and potato this evening.'

The kitchen was now empty, so once again I poured kibble into the dog bowls. Before I could serve breakfast, though, the door to the utility room opened. Arthur emerged, still in pyjamas and looking somewhat surprised to see us there. I noticed his fingers remained bare.

'No luck finding your ring, then?' I asked.

He looked from me to Birch, then to the dogs. 'What's going on?'

'Just some breakfast. I've cleaned up the mess and left the mop in the corridor, by the way.'

'The mop, yes. Thank you.'

'Is Roy down yet?' Birch asked.

'He will be soon,' Arthur replied, walking into the corridor. 'He's always late for breakfast.'

CHAPTER FIFTEEN

Roy might always be late for breakfast, but today he still hadn't emerged by nine o'clock. Birch and I had brushed our teeth, washed, and eaten jam on toast (donating a corner each to the dogs, of course), which I've always found an effective hangover cure when accompanied by strong coffee. Or maybe it's just the coffee.

Was that Roy's problem this morning, too? I wasn't sure exactly how much our host had drunk, but perhaps he'd returned to bed to sleep it off. A luxury for those without dogs to rouse one come rain, shine or hangover.

The trouble was that none of the other guests seemed particularly interested in interacting with us, and with no mobile signal, we were at something of a loss. After breakfast, we joined Arthur in the lounge, where the Christmas tree lights were on and he was engrossed in a big hardback, *Soviet Aircraft of the Cold War, Vol. 1 (1947–1970)*. With his permission we found books to read ourselves: I picked up the Harold Wilson biography Roy had been reading the night before, while Birch pulled down *Target: Spitfire*, the new Max Calibre book which he hadn't yet read. Neither had anyone else in the house, apparently.

'This copy's pristine,' he said to Arthur. 'Haven't you read it yet?'

'Um . . . no, we all read them on the computer. The books are for show. But you're welcome to read it. Enjoy.'

I looked up from the Wilson biography. 'So you buy every book in both paperback and ebook? I'm sure Max Calibre's happy about that, wherever he is.'

'Oh, yes.' Arthur smiled. 'I'm sure of it.'

We settled in with the dogs at our feet, although I kept glancing across at Paul's unfinished jigsaw, wanting to help complete it even though that would be a terrible breach of puzzling etiquette. I contented myself with merely looking at the half-formed London skyline and imagining which pieces I could place. By ten-thirty, though, there was still no sign of Roy and I grew restless. Much as nobody had expected we'd have to stay over, it was rude of him to abandon his host duties and leave us to our own devices. Besides, hadn't he wanted to talk to me about deciphering my father's notes?

'I'm going to check on Roy,' I said. 'Surely he must be awake by now. Birch, keep an eye on the dogs.'

He grunted agreement, engrossed in Jack Spitfire's latest escapades. My intention was to leave both dogs sleeping, but as soon as I stood, Spiggy leapt to his feet and wagged his tail. Given his lack of training, it seemed pointless to try and make him stay, but equally I knew that if I went into the corridor to fetch a lead, Ronnie would think it was time for another walk. So I simply scooped Spiggy into my arms, carrying him towards the stairs in silence. He responded by licking my ear enthusiastically, which was simultaneously delightful and disgusting. Ronnie watched us from his spot at Birch's feet, but didn't move to follow. I quietly closed the door behind us and, with Spiggy still in my arms, made my way up to the bedrooms.

Spiggy barked softly as we headed down the hallway and approached Roy's bedroom door. I shushed him, then knocked quietly.

Perhaps too quietly, judging by the lack of response. I knocked again, louder, and called out, 'Roy? Roy, it's Gwinny. Are you awake?'

Still nothing. I grew concerned.

'Roy! I know we all had a bit to drink last night, but it's almost eleven and we're snowed in. You really should get up.'

Silence. Now quite alarmed, I adjusted my hold on Spiggy and grasped the door handle. I wasn't in the habit of entering bedrooms uninvited, but I'd made my presence known as best I could, so he really had no excuse.

'Roy, forgive me but I'm coming in. I do hope you're decent . . .'

I turned the handle, opened the door, and stepped inside.

My imagination being what it is, I was prepared for lots of things. Roy still unconscious from booze; Roy lying in bed with headphones on, oblivious to the outside world; given his age and that terrible cough, I even braced myself to find Roy lying pale and motionless, having breathed his last during the night.

What I wasn't prepared for was no Roy at all.

I was so surprised that I lost my grip on Spiggy, who leapt down to the ground to begin sniffing. I took another step inside, making sure Roy hadn't fallen out of bed on the other side. But he wasn't on the floor, and in fact the bedclothes were neatly made. All this time we'd assumed Roy was getting up later than everyone else, when instead it looked like he'd beaten us to it.

Where on earth had he gone?

I checked the bathroom, just in case, but it was unoccupied. Spiggy followed me, reminding me of his presence with another bark, so I picked him up again and carried him downstairs into the lounge.

'He's not there,' I said to Birch and Arthur. 'His bed's made, and there's no sign of him. He must have got up before all of us.'

I suddenly remembered the odd scraping sound I'd heard in the night. What time was that, though? All I remembered was that it had been dark. At this time of year, that could be any time until about half past seven, which wasn't long before I got up myself.

'Arthur, didn't you say you saw Roy this morning?'

'That's right. He's always late for breakfast.'

'But he wasn't late, was he? He skipped it altogether.

So he got up shortly before everyone else . . . but then left after we'd all come down for breakfast, without even saying good morning. How odd.'

'He's probably out in the garden,' Arthur said, seemingly unconcerned. 'Or perhaps he's gone into town.'

'In this weather? We're snowed in, remember.'

He looked out the window and frowned. 'Perhaps he's visiting Zoe. They often have things to talk about.'

That seemed plausible, although it would have been an early visit – and a long one, if he was still there. Perhaps he'd gone to patch things up with Willie Mac, after their row last night.

I looked at Birch, still engrossed in his Spitfire book. 'Just one more page in this chapter,' he said, holding up a finger.

Frustrated, I walked to the front window and looked out at the cars and driveway. The snow remained pristine, with no visible tracks of anyone having gone that way.

'Right,' Birch said from behind me, putting the Spitfire novel down on the coffee table. 'Let's see if he's with Zoe, shall we?'

'It's good, then?' I asked in the corridor, as we once again donned boots and clipped the dogs on-lead. 'The book, I mean.'

He nodded. 'Quality's been dipping the last few years, to be honest. More politics, less action, and simpler plots. But Calibre can still write a cracking scene, and he knows his tradecraft.'

'I assume "Max Calibre" is a pseudonym. What's the story there?'

'Nobody knows. No author photos, no appearances, no radio or TV. He's a recluse, by all accounts.'

'He *or* she,' I reminded him. Feminism aside, though, no wonder I wasn't familiar with the books. If the author did no publicity for them, it was amazing they sold at all.

We stepped out into the quad garden. The sky was a cloudless clear blue, which was good news, but the temperature remained freezing and the snow underfoot had begun to harden, its crust cracking as we stepped on it.

From somewhere in the garden we heard a metallic scraping sound. Was it the same noise I'd heard last night? Hard to tell. I turned in a circle, trying to locate it – then Willie Mac appeared around a corner, shovelling snow from the garden's outer path.

'Morning, Willie,' Birch called out. 'No rest for the wicked?'

'Aye, well. Zoe can't get around in snow, and I don't fancy Paul's chances much either.'

'Have you seen Roy?' I asked. 'Arthur thought he might be with Zoe.'

'No, he's not. Try Jane's. Come on, get out of the way.'

Ronnie and Spiggy were both shying away from the advancing Scot and his snow shovel anyway. We moved further into the garden, along the paths Willie had yet to clear among the snow-covered hedges.

'That's us told,' Birch said. 'Someone should explain to him that retirement's supposed to reduce stress, not increase it.'

'Willie's not just Zoe's partner, remember, he's also her carer.' I looked between the smaller houses, trying to recall which was Jane's. 'He seems very capable but I'm sure it's not easy, especially at his age.'

Birch snorted. 'Seems to find being a rude bugger easy enough. So which one is Jane? Paul said she was next door.'

'Yes, but that could mean either house . . . Let's just pick one. It doesn't really matter.'

We did, and when we knocked on the door it was answered by Paul. He looked as surprised to see us as we were to see him.

'I didn't realise you were still here,' he said. 'Can I help you?'

'We can't go anywhere in this snow,' I explained. 'Is Roy there?'

He shook his head. 'Why would he be here? You're the first people I've spoken to this morning.'

'How strange. He wasn't at breakfast, and he's not in his own house. Willie says he's not with Zoe, either,' I added before he could suggest it.

'Then he must be with Jane. The house opposite.' He pointed directly across the quad, then closed the door. I was starting to get the impression that, despite last night's jollity at dinner, the only person who actually wanted us here was Roy himself. I was impressed he'd assembled the others at all.

We trudged back across the length of the garden, pausing at the now-frozen fountain for Spiggy and Ronnie to have a good old sniff and cock their legs, then knocked on Jane's door. She took her time, finally answering while tying her voluminous silver hair into a rough bun.

'Gwinny. Sorry, I was in the shower. What's up?'

'Have you seen Roy this morning?'

'I took one look at the weather and decided to stay in. Why do you ask?'

'Then where can he be?' I explained his apparent vanishing act to Jane. 'Surely he wouldn't have ventured out into snow like this.'

'Does Roy have a key to Willie Mac's shed?' Birch asked.

She laughed. 'Not unless he stole it. That shed's more secure than the house.'

'I do hope nothing's happened,' I said. 'One moment Roy was there, and told Arthur he was on his way down to breakfast. The next, he's disappeared into thin air.'

'Nobody can disappear into thin air,' Jane pointed out. 'Maybe he just . . . I don't know, went for a walk.'

'But I'm wearing his Wellingtons.' I pointed down at my feet. 'And the snow on the driveway is undisturbed.'

'There are four sides to the quad, Gwinny. Have you asked Zoe?'

'Willie Mac says he's not in their house.'

'That's not what I meant. Zoe's in charge of the CCTV recordings. She can check them, see what time he left.'

'You have CCTV? Why hasn't anyone else mentioned that?'

Jane shrugged. 'Arthur's often distracted, and Willie has a lot on his plate at the best of times. Are you *sure* Roy isn't just working in his study? Upstairs, on the left.'

I hadn't even known Roy had a study, let alone that he might be in there. Once again I thought how rude it was to shut himself away when he had two guests, plus dogs, in his house. But one advantage of getting older is that the more the years pile up, the less you care what other people think or do. If I already felt like that now, I could only imagine what it must be like for someone twenty years my senior.

'I'll go check,' Birch said as we walked away from Jane's house.

'No, Roy's less likely to be annoyed by me interrupting. Here, you take the dogs while I run up, I won't be a minute.'

I handed him Spiggy's lead then hurried back into Roy's house, where I slipped off his wellies and, not bothering with slippers, marched through the lounge in my socks. Arthur was still in his chair, staring out of the lounge window with the book of Soviet aircraft open on his lap. He was so lost in thought that he didn't even notice me.

I jogged up the stairs, then regretted it and had to lean on the top newel post for a moment to catch my breath. That's what I got for being both excited and relieved that my imagination had overtaken me, and in a moment Roy and I would have a good laugh about how silly I'd been. Of course he was just in his study, doing . . . whatever it was he did there. Checking his email, perhaps. For several hours. Stranger things had happened.

The first few rooms leading off from the upper hallway were the bathroom, Arthur's room, Roy's room, a storage cupboard and the guest room. All of which I checked just in case, but they were empty. At the far end of the hallway, though, were two more doors. Hidden in shadows, I simply hadn't noticed them before. Thinking about the layout of the house, I guessed these rooms were above the kitchen; the one to the left faced the garden, the other the driveway. As he'd lived here first, it made sense that Roy would have taken dibs on the room with the better view.

I knocked at the door. 'Roy? Roy, are you in there?'

There was no answer, so I turned the handle and pushed open the door.

CHAPTER SIXTEEN

The study was empty.

Actually, it was anything but. The desk looked more like it belonged to an overworked professor than a retired civil servant, covered as it was with piles of paper, books and overflowing in/out trays. A computer, a big square white thing with a large screen and matching keyboard, sat front and centre amongst this mess. Beside it were a mug with *#1 Bestseller* printed on its side, stuffed with pens and pencils; a notepad, itself half-covered by a small tower of books; and, on the other side of the keyboard, a small, neatly stacked column of copy paper. On a shelf behind the computer screen stood a framed photo of two men shaking hands and smiling for the camera. Looking closer, I recognised a much younger Roy alongside Edward Heath.

But there was no sign of Roy now, and upon reflection I should have known there wouldn't be. His cough alone would have alerted us to his presence up here, yet I hadn't heard it at all since waking that morning.

I walked slowly into the room, marvelling at the messy desk and wondering if I'd misunderstood Roy's comments about retirement. Maybe he *was* an overworked professor, having turned from the civil service to . . . something. Teaching other spies, perhaps? Somebody had to. Why not a man who'd spent decades on the job?

The bookshelves supported that notion. Seeing all the reference books on global security agencies, military history and firearms, I wondered if this was where Arthur had obtained his book of Soviet aircraft. There were lots of thrillers and spy novels, too. No surprise Roy and my father had got along. The collection included another set of the Max Calibre books.

Something felt off, but I couldn't put my finger on it.

The desk had two drawers. I pulled them open, not even sure what I was looking for, but hoping there might be something that would suggest Roy's whereabouts. It was a naive hope, of course, and there was nothing of the sort. In fact, the drawers were no less messy than the desk, so even if there had been something significant, I doubt I could have identified it.

It was then I noticed that the top sheet of the stacked paper column on the desk was printed. To the right of the desk, another bookshelf held a combined printer/fax machine, its power light glowing. I flicked through a few sheets of the stack, and saw it was a manuscript. I wondered again if Roy was working as a professor, perhaps even writing a book on his subject.

He wasn't.

Chapter Ten

Jack Spitfire ejected the Browning L9A1 clip into his sweating hands and counted the rounds. Only four bullets remaining, with not a refill in sight. He swore quietly under his breath, slammed the clip back into the pistol and braced his broad shoulders against the pockmarked concrete wall, briefly hiding a patch of anti-DDR graffiti.

Vinovych stayed on the floor. The would-be defector was bleeding badly. His skin was pale, his breath short and hurried. Spitfire considered leaving him. Whitehall would never know.

But then all those secrets locked inside the Russian's head, the secrets of their advanced nuclear programme, would be lost. Great Britain needed those secrets, needed to understand the next major Soviet threat in order to counter it. That was up to the boffins in London, men who wouldn't last a day in Jack Spitfire's world, but who relied on him all the same.

Just like Heidi had relied on him. Before someone squeezed the life out of her, with Spitfire mere yards away.

Focus, Spitfire! Focus on the half-dozen Russians between you, Vinovych and freedom.

I replaced the top page and stood stock still, my mind whirring as puzzle pieces slotted into place and at least one mystery around Roy Singleton became clear.

He hadn't been wrong to call the Spitfire books potboilers, and it was now clear that he'd know better than most. I looked again at the Max Calibre collection on the wall, and realised what had felt off: like the copy Birch had picked out to read downstairs, the spines were intact.

Almost every other paperback on the shelf, whether fiction or non-fiction, bore the telltale cracked spines and curled pages of books that had been read and re-read many times over. *The Day of the Jackal* was barely identifiable, with its battered gold spine, but I recognised the edition from my own bookshelves. Not so the Max Calibre collection. *The Spitfire Affair*, *Spitfire Unbound*, *My Name is Spitfire* . . . these and many more were all untouched. Roy had a full collection that he'd never read – because, I now understood, he didn't need to.

Roy Singleton *was* Max Calibre.

It explained so much. The collection downstairs; Roy himself, gently mocking the books as pulp; Willie Mac, laughing about the overly detailed weapons descriptions; Jane, rolling her eyes and quickly changing the subject. Roy wrote the series under a pseudonym – had done for years, judging by the number of books on the shelf – and it was the quad gang's secret. Did it also explain why Paul, the bossy authoritarian, seemed judgemental of Roy? Did he disapprove?

I took in the desk again with fresh eyes. The piles of paper were manuscript drafts. The books were reference volumes on subjects like the USSR and Cold War firearms. The trays overflowed with correspondence, likely from his publisher. The *#1 Bestseller* mug was a gift, probably from one of the other residents. It all made sense.

Roy had joked that he and Arthur were the 'lazy' ones in the quad, who did nothing but sit around all day watching old films. Obviously he'd lied, but I understood why. He didn't want us to even suspect that he was an author, because from there we might make the leap to his alter ego, Max Calibre.

My gaze settled on a wastepaper basket beside the desk, which appeared to contain discarded pages of printout. I bent down and retrieved some. If the pulpy cliché I'd just read was the good stuff, what were the pages he threw away like?

The answer was: really quite bad. Notwithstanding that I was reading things out of context, they barely made sense. A passage about Jack Spitfire's history in MI6 suddenly transitioned without warning into a conversation between two Russian spies. A romantic scene between Spitfire and an East German femme fatale was interrupted by a meditation on the SIG Sauer P220 pistol, before repeating the same romantic scene again. All the printouts from both desk and bin shared a distinctive streak running down one side of the page, presumably a fault in Roy's printer, so there was no question it was his work. Evidently, his rough drafts were just that.

However, this didn't help me find him. If he wasn't

in here, that left only one room. I left the study and knocked on the door opposite. Once again there was no answer, so I opened the door.

To my surprise, this room was another study, almost a mirror image of the one I'd just left. But despite consisting of the same base elements of desk, computer and bookshelves, it was an exercise in contrast, almost excessively neat and tidy. The shelves held another full set of Max Calibre books, along with many well-thumbed reference manuals and thriller novels, although these were more focused on the traditional British output from the likes of Ian Rankin, Peter James and Lynda La Plante. Unlike in the other room, no reference materials crowded the desk and the in/out trays were almost empty.

This must be Arthur's study. How different the men were.

So neat and tidy was this desk, in fact, that an anomaly caught my eye: the bottom desk drawer, slightly ajar. It was very innocuous, really. Surely Arthur had simply left in a hurry and not fully closed it. But set against the room's almost fanatical precision, anything even slightly off-kilter stood out like a sore thumb.

A slightly open drawer was none of my business, of course. There was even less justification for my rifling through it than there had been in Roy's study. But his disappearance was extremely odd, so perhaps anything else which seemed odd might help furnish an explanation. I reached out and pulled the drawer open, wondering what I might find.

To call my feelings 'anticlimactic' would be an understatement. It was simply a drawer of bits and bobs: ballpoint pens, pencils, sharpeners, paperclips, an unused spiral notebook, a lighter, a box of drawing pins, a pair of scissors, some envelopes. I pushed them around unenthusiastically, annoyed with myself for letting my imagination run wild again, then closed the door and looked around.

It was then I saw another small column of manuscript pages, neatly arranged next to the keyboard, like in the other study. Once again, I couldn't resist a quick flick through. After the shock of discovering Roy was Max Calibre, I thought I was prepared for any possible revelation.

I was wrong.

The pages here were another scene from *Spitfire Behind the Wall*. In fact, they appeared to be a more coherent and sensible version of what I'd found in the other wastepaper basket. In a Berlin hotel room, Jack Spitfire recounted to an East German femme fatale how he'd once overheard two Russian agents talking about a mole in MI6. The woman called him to bed. Unbeknownst to Spitfire, though, his lover had hidden a loaded pistol under her pillow.

These pages were marked by the same thin vertical streak on each page. I saw no printer in this room, so presumably Roy and Arthur shared one. But it now seemed they shared a lot more than that.

Were *both* men Max Calibre? According to the shelves, there were more than twenty books in the

Jack Spitfire series. Were they so prolific because they shared the workload?

Thinking about the pages in Roy's wastepaper basket, a theory formed in my mind. Perhaps Roy did the research and wrote a rough draft, then Arthur cleaned everything up. It had been a long time since I'd chatted to an author at a party, but I recalled that many worked by first producing an almost stream-of-consciousness rough draft, then later rewrote everything so it made sense. Perhaps that was the case here, except that instead of it being one person, they divided the tasks.

Arthur had said the paperbacks were unread because 'We all read them on the computer. The books are for show.' Now it made sense. They didn't actually buy every book in both ebook and print, as I'd assumed. They didn't need to.

I couldn't wait to see Birch's face when I told him. He'd be flabbergasted.

But in the meantime, I still hadn't found Roy, and now I was becoming concerned again. Where could he possibly be? How could he have left the house without any of us noticing – and, apparently, without even disturbing the snow outside? It seemed impossible.

CHAPTER SEVENTEEN

Although my mind was a-whirl, before leaving I remembered to look in the hallway storage cupboard. I was in luck; several fresh towels were folded and piled up on a shelf. With one tucked under my arm, I returned downstairs. Arthur was still reading in his chair.

'I hope you don't mind if we use this,' I said, holding up the towel. 'The dogs get wet every time we take them out in the snow.'

He looked up, startled. He'd been so engrossed in the book, I don't think he'd heard me enter the room.

'Sorry, what? What's going on?'

'I just wanted to check it's OK to borrow a towel. For the dogs.'

'Oh. Oh, yes, if you want.'

It seemed that was as affirmative a response as I could expect. I was tempted to ask him about 'Max Calibre', but I wanted to straighten that out in my own head first. I hung the towel on a hook in the corridor, then slipped on Roy's wellies once again and hurried into the garden. I'd been upstairs much longer than anticipated, and hoped Birch and the dogs hadn't minded waiting in the snow.

'Birch,' I called out, unable to see anything through the tall hedges. 'Sorry I took a while, but he's not there. Where are you?'

There was no answer. Not just from Birch, but from anyone else, or the dogs.

'Birch!' I yelled, walking as fast as I could towards the fountain at the centre of the garden. 'Spiggy! Ronnie!'

The only sound was my own feet, trudging through the snow. Willie had only cleared snow from the garden's outer path, and now there was no sign of him either. Was the quad some kind of black hole, swallowing people up? What on earth was going on?

From somewhere I heard a door open, followed by a call: 'This way, ma'am. Zoe's place.'

I'd never been so glad to hear Birch's voice. I hurried through the snow to Zoe and Willie Mac's house, where the former policeman stood in the open doorway with a mischievous smile on his lips.

'Saw you on the live feed,' he said. 'Zoe's got the CCTV up, come and have a look.'

'Live feed? What? Where are the dogs?' I panted, following him inside.

'Fast asleep under her desk,' he said, chuckling. 'Thought I'd come and check while you were looking in Roy's house. Is he there?'

'No, although I did find – actually, I'll tell you later.' I followed him inside, removing my boots in the hallway. Unlike in Roy and Arthur's house, this hallway was airy and open, with a set of stairs to the first floor and wide, doorless portals leading to downstairs rooms like the kitchen and lounge. There were no Christmas decorations.

'What's on the CCTV?' I asked as we climbed the stairs, passing a folded wheelchair at the bottom. We followed the unmistakeable rail of a stairlift upwards.

'Nothing we haven't already seen, I'm afraid. Zoe can explain.'

The lift chair was at the top and, as we reached the wide, airy landing, I heard someone confidently tapping a computer keyboard.

We walked into a room that, to my untrained eyes, looked like something out of a film set. Zoe sat, in her wheelchair, before a desk with a keyboard and trackball, plus other electronic gadgets I didn't recognise festooned in buttons and lights. Directly in front of her was the biggest computer screen I'd ever seen, two metres wide and curved, wrapping around her and filled with windows that seemed to display nothing but lines and lines of text.

On the wall above it were four smaller screens, arranged in a square grid. Wires snaked between them and the desk gadgets, ending in something that looked like a power strip except for cables. More went behind the desk to who knew where. And under the desk, just as Birch had said, Spiggy and Ronnie were happily curled up and resting. They both cocked an ear when we entered, but didn't move. I realised then that the room was quite warm, and the computers powering Zoe's set-up were probably under that desk. Trust the dogs to find the best source of heat.

One wall-mounted screen contained documents and web pages, none of which I recognised. Another was tuned to the BBC live news channel. The remainder displayed what I assumed, from the dazzling whiteness of snow, were CCTV images of the quad garden and grounds.

'Well, this is a far cry from World War II documentaries,' I said.

'Not everyone is content to wallow in nostalgia for the good old days like Roy and Arthur,' Zoe said, her eyes flicking down to her legs. 'Some of us prefer to focus on the future. There are large portions of my own past I'd rather forget.'

'Aye, forget but not ignore,' said Willie Mac, startling me as he emerged from a corner of the room. I hadn't even noticed he was there. He moved to stand behind Zoe, placing an affectionate hand on her shoulder and fixing us with a stern glare. Zoe reached up to pat his hand, then returned to her computer.

'There's no sign of Roy on the cameras,' she said, pressing buttons on one of her gadgets. 'Look.'

Two screens flickered and changed their viewpoints. The first showed Willie leaving the front door to trudge through the snow, then return with a shovel. The view then changed to the internal garden door, where he stepped out with the shovel and began to clear the path. The second screen showed Birch and me leaving Roy's house to walk Spiggy and Ronnie in the quad garden, then me returning inside by myself. The video time codes confirmed that these images were all from this morning, after breakfast.

'These are recordings from the door cameras,' Zoe explained, pressing more buttons to cycle through them. 'We have one focused over each door for security. Now I'll switch to the live feeds.'

'That's how I saw you come out of Roy's house just now,' Birch said.

The screens displayed images of the four internal doors in turn, looking down from a high vantage point. Nothing was happening on any of them.

'You've looked through all the footage from every camera already?' I asked. 'That must have taken a while.'

'No need,' Willie grunted. 'They're motion-sensitive. Zoe can watch a live feed, but they only record when something moves. After everyone left dinner last night, there's nothing on tape until this morning when I fetched the shovel from my shed and you two walked your dogs.'

'These cameras only show the area in front of the doors, though,' I pointed out. 'You can't see the rest of the garden.'

'That's true, but we also have cameras on the external doors,' Zoe said, pressing more buttons. Now the view switched to look out from above those doors. 'Focusing only on the doorways gives everyone a little more privacy. But it's enough for security, and, regardless, there's no sign of Roy.' She pressed another button to show Birch and me approaching Roy's front door, *sans* snow, which meant it must have been yesterday. 'There's you arriving yesterday . . . now here's you going out the front to walk the dogs . . . and one from our door of Willie coming out to talk to you. And that's your lot. The only other footage is a few seconds here and there during the night, triggered by particularly heavy snowfall or a fox wandering by.'

'Are you sure?' I asked. 'Can we see them?'

'No, I already deleted them.'

'Maybe we can recover the files,' Birch said, reaching for her trackball. 'Know a thing or two about computers myself—'

With surprising speed, Zoe grabbed a plastic ruler from her desk and *thwacked* Birch's hand with it, like a schoolteacher admonishing a naughty pupil. He yelped and recoiled.

'No touching,' she said firmly. 'All deleted files are securely erased and overwritten as a matter of course, so they can't be recovered.' She glanced up at Willie. 'Not that it matters. Unless Roy was wandering around in the night wearing a remarkably lifelike badger suit, I assure you, he was nowhere to be seen. Have you checked his study? He's in there all hours.'

I nodded. 'Yes, I think I heard him last night, but he's not there now. The fact is that Roy definitely isn't in his own house, and I expect if he was here, you'd have noticed. Is it possible he could be in Jane or Paul's place without them knowing?'

Zoe and Willie exchanged glances. 'Anything's possible. People here do tend to wander in and out at will. I'm not sure why he would, though. Unless he's with Jane— Um, I mean, to, um . . .' She trailed off, as if realising she was about to say something she shouldn't.

'Roy and Jane take care of the house business between them,' Willie explained. 'You know, bills and so on.' This was plausible, though something about the way he picked up Zoe's thread gave me pause. Were they hiding something?

'But it was Jane who suggested we check your CCTV,' Birch said. 'Unless . . . blimey, they're not wanting some, um, *extra* privacy by any chance?'

Zoe frowned, then realised what he meant and laughed. 'Roy and Jane? More chance of me and the Pope. Mind you, don't be fooled. She was a looker back in the day.'

'Weren't we all, fifty years ago,' said Willie, running a hand over his grey-stubbled tonsure.

'Regardless, unless Jane is hiding him in a cupboard, he's not there,' I said. 'Willie, could he be in your shed?'

'No. I keep it locked.'

'Perhaps he has a key,' Birch suggested. 'Let's take a look.'

'*No*,' Willie repeated. 'He's not there.'

I sensed something here was going unsaid. 'Neither of you seem especially worried about this situation,' I said.

'Look, Roy spent his career flying a desk,' Zoe said. 'He's not the adventurous type. He also knows this place better than any of us; he's lived here the longest, and supervised the extensions too. Come lunchtime, he'll pop up out of some nook or cranny and wonder what the fuss was about.'

'I hope you're right. I'm more worried we might find him collapsed in one of those nooks and crannies. Do the houses have cellars?'

'No,' said Willie. 'Everything's above ground.'

We thanked them and left, taking the dogs with us – though I'm pretty sure both would have happily stayed under Zoe's warm desk for as long as we'd let them.

'Is it just me, Birch, or do there seem to be a lot of things around here that people don't want us to see? Willie Mac's shed, Zoe's computer, Roy and Jane's clandestine meetings, Arthur's—' I stopped, realising what I was about to say. The irony that I was now the one keeping secrets from Birch didn't escape me.

'What's up?'

'Oh, fiddle. There's something I need to tell you, but let's get inside and find Arthur before I explain.'

CHAPTER EIGHTEEN

We returned to Roy and Arthur's house, removed our boots and towelled down both dogs with the fresh towel I'd acquired. I was starting to wonder if Spiggy was more sponge than Spaniel, with fur possessed of an uncanny ability to retain what seemed like gallons of water.

Of course, the one time I wanted to find Arthur reading in the lounge, he was gone. I checked the kitchen, as it was approaching lunchtime, but he wasn't in there or the utility room either.

'Rum do,' Birch said. 'Another missing resident?'

'No, I don't think so. In fact, if he's where I think he is, this will help explain. Come on.'

I led Birch and the dogs upstairs, to the end of the hallway. Spiggy barked excitedly and sniffed the ground as we passed Roy's bedroom, but I urged him along and we made our way to the doors at the end of the hallway instead.

'This is Roy's study,' I said, opening the door on the left to show Birch.

'Understood,' he replied, not yet understanding. 'Nobody there.'

'That's right.' I closed it and turned to the other door. 'This, on the other hand, is Arthur's study.' I knocked on the door. 'Arthur, are you there? Can we come in?'

'No!' he replied from within, sounding rather panicked. There was a shuffling of chairs and feet, then the door opened a crack and Arthur looked through. 'This room is private. Can I help you?'

I put on my best reassuring smile. 'It's OK, Arthur. I already know. About you, Roy and Max Calibre. I wanted Birch to see for himself, seeing as he's a fan.'

Arthur's expression froze, like a schoolboy caught in the act.

'I don't know what you're talking about.'

'Yes, you do, and I promise your secret is safe with us. We won't tell anyone.'

He looked from me to Birch, then down to the dogs for some reason, and for a moment I thought he was going to slam the door in our faces. But then he exhaled heavily and pulled the door open. He'd finally exchanged his pyjamas for normal clothes, and, as we followed him inside, I saw he'd been working on his computer. But he quickly reached for it and pressed a few keys to make whatever he'd been doing disappear. The previously ajar desk drawer was now firmly shut.

'Care to explain . . . ?' Birch leant in and murmured in my ear.

Arthur turned and said, 'How did you find out? We never told anyone.'

'I came up here earlier, looking for Roy, and found some manuscript pages on his desk. May I?' I gestured to the small stack of pages on Arthur's own desk, and he passed them to me. It was still the femme fatale scene with the gun under her pillow, which I handed to Birch. 'Look familiar?'

His expression as he read the first page changed from puzzlement, to suspicion, to amazement, and finally a gleeful grin.

'You're Max Calibre!' he exclaimed to Arthur joyfully. I couldn't help smiling at his delight, but corrected him.

'Actually, it's both of them,' I said. 'He and Roy write them together, I believe?' Arthur nodded.

'But that's – that's amazing,' Birch said, reaching out to shake Arthur's hand. 'And here we are, in your house. Amazing!' he said again. 'No wonder they're so good. All that real-life experience to draw on.'

'That's right, yes,' Arthur said bashfully. I realised belatedly that he wouldn't be used to this part of being an author. Like actors, authors regularly meet the public if they're lucky enough to be successful. But despite Max Calibre's success, the author's identity was a secret. That meant no appearances, no signings and no meeting fans.

'Does your publisher know?' I asked. 'Or do you handle everything anonymously with them, too?'

'We self-publish. Jane edits, and then Zoe puts them online for us.'

This stopped me dead in my tracks. Roy and Arthur was surprising enough, but now hearing Jane and Zoe were involved as well was completely unexpected. 'Is everyone in this house part of the Max Calibre family?'

'Willie helps us out with weapons research,' Arthur said. That explained why it was the Scot's favourite part of the books. 'Paul doesn't do anything. He's not interested.'

So five out of six of the 'quad gang' were involved in this pseudonymous, and seemingly lucrative, business. And to think I'd wondered what these retirees did all day long.

'Whose idea was it originally?'

'Roy's,' Arthur said with a fond smile. 'He's always been the ideas man.'

That fitted. Roy thought of the quad; Roy arranged the house extension; Roy invited them all to live in it; Roy had the brainwave to collectively become a popular author. Had that always been the plan, or was it something that had come to him once everyone had moved in? That was a question I'd have to ask the ideas man . . . when I found him.

'Were you working on a new book when we came in just now?' I asked.

'Ooh,' Birch said, excited. 'Any chance of a sneak peek?'

'You just had one,' I told him. 'Don't be greedy.'

'I can't tell you what we're working on,' Arthur said. 'Top secret. We only outlined the story last week.'

'Then we'll leave you to get on with it,' I said,

ushering Birch and the dogs towards the door. 'By the way, we still haven't found him.'

Arthur looked puzzled. 'Found who?'

'Roy. Nobody's seen him since you spoke to him this morning.'

'Oh. Well, I'm sure he's around somewhere. He's probably out in the garden. Or perhaps he's gone into town.'

'No, the snow's still piled up outside. And there's no sign of him leaving on Zoe's CCTV, either. I'm a little concerned, to be honest.'

'Don't worry about Roy. He's always been the brains of this house.'

With that curious non sequitur, he closed the door and left us standing in the hallway. We walked back to the stairs, with Birch still in something of a state of shock from the revelation that he was staying in Max Calibre's house, and once again Spiggy barked as we passed the door to Roy's bedroom.

'He keeps doing that every time we pass this door,' I said, stopping. 'I wonder why?'

'Shall we take a look?' Birch suggested.

'I already did. It was the first place I looked for Roy. But maybe there's something else catching Spiggy's nose.'

I opened the door and entered. The room was as I'd last seen it, with no sign of Roy and a very neatly folded bed, which I envied while also knowing I'd never have the time or energy to make my own bed look like that in the mornings.

I held Spiggy on a loose lead, encouraging him to sniff around, but he no longer seemed keen. 'You're the one who barks whenever we walk past,' I said to him, exasperated. 'Show me why, for heaven's sake.' The Cocker Spaniel looked up at me with his big brown eyes, then returned to sniffing the bed in a lacklustre fashion.

I looked around the room in despair. 'I must say, Birch, I'm quite worried about Roy.'

'Out there in the cold, you mean? Can't be easy for an old fellow.'

'Well, yes and no. You're right, if he really did decide to just up and leave, I certainly hope he's somewhere warm and not trudging around in the snow. But I still can't see why he'd have left in the first place, and there's no evidence he did. The snow was already a foot deep by the time we got up, and Arthur had spoken to him not long before. It's simply not possible that Roy could have left without leaving tracks of some kind, especially while avoiding Zoe's cameras.'

'Arthur did say Roy's the brains. He might know a blind spot where the cameras can't see.'

'He'd still disturb the snow, though, wouldn't he? Besides, this is his house. There's no reason for him to sneak around, climbing out of windows or whatever to avoid the cameras . . . is there?'

Birch twitched his moustache. 'We only met this lot yesterday. Don't know them as well as we might. Could have a reason to scarper that we're not aware of.'

'I suppose that's true. But to be honest, I'm now more worried that we're barking up the wrong tree.'

He frowned. 'How so?'

'What if Roy never left the house at all? What if something happened to him . . . or, even worse, someone *did* something to him?'

Birch pondered this. 'Everyone already looked in their houses, and Willie Mac said the shed's been locked. No sign of Roy anywhere.'

'We only have their word for that. If someone attacked Roy and then hid him, they wouldn't tell us, would they? They'd go back inside their house, pretend to look for him even though he was right in front of them, then come back out and tell us they hadn't seen him.'

He nodded, getting the gist. 'Mustn't leap to conclusions, but it's a working hypothesis. We should search the houses independently. Maybe ask everyone to search someone else's, so there's no bias.'

'Unless more than one of them is in on it,' I pointed out. 'No, I don't think we can trust anyone . . . except ourselves.'

CHAPTER NINETEEN

We made ourselves lunch and decided that whatever else was going on, we were certain Roy wasn't in his own house. Beyond that, though, all bets were off. We finished our sandwiches (saving a corner each for the dogs, of course) and decided to go around the quad in order of who was most capable of doing Roy harm. That meant a toss-up between Paul and Willie Mac, and as we'd only just recently come from the latter we decided to call on the former.

Birch raised his hand to knock on Paul's door, then stopped and held out Ronnie's lead for me to take.

'Best if you stay out here with the dogs,' he said. 'I'll look around, give it the copper's eye.'

He meant well, and I loved him dearly, but Birch's male bluster could be annoying at times. 'Absolutely not,' I said, declining to take the offered lead. 'You may have been a DCI, but you know by now that I'm no less capable of spotting the odd and unusual. Besides, you never know what the dogs themselves will sniff out.' I reached up and knocked on the door.

Birch opened his mouth to protest, then thought better of it.

Paul didn't come to the door.

'He answered very quickly before,' I said. 'What's keeping him?'

'Could be indisposed?' Birch suggested.

'Or he might be in trouble. Perhaps we should check.' I turned the door handle. 'Zoe did say the residents here often wander in and out of one another's houses,' I reminded Birch.

'We're not residents,' he reminded me.

'Details, details. I don't think it's unreasonable.'

Paul might not see it that way, but at that moment I was more concerned about Roy than social decorum. I pushed open the door and walked in. Unlike the corridor of Roy's larger house, this door opened directly into a kitchen with a dining area to one side and a door leading off. I heard a low voice from that direction, but couldn't make out what was being said.

What we should have done was call out immediately and announce ourselves, of course. But once again my concern for Roy overruled such thoughts. Instead, I put a finger to my lips for Birch to be quiet, then tiptoed towards the door and peeked around.

It opened into a carpeted hallway, with two more doors and a staircase leading upstairs. Halfway down, Paul stood by a phone table, talking into a handset that looked like it had escaped from the 1990s. His walking stick leant against the stairs, and behind him I saw a metal stand holding more sticks and a couple of umbrellas.

'Look,' he said into the phone with an annoyed tone, 'I don't like this situation, but I'm paying you a good deal of money . . . We're running out of time . . . Yes, of course things will have to change . . . We need a contingency, that's all . . . I want you to be ready as soon as— *What the hell is that dog doing in here?!*'

This final outburst was my fault. I'd been so engrossed in listening to Paul's phone conversation that I hadn't kept a strong grip on Spiggy's lead, and when the Spaniel ran towards him, it slipped from my hand.

'I'm so sorry,' I said, rushing after Spiggy as if we'd only just entered the house. 'You didn't answer your door, and it was open, so, um . . .'

'Stop!' Paul shouted. I wasn't sure if his commanding tone was directed at me or Spiggy, but it worked equally well on us both. 'Shoes off, if you please. Especially after traipsing about in the snow.'

I wasn't sure how much difference it would make, considering Spiggy's wet paws had already met the carpet and Ronnie was about to follow, but I hastily removed my wellies anyway and Birch followed suit.

While Spiggy sniffed enthusiastically at his legs, Paul said into the phone, 'I'll have to call you back,' and replaced the receiver. Then he watched us enter the hallway in our socks and frowned. 'Now. I didn't answer the door, and it was open, so . . . ?'

'So we became concerned, sir,' Birch said, adopting

his policeman's tone. 'My fault, you see. Old copper's instinct kicks in when something seems afoot.'

I retrieved Spiggy's lead and pulled him away from Paul, flashing a quick thank-you smile at Birch for taking the blame.

'What, exactly, is afoot?' Paul asked.

'Roy,' I said. 'He's still missing. We've searched every room in his own house, and everyone else claims they haven't seen him. Arthur did, before breakfast, but since then he appears to have somehow vanished into thin air. And before you ask, Zoe checked her CCTV. There's no sign of Roy leaving the house at any point since last night.'

He took all this in. 'Yes, I agree that's rather odd. But why were you concerned about me?'

Although Birch had come up with that story to cover our intrusion, it wasn't entirely a lie. I decided to come clean with Paul.

'We're worried something has happened to Roy. We thought it would be a good idea to check all the houses, just in case.'

'You mean in case one of us has him squirrelled away somewhere? That hardly seems likely.'

'*When you have eliminated the impossible, whatever remains, however improbable, must be the truth*,' Birch said. 'Sherlock Holmes,' he added.

'Thank you, I'm quite familiar.' Paul thought for a moment, then seemed to make a decision. He picked up his walking stick and leant on it. 'Very well, I'll give you the tour to satisfy your curiosity. Though you'll see for yourselves that it's hardly a palace. If Roy was here, you'd trip over him within two minutes.'

He was right. Downstairs consisted of the kitchen diner, a cloakroom, the hallway and the lounge. I'd already observed that the kitchen was meticulously neat and tidy, with utensils, pots, pans and crockery all carefully arranged and so clean they practically sparkled. A shelf of cookery books was arranged by size. The lounge was sparse and orderly, its shelves filled not with books but jigsaw puzzles. A large table in front of the sofa contained a work in progress, a pastoral scene with completed edges but lots to do in the centre. In fact, there were no books whatsoever in the lounge, and certainly nothing by Max Calibre. The stone walls and old flooring reminded me that this was part of the original farmhouse, along with Roy's place. Unlike Roy's, however, there was not a shred of seasonal decoration. Christmas was not celebrated in this house.

We checked the under-stairs cupboard at Paul's insistence, even though I felt faintly silly doing so, then went upstairs to find a bathroom, bedroom and study. The bathroom was as tidy as the kitchen, but the bedroom and study were a different matter. In those rooms, we found a morass of clutter: not messy *per se*, but simply filled with lots and lots of *stuff*. This took me by surprise, and gave me quite an existential worry when I wondered if this was how other people felt upon seeing my own house. Admittedly, not many had in recent years, apart from Birch and my best friend Tina, but that wasn't the point. It made me determined to sort things out when I returned home.

In the bedroom we found piles of clothes, boxes of old family photos, and even binders and archive boxes, overflowing with files and papers. In one corner, surrounded by this clutter, was an exercise machine: a contraption of weights and bars that would have been more at home in a gym. I looked from it to Paul, and his walking stick.

He bristled, defensive. 'Healthy body, healthy mind, or so the doctors tell me.'

After checking the wardrobes, again at his insistence, we moved on to the study and found even more clutter. More archive files and binders, either boxed up or simply stacked on top; columns of magazines ranging from *The Economist* to *What Car?* to the *Radio Times*; papers, printouts and stationery that covered the desk so fully I had to take the existence of the surface underneath on faith. A laptop sat, plugged in and charging, atop several manila files.

'Quite a contrast,' Birch said. 'Public versus private.'

'Yes, well, normally nobody else comes in here. Including Roy, as you can see.'

That much was obvious, and we would have left there and then if not for Spiggy. Since his escape act downstairs I'd kept a tight grip on his lead, but that didn't stop him from sniffing around. Now he took interest in a tower of *House & Garden* in one corner of the room, and the next thing we knew the tower was toppling like a house of cards. Magazines slid to the floor, their pages flapping open and spines colliding, and soon we stood amid a carpet of glossy paper. Spiggy scurried back to me, wearing a mildly alarmed expression but wagging his tail. I frowned at him and wagged a finger in admonishment, which allowed me to avoid Paul metaphorically doing the same to me.

But re-flooring the room wasn't the only thing bringing down the magazines had done. It also revealed something tucked into the corner: a small safe with a combination lock.

'Is that where you keep all your spy equipment?' I said, trying to make light of the situation.

Paul stiffened, failing to see the funny side. 'Legal documents and house deeds. More importantly, you'll see there is no Roy Singleton lurking in the corner. If he really is hiding somewhere, it's not in my house.'

I remembered Roy laughing about Paul's missing torch, saying his mind must be going. But standing before him now, he seemed like the very last person whose mental faculties would be a concern.

'Paul?' a woman's voice called from downstairs. 'Are you there?'

Both dogs' ears pricked up, and they pulled us along the hallway to the top of the stairs. Looking down, I recognised Jane standing in the kitchen doorway, bundled up in even more layers than usual against the cold.

'We're all up here,' I said.

'Sorry, I didn't realise you had guests. Shall I come back later?'

'Not at all. They were just leaving,' Paul said from behind us.

Taking the hint, Birch and I led the dogs down the stairs. Ronnie made a beeline for Jane, wagging his tail and sidling up against her legs. She smiled and fussed him while removing her boots.

'I didn't mean to interrupt,' she said. 'Paul and I often have a natter over lunch.'

I couldn't imagine anyone in the quad less likely to 'have a natter' than Paul. Perhaps it was more the case that Jane did the nattering while making lunch, and in exchange Paul listened to her.

'They're looking for Roy,' he explained. 'They thought he might be here.'

Jane crouched down, still fussing Ronnie. The Lab's tail rotored as if it might make him airborne. 'You haven't found him? Why did you think he'd be in Paul's house?'

'Because he must be *somewhere*,' I said, and once again explained his apparent vanishing act in defiance of snow and cameras.

'Thought we'd check everyone's houses,' Birch added afterwards. 'Started with Paul, that's all. Could just as easily have started with your house.'

Jane laughed. 'I can assure you he's not there. But I suppose you don't want to take my word for it, do you? Feel free to pop over there and take a look, the door's open.'

'Oh, we wouldn't want to look around without you being there,' I said.

Leaving Ronnie bereft, she took a step forward. She was taller than me, and as she looked down all pretence of joviality disappeared from her expression. For the first time since we'd arrived, I felt I was seeing the real Jane.

'Guinevere,' she said quietly, 'like everyone else around here, I spent forty years working with professional liars. It's plain as the nose on your face that you'd like nothing better than to poke around my house, so get over there and do so with my blessing. I can assure you that Roy is not there, and what's more you'll find nothing more incriminating than a subscription to *Weight Watchers*.' As suddenly as it had vanished, her smile reappeared. 'Just promise me you'll put everything back where you found it, OK?' She stood aside to let us pass.

Birch and I re-donned our boots in the kitchen, bid Paul and Jane goodbye, and stepped back into the garden.

'Jane aside, don't you think that was all rather odd?' I said when the door had closed behind us. 'Paul seemed more bothered by my asking what was in his safe than he was about Spiggy making a mess.'

'To be honest, I was focused on making sure Ronnie didn't knock anything else over. Interesting, though. Especially in light of what Paul said on the phone. "We're running out of time" and "we need a contingency" . . . not just passing the time of day, was he?'

'No, he wasn't. Thank you for taking the blame when Paul caught us, by the way. Very noble of you.'

Birch's bright blue eyes twinkled with mischief. 'Nobody thinks twice about a copper poking his nose in. Always a good fallback. Now, what about Jane?'

'I'm sure there's more to her than the shambolic mother hen she wants us all to see. But I'm struggling to imagine how that might connect to Roy disappearing.'

'Revenge for all those demands to cook and make tea?'

'If that were sufficient grounds, Birch, there wouldn't be a man left alive in the world. Come on, let's take a look in her house. With her rather dubious blessing.'

CHAPTER TWENTY

We took the cleared path around the edge of the garden to Jane's house. Even though we'd been invited, it felt odd walking in without knocking. At least this time we knew there was nobody else in here.

Apart from Roy, potentially, I supposed. Jane had been quite certain we wouldn't find him. Because she was innocent . . . or because he was hidden away somewhere she was confident we wouldn't look?

My resolve faltered. Did I really think one of Roy's own housemates – people who by all accounts had lived with him for many years – would kidnap him and hold him prisoner? Or worse? Suddenly, our self-appointed task seemed absurd.

'What are we doing, Birch?' I said as we removed our boots. Like Paul's single-occupant house, the garden door opened directly into the kitchen. The build was newer, with every wall and corner plumb-straight rather than slightly off as old stone-built houses so often are, but the layout was identical to the older house opposite.

'Looking for Roy,' Birch replied simply. 'Got to be around here somewhere. People don't vanish into thin air.'

His bluntness dispelled the doubts that had begun to creep into my mind. No, people *don't* vanish into thin air. Roy must be somewhere here in the quad, and unless all six of the 'gang' were playing a horrible trick on us, the fact that nobody had seen him was seriously concerning. Why not Jane, anyway? If everyone in the quad had previously worked for the secret services, then surely they were all adept at performing devious tasks in secret. Even a secretary.

Newly emboldened, I checked the cloakroom then led us through the hallway into the lounge. It wasn't quite the mess I'd expected, but it was definitely a contrast to Paul's place. A small plastic Christmas tree stood on a table in one corner, with small garlands of tinsel and lights, but that was the sole concession to Christmas. By contrast, the room was abundant with baskets of fabric and thread, buckets of yarn and wraps of knitting needles. In the centre of it all, a large sewing machine took pride of place, and nearby stood a cushioned chair upon which a work in progress was entangled around two needles. I hadn't looked at a knitting pattern since my schooldays, so couldn't begin to guess what it would be. Anything from socks to a jumper.

'I suppose this explains Jane's wardrobe,' I said, taking in the scene. 'She makes her own clothes.'

Birch didn't reply. I looked behind me to make sure he was still in the room and found him examining a series of framed pictures on the mantelpiece, while Ronnie sniffed around the fireplace. Thankfully a metal guard stopped the Lab from shoving his nose in the coals.

'Doubt she made these,' Birch said as I joined him. The pictures were old photos, their age evidenced by softness and colour tone, although some were black and white. It was mostly obvious from their subject, though: a much younger Jane, slim, beautiful and fashionably outfitted, posing and smiling in swinging London. 'She could have been a model,' he added, evidently a bit smitten, though I couldn't blame him. As Zoe said, in her day, Jane had been a catch.

'Unfortunately, a young woman in the sixties and seventies who *didn't* want to be a clothes hanger had limited job options,' I reminded Birch. 'It was hardly a picnic for my generation, but Jane and Zoe had it worse. At least she got to be a secretary in an exciting profession.'

'Must have been fairly well paid for a typist. Look at all these.' Further down the mantelpiece were pictures of Jane in foreign locations. She sat in a bustling Parisian café, gazed across the wide river flowing under a European bridge, and smiled from under a sun hat in front of the Parthenon. 'Wasn't cheap to travel like that, in those days. I think that's Berlin,' he added, pointing at the photo on the bridge.

'Perhaps she saved all her wages to go abroad,'

I suggested. 'Anyway, unless he's buried under a hundredweight of wool, Roy's not here. Let's look upstairs.'

We checked the under-stairs cupboard on the way, finding it filled with a combination of household cleaning appliances and more fabric, then mounted the stairs. The bathroom was clear. So was the bedroom, which was much tidier than Paul's but did contain a pile of clothes and underwear stacked on a chair, at which Birch blushed. Amused, I ushered him out and into the second bedroom.

In Paul's house, this had been a study, but here it was more like one of my own spare rooms in Chelsea. An open rail was over-filled with clothes wrapped in plastic, many dating back to at least the eighties, judging by the shoulder pads. Around it were boxes of accessories, ranging from scarves to gloves to berets. These gave way to boxes of fabric, skeins by the dozen, books and books of clothes patterns, and at least two more sewing machines that I could see.

'What was that about him being buried under wool?' Birch said.

Joking aside, there was no sign of Roy and it was all we could do to hold Spiggy and Ronnie back from sniffing the entire room from top to bottom, so we retreated and closed the door.

'Jane's is a bust, then,' I said. 'That only leaves Zoe's house—'

'Are you upstairs?' Jane's voice called out.

With a strong sense of déjà vu, we walked to the top

of the stairs and found her looking up at us, smirking.

'I said you wouldn't find him. Or anything else.'

We descended, letting the dogs go first. Once again, Ronnie went immediately to Jane and leant against her while she fussed his ears and shoulders. 'Come to think of it, I didn't see any *Weight Watchers* either,' I said.

'That was a joke, Gwinny. I haven't worried about that in forty years.'

'We saw the photos. You were very glamorous. Birch thought you should have been a model.' I knew he'd go red at my mentioning it, but I had a point to pursue.

Jane smiled. 'I was asked once or twice, believe it or not. But I was happy where I was.'

'Yes, a secretary at MI6,' I said. 'Except . . . now I don't think you were. It's a nickname, isn't it?'

'I'm sure I have no idea what you mean.'

'All that foreign travel, on a secretary's wages? I suppose you could have come from money, but there's a simpler explanation. People always underestimate women, don't they? I almost fell for it myself.'

Jane's demeanour changed, becoming serious once again, and a moment of understanding passed between us.

'*Plus ça change, plus c'est la même chose*,' she finally said with a perfect Parisian accent. 'Paul once said I looked like nothing more than a secretary, you see. It was an enormous help. A free-spirited young girl from London, wide-eyed at exotic Europe? The perfect cover.'

'So you weren't a secretary at all?' Birch said, catching

up. 'You were a real spy, going on missions?'

'Don't think that admins and desk handlers aren't "real" spies too,' she replied, gently admonishing him. 'Neil Armstrong may have been the first man to set foot on the moon, but it took years of work by thousands of people on the ground to get him there.'

'So why is it only Roy and Arthur who write the Spitfire stories?' I asked, enjoying her surprise at my knowing the truth behind Max Calibre. 'Arthur said they come up with the stories and write the books, then you edit them.'

'Is that what he told you?' Jane smirked again. 'Then that must be what happens.'

Evidently, Arthur had downplayed her part, which shouldn't have surprised me. Women are underestimated, yes, but even more frustrating is how frequently our work gets brushed over. I was suddenly reminded of Colin Prendergast failing to remember me. A troublesome woman, disposed of and forgotten.

'So you do work on them together. The three of you, refugees from MI6.'

'Actually, Arthur was MI5, which is why he gets a bit of stick now and then. But, unlike Roy, he did lots of fieldwork, and has significant experience to draw on. Not that the Spitfire books are especially realistic, you understand. They're about as close to operational reality as Miss Marple is to police work. If anything, we go to extra lengths to fictionalise things.'

'Apart from the weaponry, which Willie Mac helps you with.'

She smiled, impressed. 'You really have done your homework. Roy, Arthur and I work out a story; they write a first draft, with William's help on weapons; I rewrite the final draft to make it coherent and read like a single author; then Zoe publishes them online and deals with the accounts. She's a few years younger, so she knows all about computers and things.'

Given Zoe was several years older than me, this remark made me feel like a Luddite.

'Why isn't Paul involved?' Birch asked.

'He was quite senior in operations. Sometimes that meant sending officers away on missions with . . . let's say, a low chance of returning home.' A dark cloud passed over Jane's expression. 'You can imagine the effect that has.'

'Probably not as bad as the effect on the officers he sent out,' Birch said, not unkindly. Jane nodded in quiet agreement.

'This is all fascinating,' I said, 'but it doesn't bring us any closer to finding Roy. Do you really have no idea where he could be?'

'None at all. I need to find him myself, to check his arms.' Seeing my confusion, she explained: 'Sleeve length. I'm knitting him a cardigan.'

As we put our boots back on to leave, the futility of the situation struck me again.

'Hold on, Birch. Jane, can we use your front door to get out to the grounds? I'm sure the dogs would enjoy a bit of a frolic.'

'Of course. It's through the hallway, I'll show you.'

She led us to a door at the foot of the stairs and unlocked it. The deep snow outside was untouched from the house to the stream, and on into the trees. We let the dogs off-lead and they gleefully ran, revelling in the open space. Snow crystals sparkled in the drifts, at least until Spiggy and Ronnie took it in turns to colour them yellow.

Birch waited until we'd walked far enough into the field to be out of earshot, then said, 'We haven't searched Zoe's house yet.'

'I know, but really, what do we expect to find? Is it likely that a paraplegic and her boyfriend-slash-carer have knocked Roy unconscious and stuffed him in a cupboard without anyone else noticing?'

'We've noticed. The others don't seem particularly worried that he's missing.'

'Yes, that does bother me. Although I suppose, with them all being spies, they've had a lifetime of staying calm in odd situations.'

The dogs worked as a double act: Ronnie churned up snow with his nose, digging trenches which Spiggy used as launching points to hop into the drifts like a snowbound deer, before returning to Ronnie's side and doing it all over again.

The sun hung low on the horizon, and it would be dark again soon. Where had the day gone? I took Birch's hand and leant on his arm.

'I'm so sorry you missed your Christmas lunch. If I'd known, I'd never have stayed for dinner last night.'

He kissed me gently on the head. 'It was as much my

decision as yours. Should have paid more attention to the forecast.'

'At least we're together. If I'd come here on my own and got snowed in, you'd be frantic. And Spiggy wouldn't be having nearly as much fun,' I added, watching the Cocker gambol around in the snow with Ronnie.

Then, without a moment's hesitation, Spiggy jumped into the freezing stream.

CHAPTER TWENTY-ONE

Spaniels are drawn to water like moths to a flame, no matter the weather. Nevertheless, with the temperature still below zero, I worried Spiggy might spend too long in the freezing water without realising until it was too late.

'Spiggy, *come*!' I yelled, running towards the stream, hoping he could hear me and wondering if he'd obey regardless.

There was little sign of that as I reached the banks, scanning up and down the water to locate him. I found him upstream, splashing against the flow, some way behind Willie's shed. I'd only walked here once before, and things had looked very different yesterday. I couldn't see the extent of the banks for the snow, so took things carefully as I made my way towards Spiggy, who remained oblivious.

Birch jogged up beside me, having already put Ronnie on-lead to stop him following the Spaniel into the water.

'Needs training, that one,' he said, letting Ronnie pull him ahead.

'You don't say? I'll be sure to let the rescue know.'

I regretted my sarcasm a little when Birch suddenly stumbled, slipped and fell on his back in the snow. I heard the breath get knocked out of him, and he lost his grip on Ronnie's lead. Rather than immediately jump in the water, though, Ronnie instead ran back to Birch, concerned for his owner's safety.

'Are you OK?' I said, taking hold of Birch's shoulders and trying in vain to sit him upright. He weighed twice as much as me, and the best I could manage was to tug on his coat.

He caught his breath and groaned in pain. 'Fine . . . tripped . . . that's all . . .' he grunted, but it was clear from his expression that he wasn't 'fine'. An injury while stuck with no way of getting to a doctor would be the icing on the cake for this trip. I'm no more superstitious than the next actor, but it really did seem like fate wasn't keen on us coming here.

From the water, Spiggy barked. I thought he was simply excited, but when he kept going I began to wonder. Spaniels are gun dogs, bred to flush game and retrieve it. Was he alerting me to something? Birch had by now sat upright and had hold of Ronnie, which were my main concerns, so I turned my attention to the stream in time to see Spiggy suddenly dive under the water, just a few feet from where I stood. He thrashed his head around, then re-emerged and barked again.

I now saw that a stick extended over the water, near

the spot on the bank where Birch had tripped. I reached down to clear the snow and, sure enough, a short, thick branch stuck out of the ground at a low angle. It didn't look natural, but who would shove a stick into the bank like that? And, come to think of it, had it been there yesterday when we'd walked along this same bank? We hadn't come this far upstream, so I couldn't be sure.

Spiggy barked again. Following the line of the branch I saw a cord tied around its end, hanging down into the stream and pulled taut. Something was attached to that string. Something that Spiggy had found, but been unable to retrieve.

'I think I've found the stick you tripped over,' I said to Birch. 'There's something tied onto it.'

I crouched in the snow, took hold of the cord and tugged it. It moved a little. Whatever it held had weight, but didn't feel so heavy it was immovable. Making sure of my footing, I took hold with both hands and lifted.

A sports kit bag emerged. The other end of the cord tied its handles together, and the zip was closed, though it was far from impermeable. Water poured off its surface and from within. Spiggy watched it with wide eyes, as if it were prey.

I lifted the bag onto the bank and unzipped it, keeping it at arm's length. To my relief, nothing burst out, moved or made a noise, so I leant over and peered inside.

What I saw made me recoil, and I fell back into the snow. Spiggy barked.

'What is it?' Birch asked, worried. 'What's in the bag?'

I couldn't quite articulate what I saw, so I reached

178

inside and removed part of the bag's bizarre contents, holding it up for him to see.

'Is that . . . a crow?' he gasped.

It was. More specifically, a jackdaw, if I wasn't mistaken. Quite dead, and sealed within a glass jar with a watertight clip-down rubber seal, the sort of thing one might use to infuse kitchen herbs.

Inside the bag were three more jars, all with similarly deceased contents. A grey squirrel, a sparrow and a long-tailed rat with one foreleg missing.

'What . . . the blazes . . .' Birch breathed. Despite his bravado, he was evidently still in pain.

'This must be what Spiggy scented,' I said. 'We were downstream, so perhaps it carried through the water.'

I looked back towards the house, thinking again about the lack of pets. Then I replaced the jars, zipped up the bag, and dropped it back in the stream. Spiggy finally scrambled up onto the bank, his gun dog mission accomplished. After he'd shaken himself off, I clipped his lead back on and picked up Ronnie's.

'Come on, let's go back inside and sit in front of the fire. We could all do with a rest after that.'

Birch struggled to his feet, grimacing with pain. 'Dead animals in jars . . . classic sign of a psychopath,' he said, limping along beside me on what now appeared to be a twisted ankle.

'Yes, it's the sort of thing you read about, isn't it? But whose collection is it?' I didn't need to wonder why it was in the stream. That was obviously to keep it hidden.

'Perhaps best not ask or even mention it just yet. Keep our powder dry.'

'I just had a terrible thought. If someone's already using the stream to hide carrion, what if Roy's been dumped in there too?'

Birch shook his head. 'Spiggy would have found him first . . . scent much stronger than an animal in a jar. Besides, the stream's not that deep . . . we'd have seen the body.'

'Yes, you're right. I'm just being paranoid now. Come on, let's get you inside.'

My concern for Roy's safety was greater than ever. What on earth was going on here at the quad?

CHAPTER TWENTY-TWO

We finally limped inside Roy's house, and I helped Birch get his wellies off. His left ankle felt quite badly swollen, and every time he tried to bend over he clutched at his back. I dried the dogs, although with Spiggy having been literally submerged I once again could only get him down to 'damp' rather than 'dry'. I'd need to borrow another towel, too.

The lounge was empty, and Birch gratefully lowered himself onto the sofa. Ronnie leapt up beside him and flopped down with his head on Birch's lap. I wished I'd thought to put a throw of some kind over the cushions, but it was too late for that now.

'Just need to sit down for a bit,' Birch said, wincing. 'I'll be fine.'

'I doubt that. Your ankle's the size of a tennis ball.' I pointed at the offending joint, which had already swollen to a sizeable lump. 'It sounds like you did something to your back, as well.'

He harrumphed and deflected while I tried to establish what exactly he'd done, but regardless it was clear he wasn't going anywhere for a while.

'Then let's stay here. Zoe's house can wait, and I'm sure the dogs want a rest after being out in the snow.' Spiggy actually looked like he could go a few more rounds, but Ronnie had already begun to snooze. I had an idea. 'Hold on to Spiggy for a moment. I'll find some ice.'

I crossed the corridor into the kitchen and found a tray of ice cubes in the freezer. I emptied some into a dog bag from my pocket, tied it off, then returned to the lounge with it wrapped in the towel I'd just used on Spiggy; it was already wet so wouldn't make any difference now. Birch pressed the cold compress to his ankle, hissing as it touched.

'That should help. Now stay here while I fetch another towel from upstairs. We'll have to start borrowing them from the other residents at this rate.'

I made for the stairs, but turned back at a strangled sound from Birch. Spiggy was pulling at his lead, obviously wanting to come with me.

'OK, fine. Give him here.'

I took the Cocker's lead and led him upstairs to the storage cupboard. Once again, he barked as we passed Roy's bedroom.

'Yes, Spiggy, thank you, but he's not in there,' I murmured. 'We already checked.'

I was about to open the cupboard when I heard movement from the end of the hallway, and decided to mention what had happened to Arthur. I knocked on his study door and opened it without waiting. Arthur sat at his desk, staring at a blank screen.

'Is Roy's disappearing act distracting you?' I asked.

Startled, he whirled around in his seat and stared at me, then Spiggy, then me again. 'What's going on?' he said.

'Sorry, I didn't mean to make you jump. Listen, Birch fell outside in the snow, so I've had to use that towel I borrowed to make an ice compress. Can I borrow another, for the dogs?'

'Um . . . yes, yes. Whatever you need. Whose ankle?'

'Birch's.' I didn't want to mention the stick or dead animals. 'He fell in the snow. He's in the lounge, resting.'

'Of course. Is Roy with him?'

'I'm afraid not. We still haven't been able to find him. It's utterly baffling.'

Arthur stood, and once again I was struck by his size. Just about everyone is statuesque compared to me, but he really was a man-mountain. If he wanted to cause anyone harm, I had no doubt he'd do so with ease. That said, I simply couldn't imagine it of this mild-mannered, softly spoken man, although of course appearances can be deceptive. Especially when dealing with a former spy. Jane had said Arthur had lots of field experience working for MI5, and I doubted it was all picnics and flower arranging.

'I'll find him,' he said. 'He'll be about somewhere.'

We both retreated into the hallway, and I took two

more clean towels from the cupboard while Arthur walked on ahead.

Yet again, Spiggy barked as we passed Roy's bedroom door. But now something about it struck me as different, and I could have kicked myself for not realising earlier. It wasn't just a casual bark. It was the same kind he'd made fifteen minutes ago, when he found that bag in the stream. The sort of bark a gun dog made to alert its owner.

It always happened here, in this particular spot of the hallway. I'd assumed Spiggy was barking at Roy's bedroom, because it was the closest door. But now that I observed him properly, I saw he wasn't looking at the bedroom, or even anywhere in particular. His head tilted from side to side, then at me; then he sniffed the air, and finally the ground.

I turned in a circle, scanning the hallway. It was minimally decorated, and I saw nothing that might give off an odd or alarming scent. The carpet, the painted balustrade at the top of the stairs, an occasional table with a vase of dried flowers, light switches on the walls . . . above that was nothing but coving, the ceiling, a hatch . . .

Which Spiggy sat directly beneath.

'Arthur!' I called out.

He'd already begun to make his way downstairs. From halfway down he turned around. 'What's going on?'

'Does this hatch lead to an attic? Can you open it?'

'Nobody goes up there.'

184

'Every time we walk past this spot, Spiggy barks and gets agitated. I thought he was barking at Roy's bedroom door, but then I realised . . .' I pointed up at the hatch. 'We haven't searched the attic.'

Arthur walked past me to the hallway cupboard. From inside he withdrew a long metal rod with a hooked end. 'There's a ladder built in,' he said, hooking the rod through a loop in the hatch. 'Stand back.'

With a single easy pull the hatch opened and a folding ladder dropped out, automatically lowering under the effect of gravity. With a metallic scraping sound it extended to the floor in three sections.

Spiggy barked, looking up into the darkness of the attic. Arthur didn't move.

'You should probably take a look up there,' I suggested. 'For Roy.'

'Nobody goes up there,' he said again, still not moving.

'Oh, for heaven's sake. Here, hold on to Spiggy.' Losing my patience, I handed him the dog lead and placed a foot on the ladder, gripping its narrow side railings with both hands. If I'd given myself time to consider what I was doing I might have backed out, so I didn't. Instead I started climbing, one foot above the other.

It was only when my head entered the dark of the attic that I thought about adding some light. Holding on with one hand, I fumbled in my pocket for my phone and turned on the torch. Dust swirled in its beam as I scanned the space in front of me, finding nothing but cardboard and plastic packing boxes, carpet offcuts, bin liners filled with who knew what and tied off. Cobweb strands reflected the light, and I prayed there were no rats up here – with or without a missing forepaw. I turned in a circle, adjusting my footing on the ladder.

That turned out to be a mistake, because when I yelped and recoiled I only had my heels on the rungs and lost my footing. I dropped my phone and flailed my arms, somehow managing to grab enough of the railing on the way down to descend slowly, almost tumbling in slow motion until I lay at Arthur's feet, winded but intact. Spiggy whimpered and licked my face.

'What's the matter?' Arthur said dumbly. 'Are you all right?'

'I found Roy,' I gasped, closing my eyes. The image of his bloodshot eyes, so close and reflecting my phone light, remained seared into my retinas. 'I think he's dead.'

CHAPTER TWENTY-THREE

Perhaps I shouldn't have been surprised that Arthur was the only resident who seemed genuinely upset, but the others' stoic reaction felt rather odd. Maybe spies were used to seeing their friends turn up dead.

When I'd convinced Arthur I wasn't joking, he'd fallen to his knees and wept. I'd left him there, with instructions not to move, while I ran downstairs. After hastily handing off Spiggy to Birch and hanging the fresh towels in the hallway, Paul had been my first port of call. He'd fetched Zoe and Willie while I went to tell Jane.

Roy's house had no stairlift, so Willie Mac had offered to carry Zoe up, but she declined. Birch could probably have limped up the stairs, but he politely offered to stay with Zoe instead, keeping her and the dogs company.

Paul and Willie fetched the body down from the attic while Jane and I watched from the hallway below.

Upon laying him on the floor, Willie closed Roy's staring, bloodshot eyes. I belatedly realised that we were all still wearing our outdoor boots, of which Roy would have disapproved. But this wasn't the time to worry about the carpet.

'What was he doing up there?' Paul wondered aloud. 'Did he fall and crack his head open? His cough's been getting worse lately.'

I didn't see any sign of damage to Roy's head, but checking for it revealed something else entirely. I opened his collar to reveal a narrow welt of red skin encircling his throat.

'This wasn't an accident,' I said, pointing to the injury. 'Along with the bloodshot eyes, that suggests he was strangled.'

Willie clapped a hand on Arthur's back. 'Maybe you can put this in your next book,' he said jovially.

'William!' Jane admonished him.

'I'm joking, I'm joking,' he said, shaking his head. 'Christ. Who'd want to garrotte Roy?'

'A burglar?' Paul suggested. 'Some items have gone missing, remember.'

'There was nothing on Zoe's CCTV,' I reminded him. 'Besides, would a burglar really kill someone over your torch, or Willie's gloves?'

'No,' he admitted. 'We can be confident Zoe herself is innocent. She couldn't even get up to this floor, let alone the attic. It's not looking good for the rest of you, though. Does anyone feel like confessing right away, to save us the trouble?'

The residents looked at each other warily, only now realising the implications of what he meant. If this wasn't the work of a disturbed burglar, then someone in the house must have killed Roy.

Willie and Jane both turned to look at me.

'Don't be absurd,' I protested. 'You can't think Birch or I did this. We'd never even met Roy before yesterday.'

'According to you,' said Willie. 'But how do we know? You could be a pair of travelling serial killers.'

I ignored this ridiculous comment. 'Paul, you said "the rest of you". Why couldn't it be you?'

'Because I know it wasn't. Besides, while I'm nowhere near as immobile as Zoe, I'd struggle somewhat.' He lifted his walking stick in explanation.

'Nonsense. You have that one-man gym in your bedroom to stay in shape, and I imagine strangling someone requires only upper body strength.'

I couldn't help glancing at Arthur as I said this. The big man looked horrified. 'I'd never hurt Roy.' He looked at the others with panic in his eyes. 'You know that. I'd never hurt him.'

'Calm down, Arthur,' Paul said, fixing me with a disapproving glare. 'Nobody's accusing you of anything. Besides, it doesn't take much strength to garrotte someone. Just patience.'

'Patience?' I repeated.

'Aye, it's not like the films,' Willie explained. 'Strangling isn't done and over in ten seconds flat. It takes a good minute, at least, to fully choke someone.'

I stopped myself from asking how both men somehow

knew this, because, on reflection, I could guess the answer. Something else then struck me.

'It's quiet, too, isn't it? If you shoot someone, everyone will hear the report. If you stab them, they scream. But garrotting not only kills, it silences. This happened right above our heads, and we didn't hear a thing.' The others murmured agreement. I placed a foot on the ladder and climbed back up into the attic, this time activating my phone torch before I reached the top.

'What are you doing?' Paul called up to me.

'Looking for a garrotte,' I replied. 'Or anything else that might give some idea of what happened.'

There was no garrotte, at least not that I could see from my position on the ladder. I wasn't about to climb all the way in and start searching the spider-infested space. But before I could climb back down something glinted in the torch beam. It lay on the attic floor, a few inches beyond my reach.

'Can I borrow a handkerchief from someone?' I called down.

Paul took one from his pocket and held it up for me. 'If you're going to sneeze, better to do it down here so you don't contaminate the crime scene.'

'No, it's not that. Hang on.' I climbed another step and placed one knee on the attic boards, stretching out to retrieve the object in Paul's handkerchief. Then I returned down the ladder and held it out for all to see.

A golden signet ring, engraved with the initials *AH*.

Paul took one look at it and turned to Arthur. 'That's yours, isn't it? What's it doing up there?'

Arthur looked very confused. 'Yes, that's mine. Thank you,' he said to me, reaching for it. I held on to it.

'This morning you said you couldn't find your ring,' I said. 'What's it doing up there, near Roy's body?'

'Maybe Roy was the thief after all,' Paul suggested. 'My torch, Arthur's ring . . .'

Willie rolled his eyes. 'Don't be daft. It must have come off in the struggle. Arthur strangled him.'

'No!' Arthur protested again. 'I'd never hurt Roy.'

'Then why was your ring up there?'

Something didn't make sense. 'If Arthur had killed Roy, why tell us his ring was missing at all? He could have said nothing, then gone back up to the attic and retrieved it at his leisure.'

'But he always wears it,' Jane said. 'He might have been worried one of us would notice it wasn't there before he could retrieve it from the attic.'

'Did any of you? Notice?' I asked. A collective shrug passed through them like a football stadium wave. 'That's what I thought. So perhaps Paul's right, and Roy was your petty thief all along.'

'Or it's a double bluff,' Willie said. 'Roy can't defend himself any more, can he?'

He had a point. Arthur could have deliberately left the ring there, calculating that we'd assume Roy was the thief and thereby throwing us off the scent.

'Can I have it back?' Arthur said, reaching for it again, but once more I held on to it.

'I don't think so. The police will want to examine it.'

'That could take a while, considering there's no

chance they can reach us until this snow starts to thaw,' Paul said. He held out his hand. 'Perhaps I'd better hang on to it.'

'Or maybe Zoe should keep it,' I suggested. 'She's the one person who definitely couldn't have done this, after all.'

Paul looked peeved, but nodded in agreement.

'We should preserve the body until a pathologist can attend. Fortunately, we have as much ice as we could ever need.' He turned to Willie. 'As well as somewhere to store it where we know it won't melt.'

'You must be joking. It's my tool shed, not a mortuary.'

'Would you rather we leave him here? Come now, Willie. You've improvised more with less, and between the four of you it'll be easy going.'

It took me a moment to realise Paul included me in that 'four'.

'I can't possibly,' I protested. 'I'm half your size.'

He gestured at his walking stick again and shrugged. 'With twice the number of working legs. I'll walk ahead and clear the way for you.'

It made sense, but Paul's cold, detached logic gave me chills. You'd never have known he was talking about carrying the body of a decades-old friend.

Arthur and Willie took a shoulder each, while Jane and I lifted the legs. Upon first meeting Roy, I'd noticed he was a bag of bones, and now I admit I was grateful. If it had been Arthur we'd found dead, I'm not sure eight of us could have carried him.

CHAPTER TWENTY-FOUR

Like a surreal funeral procession, we left the house and crossed the garden, into and through Zoe's house opposite, then finally out across the snow towards the shed. By now the sun had set, but dim moonlight reflected off the snow and the path to Willie's shed was already well trodden.

Puzzle pieces formed in my mind as we walked. I tried to fit them together to make a coherent image, but they resisted. Too many things didn't make sense.

The cause of death was obvious enough, unless someone had poisoned Roy and then throttled him to cover it up. But why was he in the attic to begin with? He hadn't appeared to be carrying anything, and none of the stored boxes or bags I could see were open. Still, there he was, and there was only one way up.

The ladder! It must have been the metallic scraping noise I'd heard. So Roy had gone up into the attic last night for some reason, followed by his killer, who took advantage of the internal doors always being unlocked. They strangled him, left his body there, replaced the ladder, then returned to their own house. In the morning, Roy was nowhere to be seen—

Wait. No, that wasn't possible. Arthur had seen him this morning, coming out of the bathroom. And nothing had tripped Zoe's cameras, so nobody had entered or left Roy's house between us walking the dogs last night and again this morning. Meaning Roy had woken and showered, then gone up into a dusty, cobwebbed attic. Why?

I imagined three possible solutions, each quite different but plausible.

One: Roy had gone up into the attic during the night, but come down again still alive, then for some reason returned to the attic in the morning followed by his killer. Though it still didn't explain why there was nothing on Zoe's CCTV.

Two: Arthur and Zoe were in on it together. Arthur had lied about having seen Roy this morning, and Zoe had lied that there was nothing on camera. Perhaps the other residents were part of the charade, too. The whole affair had been meant to deceive Birch and myself until we departed, which we'd intended to do this morning. If not for being snowed in, which led to me finding Roy's body, we'd have been none the wiser.

Three: Arthur killed Roy. This was horrible to contemplate, especially given his emotional reaction to the news of Roy's death. The men were obviously close. But Arthur had shown little interest in Roy's disappearance this morning and, being already in the house, wouldn't have been seen on Zoe's CCTV. He could have simply killed Roy, then carried the body into the attic. He was certainly strong enough. Were his tears born of guilt?

The most elusive puzzle piece of all remained one of timing. Why now? Assuming he wasn't killed by a random assassin (who'd somehow evaded Zoe's cameras, then lured Roy into the attic between bathroom and breakfast), the culprit must be one of the quad residents. So why not wait until Birch and I were gone, and the snow melted, to make it seem as if Roy had left of his own accord?

Unless they hoped to frame one of us for the murder, of course.

I failed to make the pieces fit in my mind before our unusual party finished traversing the grounds. I put them aside for a moment while Arthur took the strain and Willie unlocked the shed's heavy-duty padlock.

Although that was how everyone referred to this outbuilding, when the doors opened I saw it was quite a bit larger and better-equipped than the name suggested. Paul switched on the overhead light to reveal a space filled with tools and devices. A ride-on lawnmower, ladders, spades, strimmer and shears, handyman tools, paints and brushes . . . even a chainsaw hung on one wall. Against another stood a workbench with clamp and cutting board, and in the shadows of a far corner I spied a turning lathe. The LPG tanks Willie had mentioned stood nearby, surrounded by potted plants.

'You have electricity in here?' I said, impressed by the light.

'Ran it myself from the house, three feet down in a trench,' Willie replied.

'We need something to put Roy on,' Paul said, walking towards the back of the shed. In the shadows stood a fixed ladder leading to a narrow upper floor, like a hayloft.

'No, you stay right there,' Willie said sternly, putting out an arm to gently, but firmly, halt his progress. Paul looked aghast that anyone would lay hands on him, but Willie was determined, and pushed him back towards the doors. His voice took on a warning tone. 'This is my shed. I don't need you eejits blundering about and knocking things over. Stay there and I'll fetch a couple of pallets.'

Willie walked past the hayloft ladder, further back into the shadows. I couldn't make out what he was doing, but there was much grunting and crashing before he eventually stood up and tossed two wooden pallets, one after the other, towards us. Then he followed, carrying a piece of tarpaulin.

'Let me take him,' Arthur said. With ease, he gathered Roy over his shoulder, bearing all of the dead man's weight.

Paul laid the pallets down side by side, then placed the tarpaulin on top. Meanwhile, Willie removed two spades from hooks on the wall. He and Paul then spent a couple of minutes bringing snow in from outside, packing it on top of the tarpaulin until they'd built up a two-inch-high frozen bed. Finally, Arthur carefully laid Roy down on the packed snow and folded his arms across his chest.

For a moment we stood in silence, gathered around the body like mourners at a grave. Then, with unspoken synchronicity, we turned and walked back to the house while Willie locked the shed behind us.

CHAPTER TWENTY-FIVE

'We really should call the police,' I said, handing Arthur's ring to Zoe. It was still inside Paul's handkerchief.

'Absolutely,' Birch agreed. 'Have to start a case record.'

'Absolutely *not*,' Paul replied. 'As I already said, they can't get here anyway. More importantly, this is an internal matter and it'll go more easily if we keep it that way. Between us, we're quite capable of conducting an investigation.'

'Internal matter?' Birch protested. 'I'm former Met. Have to follow procedure.'

'Nonsense. You and I both know the Met bends its own rules whenever it suits them. These are extraordinary circumstances, and I have no doubt the Somerset police will be glad of us taking the initiative.'

I took out my phone. 'I still think they should be informed.'

'Good luck,' Willie Mac said.

I didn't understand what he meant until I remembered the lack of signal out here. I looked to Birch, who shook his head. Presumably this was why Roy hadn't owned a mobile. The only phones I'd seen in the quad were the landlines that everyone kept.

I stood up. 'I'll dial 999 from the house phone.' But Paul and Willie both moved in front of the door to the corridor, blocking my way. 'What on earth do you think you're doing?'

Willie folded his arms. 'The boss said you're not calling the police.'

'So you'll just do whatever he says, will you?' I protested, but it was clear from the Scot's expression that he probably would.

'There's simply no point,' Paul insisted. 'They won't be able to get here.'

Birch got to his feet, then immediately regretted it and winced at the pain in his ankle. 'You don't have the authority,' he insisted.

'Don't we? You're on our property,' Jane said.

'I don't care if it's owned by the Queen of Sheba,' I said. 'You're not above the law.'

'And you're not the law.' Paul loomed over me. 'Neither are you, Birch, unless you lied about being retired. We're always told the police are underfunded and short-staffed these days. Don't you agree we can save them the time and bother by sorting this out ourselves? After all, we have a prime suspect.' He looked meaningfully at Arthur.

'The forecast said the snow will only last another day

or so,' Willie said. 'At some point tomorrow it's back to rain as usual, so let's hold our horses and then we can walk to the nearest cop shop if we have to, eh?'

'Especially as the body will start to decompose in warmer weather,' Birch pointed out.

The Scot groaned. 'Christ, you're right. We'll need to get him out of the shed when that happens. I don't want that smell every time I go to fetch a hammer.'

'If the snow melts, then by definition the police can come and fetch him,' I pointed out. 'Tell them there's a dead body in the shed – I'm pretty sure that'll motivate them to get here quickly.'

'And you'll be off just as quickly, no doubt,' Paul said. The knuckles gripping his walking stick were white. 'How do we know you won't take the chance to escape?'

'Escape from what?' I said. 'I already told you, until yesterday, neither of us had even met Roy, let alone been here.'

'So you say, but until you knocked on our door everything was fine. Less than twenty-four hours later, one of my oldest friends is dead.'

'Actually, sir, we don't know when the victim was killed,' Birch said. 'Impossible to truly pin down time of death, given the deceased had been missing for some hours before the body was located.' He was trying to be helpful, but, unsurprisingly, Paul didn't appreciate the clarification.

'Bloody woodentops,' he said, seething, and turned on Birch. 'Of course, that's assuming you really are ex-police to begin with. For all we know, you're both hostile agents working undercover identities.'

'No, they're not,' Zoe said loudly. Everyone stopped and turned to look at her. 'I checked them out after they arrived. Gwinny's been on TV since the eighties, and Birch retired from the Met about five years ago.'

I stared at her in disbelief. 'You "checked us out"? Why?'

'Standard procedure,' she said. 'I told you, I did it for decades. It's even easier these days, with the internet.'

'It's also easier to fake a legend,' Willie said. 'Anyone can put whatever they like online.'

Zoe tutted. 'Give me some credit. You know I'd see through that sort of thing. No, unless they're masters of disguise, they're who they say . . . and Gwinny's also some kind of amateur detective.'

'Hardly,' I demurred. 'I don't like being lied to, that's all. I want to know the truth. We both do,' I added, indicating Birch.

The 'woodentop' twitched his moustache and turned to Arthur, who'd taken his usual chair by the fireplace and now silently stared into the flames.

'Arthur, we only have your word for it that you left Roy alive after he came out of the bathroom. By the time Gwinny and I came downstairs, you were already in the kitchen. Plenty of time between those two events for you to kill Roy and carry him up into the attic. Did you finally lose your temper and lash out? It's obvious the others here treat you with contempt.'

'Hey, hang on—' Zoe protested, but it was impossible

to deny. Since we'd arrived, the others had regularly ribbed Arthur, gently mocking him and putting him in his place. I hadn't thought anything of it because every community has a pecking order, but Roy's death threw a different light on matters. Arthur was undoubtedly strong enough to have killed his housemate.

Then again, the others hadn't seen the big man weeping in the hallway upstairs.

'Arthur,' I said quietly, 'what about the books? Will you be able to carry on writing without Roy?'

He looked up from the fire. 'What do you mean?'

'From what I saw yesterday, it looked like Roy wrote the initial rough drafts, and you sort of cleaned them up into something that made more sense. Or have I misunderstood?'

He blinked. 'We write alternate chapters. Jane makes it sound like a single author, that's all.' From the corner of my eye I saw her roll her eyes at this casual dismissal of her contribution. 'We write a lot like each other, anyway.'

I declined to mention the nonsense rough draft I'd found in Roy's bin, but it got me thinking.

'Did you notice any . . . change in Roy recently? Had he become absent-minded?'

Arthur seemed offended. 'Roy's always been sharp as a tack. It was his idea to buy this place, you know. He thought of Jack Spitfire, too. Although I came up with the name,' he added, with perhaps misplaced pride.

'You're absolutely certain you saw Roy before breakfast this morning? Coming out of the bathroom?'

'That's right. He's always late for breakfast.'

We seemed to have reached an impasse. No matter how much I doubted it, Arthur was the obvious suspect . . . but he flatly denied it and we couldn't prove otherwise. Absent further evidence, things were going nowhere. There was also a risk that by focusing so much on Arthur, we might miss clues to a different killer.

'All right,' I said, looking about the room. 'No police for now, and we'll try to figure it out ourselves. But the moment the snow clears, we call them, yes?' Everyone nodded. 'At least this way the police can't tell us *not* to do anything, and I suppose nobody knows your little "gang" better.'

Birch looked at me with an expression that I knew said, *Are you sure about this?* I nodded at him silently.

'Certainly we know our own better than you,' Willie Mac said.

'Then we'd all better get our thinking caps on,' Paul said. 'Maybe it was Arthur, maybe not, but someone here killed Roy. For all we know, they're planning to kill again. I'll be damned if they get away with it while I'm still standing.'

CHAPTER TWENTY-SIX

By now evening had drawn in, but tonight there would be no communal dinner. The residents returned to their houses, silent and suspicious. All except for one, anyway. Roy's murderer had done a great job of hiding so far.

Arthur, Birch and I were left alone. Even the dogs were eerily quiet, perhaps sensing our tension.

'I understand why you don't like it,' I said to Birch, while switching on the lounge's Christmas lights. Somehow, I felt Roy would have wanted us to. 'But one of the quad residents killed Roy, so to find out who, we need them all on-side. Antagonising them will just make them clam up.' He grunted a half-hearted agreement. 'Look on the bright side,' I added, nudging him. 'Next time you get together with your old Met colleagues, you'll have a heck of a new story to tell them.'

The hint of a smile passed over his lips. It was the best I'd get for now.

'I should take the dogs for a walk before they eat,' I said. 'Will you be OK here, with . . . ?' I nodded in Arthur's direction. The big man had picked up his book of Soviet aircraft to read, paying us no attention at all.

'If you come back and find me dead, at least you'll know who did it,' Birch grumbled. 'What I need is a stick to get around, like Paul's.'

'That's an idea. In fact, he's got a whole stand of them. I'm sure he'd let you borrow one. Hang on to the dogs for a minute, I'll go and ask him.'

I crossed the quad to Paul's, wondering about what Roy had planned to tell me this morning. He said he'd deciphered my father's notes on the Gerber file, but unless he'd written it all down somewhere (highly unlikely given Roy's 'cloak and dagger' nature), it was now gone for ever. Like so much about that part of my father's life.

Standing outside Paul's door, I heard a phone ring from inside then stop shortly after. Because the caller had rung off, or because Paul had answered? Was one of the other residents calling him from the safety of their own house? Could they be *threatening* him?

All these thoughts and possibilities ran through my mind as I quietly opened the door and sneaked inside, straining my ears to listen.

'Yes, that's right . . . With Roy gone, there's nothing to stop me . . . No, we stick to the plan . . . The others are completely unaware, I'm sure of it . . . Don't worry, Arthur will get what's coming to him.'

My eyes were practically on stalks hearing this. Who was Paul talking to? What did he mean that, with Roy gone, there was nothing to stop him? Had his self-righteous declaration about finding the killer all been an act to throw us off the scent?

If he knew I'd overheard this conversation, things could turn very nasty. I hastily retreated outside as quietly as I could, then knocked loudly before opening the door again and calling out, 'Paul? Are you there?'

This time I heard him say, 'I'll call you back,' and put the phone down. When I rounded the doorway, he stood by the phone in the hallway, just like earlier and looking no less annoyed.

'I'm here, Gwinny. What is it?'

'Nothing to do with Roy. I wondered if I could borrow one of your walking sticks for Birch to use. His ankle is still sore.'

Paul seemed surprised. Perhaps he'd expected me to accuse him of something.

'By all means. Take your pick.' He gestured at the stand behind him, then thought better of it and said, 'Actually, no, don't come in here with your boots on. I'll bring one over. Your chap's about the same height as me, I think?'

'That's right.'

Paul hovered over the umbrella stand for a moment, then selected a stick with a moulded grip and large rubber foot.

'Given the weather, this should see him right. We don't want him slipping again.'

'No, quite. Thank you.' I took the stick, ready to leave, but hesitated. Something was bothering me. 'Paul, I've been wondering: why are you the only person in the quad who doesn't take part in the Max Calibre stuff? You and Roy were the first people here, so you must have been good friends.' I decided to lay on a little flattery. 'Surely, with your background, you must have a wealth of valuable knowledge and experience you could draw on.'

To my surprise, he chuckled. If I hadn't seen it with my own eyes, I might not have believed Paul was capable of it.

'Yes, we were good friends. In fact, Roy and I tried to write a book together, shortly after we retired. Personally, what I learnt from the experience is that there's no greater threat to friendship. I don't know how he and Arthur never fell out. Or perhaps they did, of course.'

'After twenty books? Do you really think that this far in, Arthur suddenly snapped and killed Roy over a semicolon?'

'It does seem unlikely,' Paul conceded. 'Nevertheless, there's your answer. Before we built the extension and invited the others to live here, we tried, but it didn't work. Then along came Arthur, who was already thinking of trying his hand at writing, and before you knew it Max Calibre – and Jack Spitfire – was born.'

'Did you carry on writing alone? The fabulous adventures of "John Hurricane", perhaps?'

He grimaced. 'Nothing so tawdry. I've actually been

writing my memoirs, though I doubt I'll ever finish them. It's harder than it looks.'

I thanked him for the walking stick and left, trying to decide if this new information was an important piece of the puzzle. Had Paul grown jealous of Roy's success, knowing it could have been his if they'd been able to work together, and so killed him for it? Or had Arthur grown tired of carrying Roy, with his messy first drafts, and figured he could do just as well on his own?

But these felt like motivations for arguments and acrimony, not murder. Writers didn't kill one another out of jealousy . . . did they?

Lights were now on in every house, illuminating patches of the quad. Roy and Arthur's lounge, with its curtains open; Paul's lounge behind me, with curtains drawn; Jane's kitchen, the blind down over the window; and in Willie and Zoe's house an upstairs light, presumably her computer room. Through the winter hedges I saw her kitchen was also lit. Perhaps Willie was preparing dinner.

Walking stick in hand, I was ready to make my way back to Birch when I heard the sound of a door opening, followed by a woman's voice whispering, 'Willie!' and the door closing.

My first assumption was that it was Zoe, of course. I'd been mistaken; she wasn't in her computer room, she'd been in the garden. But why would she whisper when entering her own home? And if Willie was downstairs, who had switched on the upstairs light?

The answers became clear when I crept through the

hedges and saw that it was Jane, not Zoe, in the kitchen with Willie.

Doing, to my surprise, a little more than just talking.

I wasn't exactly shocked to see them embracing. Septuagenarians they might be, but Birch and I were hardly spring chickens ourselves. It was, though, unusual to see that Jane was the one bending down to kiss. As a shortie myself, being taller than a male lover isn't something I've ever had to deal with. Evidently, it didn't bother Willie Mac one bit.

Regardless of stature, Jane was clearly the one needing consolation. As they held one another close her face turned towards the window, filled with anguish and upset. By now, I was peeking out from behind a hedge, as close to them as I dared get, and it looked as if she'd been crying.

So I was right the first time. Zoe was upstairs, unable to return downstairs without a lot of noise and prior notice, which allowed Willie and Jane to snatch an illicit kiss without fear of discovery. Even if she saw Jane entering on the CCTV, Zoe had told me herself that the residents often wandered in and out of one another's houses. Explaining away Jane's presence would be easy.

Unless I spoke up.

This was a real dilemma. On the one hand, I felt a natural duty to tell Zoe what was going on under her nose. The fact that Jane had whispered his name, and they were carrying on discreetly while Zoe was upstairs, meant Willie was obviously cheating on her. On the other hand, what business was it of mine?

Could it be connected to the murder? Had Roy found out and threatened to tell Zoe, prompting Willie to kill him? The Scot had seemed as shocked as everyone else by Roy's death, but that meant nothing. I've worked opposite many great actors, and the killers I've met put them to shame.

Lost in thought, I hadn't noticed Jane leave the kitchen. Now I heard the garden door open and watched her step out into the dim twilight. She looked left and right but didn't see me, hidden behind the hedge. I followed her through the garden, not entirely sure why. For some reason, it felt important to see where she went next.

I crept along behind her, holding back and flattening myself against the tall hedges. Jane made enough noise walking through the snow to mask my own footsteps. However, it soon became obvious she was returning to her own house, and I relaxed. Which was a mistake, because I stopped paying attention to the walking stick in my hand and it struck a garden bench.

Jane whirled around, peering into the near-darkness. 'Who's there? Who is it?'

I decided to bite the bullet and stepped into view. 'It's me. Gwinny.'

'Were you following me?'

'Can you blame me, after what I just saw?'

Her eyes narrowed. 'I don't know what you mean.'

'Yes, you do. I was outside Zoe's kitchen.'

She looked shocked, then quickly regained her composure. 'Not here. Come inside.'

Jane led me into her own kitchen, where she flicked on the kettle and turned to face me. I stood in the doorway, waiting for her to talk.

'You may find it hard to believe, but back in the day I was rather good-looking. So was Willie.'

'I've seen the photos in your lounge. What happened between you?'

'Nothing,' Jane said with a rueful smile. 'That's the point. We were both married, and you're not too young to know what it was like in those days. One whiff of impropriety, especially with a colleague, and I'd have been out on my ear. Only me, mind. They always blame us.'

Show business is less draconian when it comes to affairs of the heart, but she was right; if there's blame to be apportioned it will fall squarely on the woman's shoulders. Some things never change.

'So Willie's been married to Zoe all this time?' I asked.

She laughed. 'God, no. His first wife was a squaddie's bride, you know the type.'

I didn't, but asked, 'What about your husband?'

Jane looked wistful. 'James. Fifth child of an earl, devastatingly handsome. A real charmer. It wasn't until later that I discovered he was a louche, and the family had disowned him completely. Wine, women, cards, you name it. But again, it was different in those days. Divorce was out of the question.'

The kettle had boiled, so Jane put a teabag in a mug and poured. She didn't offer me one.

'Anyway, Willie's wife divorced him soon after he returned from Minsk. Pancreatic cancer did for James. When the Cold War ended I was reassigned, so Willie and I completely lost touch. Then, ten years ago, Roy invited us all here and we realised we had the opportunity to make up for those unrequited years.'

'I suppose that's one way of putting it. How long did it take for you to seize that opportunity, exactly?'

She squeezed the teabag and looked sideways at me with a mischievous glint in her eye. 'Not long at all. And before you pass judgement, it *is* different to when we were younger. Willie loves Zoe deeply, as anyone can see. But we all have needs, and time is ticking on. You know that as well as I do.'

'What about Zoe's needs? Or does being in a wheelchair turn someone into a zombie?'

Jane took a sip of tea and looked over the steaming mug at me. 'It was a car accident, you know. Drunk driver, completely random. Zoe was paralysed instantly from the waist down, no sensation at all. You could stick a knife in her leg and she wouldn't feel a thing.'

This really was none of my business, and I was beginning to regret getting involved. However, one question remained.

'Did Roy know about you two?'

Jane laughed. 'You think we plotted to kill him because he threatened to tell Zoe, is that it? Well, I suppose Willie does have a temper. But no. The truth is, we're not normally as much of a community here as you've seen in the past couple of days. There are only so many group nostalgia sessions one can take.'

'But Roy's lounge, with all the chairs, and Paul's jigsaw . . .'

'The one he's been working on for the past three years? That gives you an idea of how often we get together. Roy simply wanted to put on a good show for you. He was always good at that. Mister Politics, the great fixer. Nobody could smooth things over with Whitehall like Roy Singleton.'

'But then why do you all live here together? Why did everyone agree to be part of this . . . commune?'

Jane sighed. 'You're an actor, aren't you? And yet you've hardly talked about it since you arrived.'

This change of subject caught me off guard. 'Why would I? It's not why I came here, and none of you are in show business.'

'Precisely. We wouldn't understand. But when you get together with your actor friends, I expect it's very different, isn't it? Then you're all about the gossip, talking shop and telling old war stories. Because you have those experiences in common.'

'Oh. I see.'

Roy had said he wanted to save them all from lives of isolation in dismal flats. Lives where they couldn't talk to anyone about the things they'd done, or the work to which they'd dedicated themselves for decades. Real, crushing isolation. But here in the quad, whether or not they were one big, happy family, everyone had shared history. They could relate to one another on a fundamental level in a way outsiders never could.

As I turned to go, Jane reached out and grabbed my arm.

'Please don't say anything,' she said. 'We're not hurting anyone, and until now nobody's found out. All you'd do is cause pain.'

I resented the implication that by merely telling the truth I'd be the one at fault, but I also understood. I'd kept quiet about many on-set affairs between actors in my career, and Jane and Willie had been lovers for years without anyone knowing. Why rock the boat now?

I freed myself from her grip, stomped outside, and hurried back to Roy and Arthur's house. The dogs still needed to be walked, and I needed to talk with Birch.

CHAPTER TWENTY-SEVEN

Arthur wasn't much help finding things in the kitchen, but I managed to locate some white fish and a bag of potatoes and set about cooking them for the dogs' dinner. I thought it would be compensation for making them spend all this time in a strange house, although, despite Birch's concerns about Ronnie's 'routine', neither he nor Spiggy seemed bothered. Being surrounded by snow to play in probably helped.

Given the day's events, neither of us felt particularly like cooking something for ourselves, so while I sorted the dogs, Birch prepared us a couple of frozen microwave meals.

After polishing off dinners, both canine and human, we went for a walk, this time opting for the exterior grounds. The quad garden felt oppressive, as if everyone was watching us. Perhaps they were.

The first order of business was, well, the dogs doing their business as soon as we got outside. With that achieved, and Birch limping along on Paul's walking stick, I suggested we simply let them off in the back field again to tire themselves out while we stood and watched. The snow was disturbed from our earlier stroll but still deep enough to be treacherous, especially as it was now almost completely dark. It didn't look like anything had melted at all during the day.

While we watched Spiggy and Ronnie run and leap around, I told Birch what I'd learnt at Paul's and seen in Zoe's kitchen.

'You should tell her,' he said, meaning about Willie's affair. 'Truth is always better in the end.'

'Normally I'd agree, but in this case I truly don't know. I need some time to think it over. Promise me you won't say anything before I do.'

He obviously didn't like it, but grunted in agreement. 'Suppose you still don't want to call the police, either. Despite murder and dead animals.'

I took his arm and leant in to reassure him, then remembered it was the one keeping him upright on a walking stick and let go again.

'Paul's right. They wouldn't be able to reach us anyway, and what advice could they give us that you can't already?'

His moustache twitched at this obvious flattery. 'Not the first time you and I have found ourselves dealing with a murder, I suppose. Not much time to investigate before all this will melt, though.'

'No, but in a way we've been investigating since this morning, haven't we? We may only have thought Roy was missing, but it took us around everyone's house, and we've already learnt that plenty of the residents are keeping secrets.'

'You mean Max Calibre?'

'That's one, yes. But also we know Willie and Jane are having an affair; Paul's making those odd phone calls; Arthur's ring somehow found its way into the attic; and let's not forget that someone, heaven knows why, is storing jars of dead animals in a bag underwater. I think even Zoe's hiding something. She seemed very defensive when you tried to use her computer.'

Birch nursed the back of his hand. 'I only wanted to recover the deleted CCTV recordings.'

'Exactly. Is she just overly protective of her gadgets? Or is there something in those deleted files she doesn't want anyone else to see?'

'Arthur's still the prime suspect, though. Ring found in the attic, as you said, and near the body to boot. Could have come off in the struggle.'

'It could, but if so, why would he tell us that it was missing? All those people who've known him for years were stood within a few feet under the attic hatch, and not one of them noticed he wasn't wearing it.'

'Be fair, they had something more pressing on their minds. Dead body and all.'

'I know, but it still doesn't sit right. What reason would Arthur have to kill Roy? And how? He'd have had precious little opportunity. Awfully risky to kill someone when we might have stumbled out of the guest room at any time. Mind you, the same goes for everyone else too.'

Birch shook his head. 'Been thinking about that. What if Arthur's lying? We only have his word for it that he saw Roy this morning. Could have killed him during the night, then claimed to see him leaving the bathroom to throw us off.'

It was a good point, and made it all the more frustrating that neither of us had also seen Roy. If we had, surely Arthur must be innocent; but if Arthur was lying, he must be guilty.

'Rum do,' Birch murmured. 'Fact is, someone in this house killed Roy and whoever it was is lying to us through their teeth.'

'I can't shake the feeling that they're *all* lying to us, one way or another. I intend to find out why.'

As if to punctuate my words, Spiggy woofed from somewhere in the field, a sound quickly followed by the familiar splashing noise of a Spaniel in the water. I groaned and wondered just how many more spare towels there were in that cupboard.

None, it turned out. A typical man's household, I supposed; the minimum required of everything, reused until it falls apart, forcing a long-overdue new purchase. I didn't relish the thought of calling on any of the others to borrow a towel and risking accidentally snooping on Paul yet again, or catching Jane and Willie *in flagrante*.

After we wiped Spiggy and Ronnie down with the last clean towels, Birch and I made our way to the guest bedroom. Arthur had already retired for the evening.

Once again, we donned the badly-sized pyjamas

and climbed into bed, albeit Birch took twice as long owing to his still-sore ankle. I hoped it wasn't a serious injury. I'd once known an actor who did three weeks of *Coriolanus* with what felt like a sore foot but turned out to be a broken toe.

'How's the war wound?' I asked Birch when he finally settled in and pulled up the covers.

'Feeling much better,' he said. 'Come the morning, I'll be right as rain— *aaah*!'

The brave face he'd been putting on was quickly dispelled by Ronnie, who eagerly leapt up onto the bed and landed on the ankle in question. Birch whimpered in pain and shifted his leg to protect it from the dogs.

When Ronnie and Spiggy finished circling on the bed and were both happily curled up at our feet, Birch resumed reading the Spitfire novel.

'You've almost finished that,' I noted. 'I assume you're enjoying it?'

'It's fine,' he said with a shrug. 'Still something missing compared to the early books, but can't put my finger on it. Don't tell Arthur I said that,' he added hastily.

'Your secret one-star review is safe with me,' I said, snuggling up to him for warmth.

CHAPTER TWENTY-EIGHT

Once again, Birch woke before me, but this time he remained in bed. When I opened my eyes, I found him sitting up, pillows stacked behind his head, reading the last pages of the Spitfire novel.

'Well?' I asked when he closed the cover. 'Still only one star?'

'Perish the thought,' he said, closing the book and replacing it on the bedside table. 'Even an average Max Calibre book is still worth reading, and it picked up by the end. Solid four stars. Pity there won't be any more, I suppose.'

'You never know. From what I saw, Arthur is the better writer of the two, and they were already working on the next. Maybe he'll finish it solo.' I sat up myself, careful not to disturb the dogs. 'Any improvement with your ankle?'

'Feels better,' he said. 'Throbbing pain's gone, for one thing.' He pushed back the covers and swung his legs off the bed. 'Might need Paul's stick again, but I'm sure it'll be f—*aaah-ah-ah-ah*!'

This time the cry of pain wasn't from a dog sitting on his ankle, but from simply putting his own body weight on it. Birch's leg collapsed under him and he toppled sideways onto the bed. To avoid landing on the dogs he twisted his body as he fell; unfortunately, this sent him crashing down on top of me instead, with his face buried in my chest. In better circumstances I might have encouraged such spontaneity, but this was hardly the time. Not least because Ronnie and Spiggy immediately leapt up, finally roused from sleep and wondering what was occurring.

'Perhaps that throbbing pain isn't quite as gone as you thought,' I said, squirming out from under Birch and getting to my feet. 'Stay in here and rest for a while. I'll take the dogs out, then decide what to do next. I still haven't had a proper look around Zoe's house.'

'She couldn't have done it,' Birch grunted, teeth gritted in pain. 'Not in that wheelchair.'

'No, but she might be protecting whoever did. She seemed awfully keen for us not to look at any of those CCTV recordings. I wonder if I can sneak in and take a look at her computer.'

'Beg pardon, ma'am, but you'll need me for that. *Ooooh*,' he whimpered as the dogs kept stomping around the bed, anticipating a walk now they could see me getting dressed.

'Well, that's not going to happen, is it? You'll have to tell me what to look for.'

He groaned and leant back on the pillows. 'I'll be bored out of my mind.'

'I'll bring you another Spitfire book to read, if you like. Better still – I wonder if Arthur would let you read the manuscript they've been working on? He knows you're a fan, now.'

Birch tried to look nonchalant, but I could tell he was excited by the prospect. Everyone loves a sneak peek at something, especially when it's exclusive.

'I'll ask him after I've walked these two,' I said, now dressed. I clipped on the dogs' leads. 'In the meantime, let's hope nobody else has vanished overnight.'

It would have been hard to tell, as we appeared to be awake before everyone else in the quad. I toileted the dogs at the front of the house, then kept them on-lead and walked around to assess the situation. The steep driveway was still impassable, and from down here in the valley I couldn't tell if the road above had been cleared. I tried walking up the drive to take a look, but by now an icy crust had frozen over the snow, making the going underfoot treacherous and slippery. The dogs didn't mind and would happily have kept going, but I had no desire to join Birch in the invalid ward, so we retreated and returned to the house. There, I did my best to dry the dogs and fixed them a kibble breakfast.

Afterwards, I entered the lounge to find Arthur sitting in his usual fireplace chair, in his slippers and dressing gown, still reading the book of Russian aircraft.

Upon realising I was in the room, his head snapped up in surprise.

'Sorry, I didn't mean to startle you,' I said. 'I've just taken the dogs out. I'm afraid you'll need to put a towel wash on, I've used all your clean ones. Sorry.'

'Oh. Um, yes, all right.'

I was going to ask him about the manuscript, but he returned to his book and seemed quite preoccupied. It could wait while I brushed my teeth, so I left him to it and returned upstairs, only to find Birch had fallen back asleep. The dogs settled down on the bed with him while I washed myself, then I quietly closed the door and crept back downstairs.

Arthur was still in his chair, the open book on his lap, gazing out of the window into the garden. I made myself coffee and toast in the kitchen, noting there was no washing machine in there. Then I saw the door beside the fridge and remembered the utility room, from which Arthur had emerged yesterday morning. Inside was a washing machine, tumble dryer and ironing board. The mop I'd used leant against a wall.

A quick peek confirmed the washer was empty so I took matters into my own hands, gathering all the damp towels off the corridor hooks and stuffing them into the machine. I wondered cynically if the quad's ageing bachelors had invited Jane the 'secretary' here simply in order to do their cooking and cleaning, but that was unfair. I had no evidence of that, and Arthur had just lost his best friend. No wonder he was distracted.

Besides, if Jane did the laundry in here, no doubt the detergent and conditioner would have been easier to find. They weren't out on a shelf, so I began opening cupboards and rummaging through baskets of rags, bottles of out-of-date floor cleaner, open bags of J-cloths and more. I found the conditioner in a wall-mounted cupboard, but for some inexplicable reason the detergent wasn't with it, so I kept searching. Under the sink I found surface cleaners, a plunger, wire wool, balls of string . . . there was even an old toolbox here, which I pulled out in order to get a better look behind it, only to discover that the lid wasn't secured. Before I knew it, the contents had spilt over the floor. I cursed myself for not checking, and the box's owner for not closing the lid properly, then began to retrieve its contents.

Which weren't tools.

A roll of Sellotape, a silver spoon, a pair of nail scissors, several ballpoint pens, an empty salt cellar, an LED torch, a porcelain squirrel ornament, a pair of gardening gloves . . . I wondered why anyone would keep such a bizarre collection of things in a toolbox under the sink.

But as I gathered them up, my eyes returned to the torch. LED, black aluminium, four inches long . . .

'What's going on?'

Startled, I looked up to see Arthur standing in the doorway. Even in his slippers and dressing gown he was a big, imposing man. His eyes widened upon seeing the box's scattered contents on the floor.

'What are you doing? Those are my things!'

'Are they?' I said, picking them up. 'An LED pocket torch, like the one Paul said had gone missing? A pair of gardening gloves, like the ones Willie Mac couldn't find? Something tells me neither you nor Roy had much use for a pair of nail scissors, either. You're the petty thief who's been taking things, aren't you? Why?'

His expression changed from shock to anger to hurt. The big man whimpered like a child. 'They're my things.'

I took the gloves and torch, as I knew who those belonged to. Everything else I replaced in the toolbox, then closed it.

'They are very much not yours. Once I've returned these items to Paul and Willie, we can begin repatriating the others, too.'

'Where's Roy?'

'Still in the shed, as far as I know. Why?'

'What's he doing in there? I'm going to fetch him.' Arthur looked on the brink of tears.

'We put him in there to keep, remember? Until the police get here.'

His expression turned to pure fear. 'Don't call the police! It's just a few things, that's all. Nothing important. I'll put them back, I promise.'

'No – no, Arthur, the police aren't coming for . . . this.' I held up the torch and gloves, then stuffed them in my pockets. 'I mean, for whoever killed Roy. Once the snow clears, we'll call them.'

'Someone killed Roy?!'

Three words. Three words that said so much, and opened a pit in my stomach.

'Who did it?' Arthur looked around, worried. 'Was it those dog people? They seemed so nice. I recognised the copper, from when we used to liaise with the Met. What was his name . . . Larch, that's it. It must have been them! Where did they go?'

'Arthur,' I said quietly, taking his hand. It swallowed mine. 'Do you remember what happened yesterday?'

'Of course. Roy was late for breakfast – he's always late for breakfast, you know – then we sat and read in the lounge. I think . . . did it snow? I think we all went out for a walk in the snow. Yes, that's right. Then we had dinner. And Willie was cruel to Roy. He's always been like that, ever since he moved in. I wish Roy had never invited him. Where is Roy?'

His eyes darted from side to side as he spoke. I remembered all the times he'd avoided a question, or looked surprised to see me. How he'd seemed to forget why he'd put out a mop for us. His habit of greeting me by asking, 'What's going on?' instead of using my name.

'When did Willie move in, Arthur? How long have you lived here?'

'Roy and Paul bought this place five years ago. Then Willie and Zoe moved in, then me, then Jane.' He looked around again, searching for a familiar face. 'You should ask Roy, he's in charge.'

'He was called away for something important,' I said, improvising. 'Top priority, you know. Very hush-hush.'

Arthur nodded as if this made perfect sense, and my heart broke.

I'd assumed his vagueness was down to either guilt or grief. But now he couldn't take in that Roy was dead, and seemed to think I was someone else entirely,

226

not one of the 'dog people' who had visited his house. During that first meeting in the lounge, Arthur had said they'd all been telling Roy what a good idea the quad was for the past five years . . . because he thought that was how long they'd lived here. But Jane had told me Roy and Paul brought the others to the quad ten years ago, and that was after it had been renovated and extended.

Perhaps he had good days and bad days, but there was an unmistakeable fog in Arthur's brain.

I walked him back through the kitchen, into the lounge, where he sat in his usual chair and once again picked up the aircraft book. How many times had he read that same book? Did it matter, so long as it made him happy?

The room was still cold, so I built a fire, scrunching up pages of an old newspaper kept by the fireplace for kindling. It made me think of the nonsense manuscript pages in Roy's wastepaper basket, and how they now meant something completely different. Repeated conversations, sudden changes in direction, long digressions unrelated to what had gone before . . . They weren't Roy's first drafts. They were Arthur's attempts to keep writing despite his growing dementia, sent from his room to Roy's wireless printer. I could picture the scene clearly: Roy would see them, discard them, then rewrite them coherently in a new version. This he would print out, and place on Arthur's desk as if they were the original pages. Nobody, including Arthur himself, was any the wiser.

How long had Roy been covering for him like this?

As Birch had noticed, the other quad residents treated Arthur like a child anyway, some kind of snobbery down to him being former MI5 instead of MI6. And Jane had said they weren't the close community Roy had wanted me to think. So perhaps it wasn't surprising that nobody else had noticed Arthur's vague manner or occasional non sequiturs. So long as the Spitfire books kept appearing on time, they didn't question how much of them was his work.

But what now? How much of Arthur's day-to-day life had been managed by Roy without the others knowing? Who would look after him now?

This discovery didn't exonerate him per se. Arthur unquestionably had the strength to kill Roy, and we'd found his ring near the body. If anything, Willie's theory that he'd lost it in the struggle with Roy now made more sense, as the big man might have simply forgotten where it was. Did he even remember murdering his friend? Surely an act so remarkable, and presumably emotional, would stick in his mind. Wouldn't it?

Then again, these people had spent decades working in the murky world of spies and intelligence. How many had taken lives before in the name of Queen and country?

With the fire lit, I stood back to enjoy its warmth. Arthur had lost focus on his book again, and was now staring out at the quad garden. I departed without disturbing him.

CHAPTER TWENTY-NINE

I made my way upstairs to Roy's study, then Arthur's, gathering the manuscript pages from their desks. I was sure Roy wouldn't have minded, while Arthur might not even notice.

Once again, I was struck by the neatness of Arthur's study compared to Roy's. I wondered if it was a coping strategy – keeping everything tidy and in its place so Arthur could find things without having to think too much, or rely on new memories.

Spiggy and Ronnie both wagged their tails at me when I entered the guest bedroom, though neither actually stirred from their warm spot on the bed. I gave Birch the manuscript pages and told him what had happened in the utility room.

He grimaced. 'Sounds familiar. Poor bugger, I should have realised.'

'My father was fortunate, I suppose. He stayed sharp until the end. When you say "familiar" . . . ?'

'Beatrice,' he explained. 'Hardly recognised me some days.'

Birch rarely talked about his late wife. When we first met he'd been in mourning for several years, still wearing his wedding ring and unable to even contemplate a new relationship. Things had improved since then, obviously, but I still avoided the subject wherever possible, so hadn't known she'd suffered from dementia.

I took his hand and gently kissed it. 'You realise this puts everyone's alibi in doubt. We thought Roy must have been killed during a very short window of time, because Arthur had seen him that morning. But if he misremembered the whole thing, then Roy could have been killed at any time during the night.'

'Including by Arthur himself,' Birch pointed out. 'He could be lying.'

'You mean pretending to have dementia? I don't know. It seemed genuine.'

'People have done stranger things to get away with murder.'

That was certainly true. 'I'm going to return these gloves to Willie and take a peek at Zoe's computer while I'm there. What do I need to look for?'

Birch hesitated, then opened his mouth to speak, so before he could protest I pre-empted him.

'Don't tell me it's too dangerous, or that I shouldn't go without you. I've done my share of sneaking around before, as you well know. You weren't even in Hendale,' I reminded him, referring to the last time I'd unmasked a killer. 'And I'll grant you that was a little dangerous, but it all turned out well, didn't it? So don't mollycoddle me.'

Throughout this tirade, the end of Birch's moustache had begun to rise, and by the end he wore a bemused smile.

'I was just going to say be careful. Wouldn't dream of standing in your way.'

I exhaled, feeling foolish. Still, it didn't hurt to reiterate these things.

'Now, about the computer . . .' He launched into a lengthy explanation of what computer system Zoe used, and how her 'interface' wasn't like the computers I was used to, and how some systems kept 'activity logs' in their memory – like a diary of everything they'd done – that I could look through if I clicked *this*, and scrolled *that*, and—

'Birch!' I held up a hand to interrupt him. 'Just write down the steps for me. I'll never remember it otherwise.'

I rummaged around in the emergency dog bag until I found the pen and notepad I kept in there. Not that I'd ever thought I'd be using it to make notes on how to break into a computer, but it shows the value of preparation.

Birch grumbled, but took the pad and wrote down instructions. 'There might be nothing there, mind you. It all relies on Zoe keeping her shell window open between sessions.'

'I don't know what that means, but is there a reason she wouldn't?'

'Depends how likely it is that anyone else in the house would look through it, and whether she cares.'

He handed me the note and I read the directions, hoping they'd make more sense in situ. 'I think the latter is more likely than the former. None of this lot seem even as tech-savvy as you, let alone Zoe.'

'Thank you. I think. Now, be careful.'

I kissed him on the cheek, at which point Spiggy leapt to his feet, so I kissed him on the head too.

'Sorry, Spiggy, but this is a one-woman mission. Look after Birch and try not to bounce off the walls while I'm gone.'

Birch turned a sceptical eye on the Spaniel and held on to his collar as I left the room.

Letting myself into Willie and Zoe's house, I listened for voices or sounds of movement. At first, I heard nothing, but as I moved further inside, silently closing the door behind me, I recognised the sound of the house boiler working. I put a hand to a radiator but found it only lukewarm to the touch; ergo, someone was running hot water. The lift wasn't at the foot of the stairs, so I guessed that meant Zoe was in the bathroom. Which in turn almost certainly meant Willie was with her, too.

I crept upstairs, keeping to the outer edges of each step so they wouldn't creak. I'd read that in a book once, but had never tested it in real life before. It seemed to work, though I wasn't about to tread in the middle of a step to test the theory.

Upon reaching the top, I heard the sound of running

water. A shower, if I wasn't mistaken. Even better. I tiptoed along the hallway into the computer room and wasted no time wheeling over a chair to sit at Zoe's desk. The grid of screens mounted on the wall were no longer showing CCTV images, but instead all joined up to display a recording of a burning yule log in a winter fireplace. Evidently, it was the closest this house would get to anything festive.

It suddenly occurred to me that Zoe's computer might require a password to use, which would stop me before I'd even started. But when I touched her trackball the screen sprang into life. Presumably, she wasn't worried that anyone else would come in here to use it, and why would they?

Birch's instructions were a godsend, and I'd have been completely lost without them. I still made a couple of mistakes, but eventually I found the right window – one of those filled with text that seemed gibberish to me – and scrolled up, which Birch assured me was like going back in time through all the things Zoe had done. It didn't take long to find what I was looking for: the commands she'd typed to delete video files yesterday morning. They all had names with a timestamp of the night before. The night, we now believed, that Roy was killed . . .

The shower had stopped.

I'd been so engrossed in the computer, I couldn't remember when the sound of running water had ended. How long did I have before Willie and Zoe emerged from the bathroom? Impossible to say, so I quickly took out my phone and snapped a photo of the list. It wasn't proof of anything, of course. Maybe they really were all completely innocent five-second clips of rabbits and foxes wandering around at night. But maybe they weren't.

I scrolled the computer window back down to the present time and shoved my phone back in my pocket. In my haste, I knocked the note with Birch's instructions on it off the desk. I dropped to my hands and knees and scrabbled around underneath, reaching for it—

'Gwinny? What are you doing in here?' Zoe asked.

Startled, I jerked upwards and banged my head on the underside of the desk.

Seeing stars, I barely maintained enough presence of mind to retrieve the note and crumple it in my hand as I shuffled backwards out from under the desk on my knees, rubbing my sore head.

'Sorry, I thought I'd lost an earring,' I said, standing up. To my surprise, Zoe was almost naked in her wheelchair, sitting on a towel and wearing a sort of half-length bathrobe. She didn't seem the slightest bit bothered by this, but I felt rather uncomfortable looming over her so sat down in the desk chair again and put my hands in my coat pockets, depositing the scrunched-up note safely out of sight.

'You're wearing them both,' she said, eyes narrowed with suspicion.

I looked over her shoulder. 'Is Willie with you?'

'Don't change the subject. Why are you in here?'

Trying to remain calm, I said, 'When I came in it

was obvious you were upstairs, and I heard the shower going. I didn't want to make you go all the way back downstairs, so I came up and waited in here. This is the only room I've been in before, and I didn't want to pry elsewhere.'

Considering that until thirty seconds ago 'prying' was exactly what I'd been doing, this was quite barefaced, and Zoe was obviously suspicious. But actors lie for a living, and there was enough truth in what I said for me to sound convincing. She couldn't prove otherwise.

'You like snooping around, don't you, Gwinny?' she said. 'No, don't deny it. I monitor the cameras, remember. I saw your little act with Paul last night, sneaking in then back out again to pretend you'd only just arrived.'

'Well, if you all locked your doors like normal people, none of this would matter.'

Unexpectedly, she laughed. 'There's nothing normal about this place. Even you must have noticed that by now. Do you think Paul killed Roy?'

'Everyone's still a suspect at the moment,' I said warily.

'What, even me?' She gestured at her legs. 'How stupid are you and your copper boyfriend?'

I almost confronted her with the photo I'd taken of the computer log, but stopped myself when I realised: that's what she wanted. Zoe was goading me, trying to make me angry so I'd slip up and reveal something I shouldn't. I was tempted to tell her about Willie's affair instead, but still didn't know if it was really my place to do so.

'Where's Willie?' I asked again.

Zoe sighed. 'Not here, obviously. If he was, I'd be dressed properly by now.' I admit, I hadn't considered the logistics of how Zoe dressed herself (or not) after a shower. Now the towel made sense.

'Is he in the shed? We left Roy's body in there.'

'Oh, so now Willie did it? What do you think he's going to do, burn the corpse? For God's sake, Gwinny, give me a straight answer. What are you doing in my house?'

I took the gardening gloves from my pocket and showed them to her.

'Are these Willie's?'

She nodded, recognising them. 'They're his favourite pair, he's been looking for them for months. Where did you find them?'

Now we were on firmer ground. I told her about Arthur's box of stolen items, and his dementia. When I finished, Zoe looked faintly guilty.

'Willie swore he hadn't mislaid his gloves, but I thought he was having a senior moment. I even made fun of him for it.'

'You didn't believe there really was a thief among you?'

'Who'd steal a pair of ratty old gloves? Or a lighter, or torch, or salt cellar?'

'Fair enough, when you put it like that. But Arthur

wasn't thinking straight. I doubt he could explain it himself.'

Zoe held out a hand for the gloves. 'Thank you for finding them. Once this business with Roy is dealt with, we'll have to work out what to do with Arthur. Perhaps Jane can take care of him.'

But while Zoe's manner had now thawed, I still didn't entirely trust her. She might not have been able to carry Roy into the attic, but from the way she wheeled herself around she clearly had plenty of arm strength. She could have garrotted him, then had Willie dump him in the attic.

A possibility which made her joke about him burning the corpse significantly less funny.

'What is it you do with all this?' I asked, indicating the computer equipment. 'I thought spying was about men wearing trench coats in dark alleyways.'

'Not any more. The real threat these days is hacking and misinformation. China, Russia, North Korea, they're all at it. I used to watch out for such things. Retaliated where possible.'

'Isn't that dangerous?'

Zoe grinned. 'Of course it's dangerous. That's why it was fun.' Her smile faded. 'Gwinny, I know you've been involved in this sort of thing before. Murders, I mean. Do you really think one of us did it?'

'Who else?' I said, standing. 'Your own cameras show that nobody came or went from the house. Unless . . . you've deleted some footage?'

If I'd hoped she might take the opportunity to explain what I'd found in the computer log and come clean, I was to be disappointed. Instead, her expression grew cold.

'I told you, the only recordings I deleted are inconsequential. Foxes, rabbits and so on.'

'We only have your word for that.'

'Then that will have to suffice, because it's all you're going to get.'

Her icy, hostile attitude had returned. I'd get nothing more out of Zoe.

'I'll take these gloves to Willie,' I said, making my way to the door. 'From what you say, it should brighten his day a bit.'

'No, leave him. He said he didn't want to be disturbed.'

'All the more reason why I intend to.'

CHAPTER THIRTY

By now the path to the shed through the snow was well worn enough that I stayed off it for fear of slipping, crunching a parallel track through fresh snow instead.

Did I really think Willie might destroy Roy's body in order to hide evidence? It seemed unlikely, if for no other reason than it would very firmly implicate him in the murder. Still, there might be other things he could do to conceal his involvement. The thought that he and Zoe might have conspired in this was a compelling one, though for the life of me I couldn't think why . . . or why *now*. Why would anyone kill Roy now, with guests in the house? Getting snowed in was rotten luck that couldn't be accounted for, especially if Roy was killed during the night rather than in the morning, as I now suspected. But still, why didn't the killer wait until Birch and I were gone?

I remembered Willie suggesting Birch and I might have come here to kill Roy. I had to admit, from the outside in, that seemed much more likely than another member of the 'gang' deciding they simply couldn't wait another day to see the back of him. But, of course, I knew that wasn't true. It had to be one of the five remaining housemates.

The shed door was unlocked and slightly ajar. Despite the day being cold and bright, a light shone from inside.

I raised my hand to knock, then changed my mind and peeked through the doorway, in case I caught Willie doing something red-handed.

But I didn't, because he wasn't there.

Willie had been absolutely clear that when he wasn't here, the shed was always locked. Had someone broken in? There were a lot of tools and supplies in there, which might be worth something. But who would come all the way out here, on foot through deep snow, to steal a spade or two?

Quite what I expected to do if I encountered a burglar I didn't know. I wasn't carrying any kind of weapon to threaten someone with, let alone defend myself. I considered going back to the house and fetching the dogs, but that would take too long. If there was someone in here, they could be gone before I returned with canine companions. Not that either Spiggy or Ronnie were exactly the Hound of the Baskervilles, anyway.

I slipped inside, pulling the door to behind me. Nothing seemed amiss. As far as I could remember, all of Willie's tools were where they'd been yesterday. The lawnmowers and strimmers remained in place. The spades he and Paul had used to shovel snow were back on their hooks, and Roy lay atop his improvised table of snow and ice with no obvious tampering.

On the corner workbench, however, were three objects that froze my blood. Glass jars with clip-down rubber-sealed lids.

I didn't particularly want to look, but how could I not? My eyes were drawn irresistibly along the line-up. A rabbit, a hedgehog, a small owl. All quite dead.

The door behind me opened, scraping against the snow. I turned to see Willie Mac, his heavy breath misting in the air as he snarled, 'What the hell are you doing here, you nosy cow?'

'It's you, isn't it?' I said, ignoring his insult. 'That bag in the stream is yours. You're the animal killer.'

He took a step towards me, his hands flexing into fists by his side.

'You don't know what you're talking about. And if you do talk to anyone about this, I'll kill you.'

The Scot wasn't much taller than me, but if he attacked, there was no way I could fend him off. A former soldier, former spy, and killer of wild animals? I was now glad I hadn't brought the dogs with me. There was no telling what might happen if they defended me.

'What have you done, Willie?' My voice shook. 'You're not a taxidermist. I haven't seen a single stuffed animal in any of the houses. Did Roy find out what you're up to in here, so you killed him to keep him quiet?'

He faltered. 'What? No, you— You can't think— Arthur killed Roy, didn't he? This has nothing to do with it.'

'Really? It's hardly normal behaviour, is it? No wonder Spiggy and Ronnie were so keen to get in here that first day, and why you shooed us off. Tell me what's going on.'

Willie's eyes widened, like a cornered animal in the throes of panic. 'I mean it. You can't tell anyone about this. Especially not—' He stopped himself.

'Especially not who? Zoe, your official partner? Or Jane, your secret lover?' He looked horrified. 'Yes, I know about you two. "Nosy cow", remember? I saw you last night, in the kitchen. Does she know about this?'

He rushed over to me and grabbed my coat by the lapels.

'Nobody knows. Not a soul. Now you listen to me, you don't understand—'

'Willie, I understand perfectly well what an affair looks like, and to be perfectly honest, I don't care. But I do care about finding out who killed Roy. Don't you? Unless you did it, of course. This macabre collection proves you're not averse to a bit of death.'

My words sounded brave, but inside I was a bag of nerves. We were alone and far from the house. Roy's body lay just a few feet away. If Willie really had killed him, there was nobody to stop him doing the same to me. His grip on my coat tightened . . .

Then he began to sob.

Willie released me and stepped back, staring at the ground with his head in his hands. 'You don't know – the things they did, what I did to survive – I'm not hurting anyone,' he said through tears.

'The local wildlife might disagree.'

'No! No, I don't . . . for God's sake, they're already dead. I save them, don't you see? From becoming worm food or eaten by their own. With me, they're . . . safe.'

'What happened to you, Willie? Is this what you and Roy argued about at dinner?'

I'm the least maternal person you'll find, but he looked up at me with an expression so pathetic, like a little lost boy, that I felt a sudden urge to take him in my arms and comfort him.

'The Russians got me,' he said quietly. 'In the seventies, when things were really bad. The worst. They took me to Minsk and . . . *questioned* me . . . until Roy arranged a hostage swap. It took two years.'

Now the argument made sense. Roy's comments that 'patience is a virtue', and telling Willie not to 'drag up the past', were about him waiting to be released. Two years like that must have been hell for a captured spy.

'So this is how you cope with your trauma? Didn't you visit a psychiatrist when you returned?'

He snorted, and his regular sardonic expression returned. 'In the seventies? They'd have put me on zombie pills for the rest of my life. Besides, I'd come to the service from special ops. Nobody talked about *mental health* back then.'

'I remember,' I said. 'But we've come a long way,

Willie. You should consider it now. At least you wouldn't have to keep that a secret from everyone, like these.' I gestured at the glass jars.

'Everyone else knows better than to come in here,' he said. 'But so long as those bloody dogs were in the house, they'd keep sniffing around. That's why I started moving things. And now with Roy in here too, everyone's all up in my business, so, because it's not exactly gardening weather, I have to sneak out when nobody's looking and do them one at a time.'

I glanced back at the door, understanding now where Willie had been and why I hadn't seen him on my way from the house. The stick marking the position of the sports bag was out of sight, behind the shed.

'Willie, how many bags are there in the stream? How long have you been doing this?'

'Three so far,' he said sheepishly. 'I only put the first one out the night you arrived. This was going to be the last bag.'

'The night we arrived? When, exactly?'

'I don't know, about two in the morning,' he said, his anger returning. 'I'm serious, Gwinny. If you tell anyone about this, there'll be consequences. You've no right to be coming here and sneaking around, anyway.'

'Heavens, I almost forgot.' I produced the gardening gloves from my coat pocket. 'I didn't come here to "sneak around". I wanted to return these.'

Willie's face lit up. 'Where'd you find them?'

I hesitated to answer, knowing that one explanation

244

would lead to another. But surely Zoe would tell him, if I didn't. So I explained about Arthur, his dementia and the box of stolen items. Willie's deep-lined face crumpled in sympathy as he realised what I was saying.

'Christ, poor Arthur,' he said. 'Prison will be impossible for him.'

'You mean for killing Roy? I don't know. I'm not sure he did it.'

'Who else? Nobody else went in or out of their house all night, remember?'

'Is there really no way through from one house to another without going outside? I don't know, maybe there's a secret passage behind a bookcase or something. I've come across them before, you know.'

The Scot laughed. 'If it's blueprints you're after, you'll need to ask Paul. Good luck getting the boss to open that safe, though. You'd have an easier time breaking into Fort Knox.'

'That's a bit rich, considering you've got an entire shed you keep locked up from everyone.'

Willie grimaced. 'Didn't stop you getting in here, did it?'

'You left the door unlocked. I suppose it's too much to hope that Paul might do the same with his safe?'

He snorted. 'Not a chance, and don't bother trying to guess the combination. The man has a mind like a steel trap. He's not stupid enough to use his son's birthday or something. It'll be a randomised sequence that he changes every week and memorises.'

'Paul has children?' I had trouble picturing it, to be honest. He seemed even less inclined to family life than me.

'Oh, yes. Three marriages, three divorces, two kids who both ran off to America the first chance they got. Not exactly a unique story for service personnel.'

'Including you? I gather your wife left you after . . .' A puzzle piece slotted into place in my mind. '*After Minsk*, that's what Jane said. Of course.'

Willie exhaled heavily. 'Aye. But this is all the family I need, now.'

Considering his relationship with both of the quad's female residents, I wasn't inclined to analyse that statement too closely. I gave him the gloves and left, nodding politely at Roy as I went. If the dead could talk, what liars they'd surely make of us all.

I'd been intending to return Paul's torch, but something Willie said had stuck in my mind. Instead, I made my way back around the front, past the snowed-under cars and into Roy and Arthur's house. I wanted to discuss things with Birch.

CHAPTER THIRTY-ONE

'Do you believe him?' Birch asked after I related my conversation with Willie Mac. 'Psychopathic killers often start small, harming animals. He didn't like the idea of storing Roy in the shed at first, remember. Guilty conscience?'

I fussed Spiggy's ears, to groans of contentment. He'd leapt to his feet when I opened the bedroom door, his tail wagging vigorously. When I sat on the bed to talk to Birch, the Spaniel had immediately flopped onto my legs and demanded skritches, which I was very happy to supply. We'd barely been together forty-eight hours but he seemed to have taken a liking to me, and I wasn't complaining. For all that I found his lack of obedience frustrating, he was a delightfully friendly dog.

'Willie didn't seem particularly guilt-ridden by Roy's body being there. He was much more concerned that I didn't tell anyone about his specimens, or his affair with Jane. But there was one thing . . .'

I took out my phone and showed Birch the list of deleted files I'd found on Zoe's computer.

'The recordings from Tuesday night were deleted on Wednesday morning, before we spoke to Zoe. That matches what she told us. But all the files are named for the times they cover. Look here.'

I pointed out two files from that night, labelled 2.01 a.m. and 2.15 a.m.

'Willie said he put the first bag in the stream that night, at "around two in the morning". I think this is why Zoe didn't want you poking around, looking at the deleted files.'

Birch nodded. 'She reviewed the recordings that morning, saw Willie going out and coming back again in the dead of night, and decided whatever he was up to wasn't something anyone else needed to see. She might even think he killed Roy, and is covering for him.'

'Exactly. There are other deleted recordings from that same night. Who's to say one of them didn't show Willie leaving his house and entering Roy's?' I shuddered a little to think of Willie wandering around in the dark hallway, yards away from us while we slept. 'He might claim that at two o'clock he was merely hiding those jars in the river, but he could be covering one lie with another. What if he was actually disposing of a murder weapon? I didn't find a garrotte in the attic, remember.'

'Ah, yes. Speaking of which . . .' Birch's moustache twitched and his bright blue eyes glinted. To be quite honest, at that moment things felt so hopeless that I would have happily leapt under the covers with him and stayed there, forgetting all about Roy, Arthur and the 'quad gang' with their quarrels and secrets. But my very own former policeman had something else on his mind.

He held up the manuscript pages I'd collected from Roy and Arthur's desks.

'Gave this a read while you were out. More a collection of scenes than a proper book at the moment, but still exciting to get a sneak peek.' His face suddenly fell. 'Could be the only peek, come to think of it. Roy's gone, and Arthur's obviously not capable. Perhaps Jane could carry on writing them herself?'

I shook my head. 'She's the editor, not an author. From what I can tell, she takes what they write and whips it into shape. It would be quite a step up for her to also write them in the first place.'

'Pity. Didn't you say they're inspired by old missions they went on, too?'

'Arthur told me they sometimes are, though Jane insisted they're not very realistic, so I don't think they're accurate in terms of what really happened. All the more reason to bemoan his loss of memory, though.'

'Was Arthur ever in Munich? No, wait – silly question. He was MI5, not MI6.'

'That's right. Why do you ask?'

Birch tidied the sheaf of manuscript pages and passed it to me. 'I wonder if it was Roy, then. He claimed to be a desk jockey, but if there's one thing you can rely on with spies, they always lie.'

I placed the pages on the bed. 'Not for me, thanks. Jack Spitfire's much more your kind of thing. Now, again: why were you asking about Arthur?'

'Just read from that page,' he said, handing me the manuscript again. 'You'll see.'

The bar on Dunkelrossstraße was somehow darker inside than the night outside. That night had barely begun, but nobody had thought to tell the barflies of Berlin, who already filled the dank, smoky space with a mass of winter-coated bodies. Jack Spitfire manoeuvred his way to the bar, ordered one of the odd, pale German lagers, and waited. He glanced at his Omega Speedmaster. Three minutes to nine. Heidi would be here soon. Wouldn't she?

Spitfire surreptitiously checked the room, in case she'd beat him to it. But few women frequented a bar like this, and of the half-dozen in sight, none could hold a candle to Heidi. Of course, first there was work to do. This was a dangerous city for him – and now for her, also. But later tonight, after they could both declare 'mission accomplished', he would take the Bavarian girl to bed and show her a real Englishman's stiff upper lip.

'Really, Birch?' I said, trying not to laugh. 'Why on earth are you making me read this?'

He reddened. 'Keep going. I promise you'll see soon enough.'

Nine o' clock came and went without sign of Heidi. Five past – ten past – a quarter past.

Something was wrong.

Every man knows that women are always late. Clothes, make-up, a natural lack of punctuality; Spitfire had heard all these reasons and more. But this was no game. Tonight, of all nights, Heidi should be here.

He finished the lager, grimacing at its hoppy aftertaste, and pushed through the bar crowd to return outside. On the street he took a deep breath of cool air and looked both ways. There were other bars on this street, further along on either side. He mentally tossed a coin and turned right, hoping the girl had merely been so stupid as to enter the wrong establishment.

Fewer people than he expected were on the Straße. Couples, braced together against the cold; single men, either making for a bar or leaving one; the odd car drifting by. Nobody seemed to be in a hurry.

Nobody except the man Spitfire saw dash out of an unlit archway, one hundred yards ahead.

Years of training and experience told him this wasn't normal. Whoever it was moved like someone trying to quickly put distance between himself and the archway. Spitfire was running before he consciously realised it, closing the distance between them. The escaping man rounded the corner of Dunkelrossstraße, and

Spitfire followed. But directly he turned the corner himself, the only movement he saw was a taxicab speeding away. He whirled round, looking for another, but the road was empty. He could hotwire a parked car but by then the cab would be long gone.

Instead, Spitfire returned to the archway. It led to a courtyard, as was common in this part of Berlin. With both hope and fear rising, he found an internal space divided between parking on one side and a garden on the other. On one stone path stood a wooden bench, and on the bench sat a woman, her head bowed as if sleeping.

But Heidi wasn't sleeping.

A thin red line bruised the Bavarian girl's neck. Spitfire checked for a pulse, but found none. All his work, ruined by a Russian garrotte! And he'd let her executioner escape into the night, unidentified.

'God damn you, you poor, stupid girl,' he whispered to her corpse. When he called this in to London, they would abort and demand his return. But Spitfire wasn't ready to go home. As far as he was concerned, there was still a mission to complete, and he intended to do so with or without Heidi's help.

'You there! What are you doing in here?' A voice called out in German.

Spitfire looked up into the cold, suspicious eyes of an approaching Schutzpolizei.

I put down the pages, bewildered. My mind filled with a jumble of puzzle pieces, all vying for space as I tried to fit them together. The victim in this story was a woman, not a man, but still . . .

'Can't be a coincidence, can it?' Birch said.

'No, I don't think it can. Is this why Roy was so keen for me to send him a copy of the Gerber file? He said it was my father who found Gerber's body. Do you think it happened just like this? He described it so vividly.'

'Remember, it was Roy who ran the mission from London – or so he claimed. I wonder if he was in Munich after all.'

'But why would he lie about that?'

Birch said nothing, because of course I knew the answer was both obvious and impossible to know. Obvious because, as he'd said, spies lie like they breathe; impossible to know because there were any number of reasons Roy Singleton might have omitted his presence in Munich from the official report . . . and from what he told me.

Had he been there to keep an eye on my father? Had Roy witnessed everything? A horrid thought came to mind: had killing Gerber been the plan all along? Was my father a decoy, sent to flush out the German so he could be assassinated? Could Roy have been that assassin? No, everyone agreed that Roy had spent his career behind a desk, not running around Europe killing people.

Or was that another lie?

'I wonder what Arthur might know about this?' I said. 'He's the co-author, after all.'

'Surely *knew*, past tense. Even if he did at the time, he won't remember now.'

I shuffled off the bed, taking the pages with me. 'You might be surprised. Sometimes people with Alzheimer's can't remember what they did last week, but will recall their youth like it was yesterday.'

'Arthur would have been around forty when this happened. Hardly his youth.'

'Still in his prime, though. If he was involved, it might still be in there somewhere.'

CHAPTER THIRTY-TWO

When I knocked on Arthur's study door, he called out, 'Come in!' with a firm, confident voice. I entered to find him sitting at the computer, as if mid-writing.

'I'm sorry to disturb you,' I said.

'It's fine, it's fine,' he said, turning to face me with a smile. 'I need to take a break, anyway. Have a . . . um, seat . . .' His arm hovered mid-gesture as he realised there were no other seats. Then he got up and offered his desk chair to me. 'Take this one, I'll stand.'

Not wanting to risk upsetting what appeared to be a moment of clarity and confidence for him, I took the seat while he leant against a filing cabinet. I stole a glance at the computer screen as I sat down. An open Word document with nothing on it. Either he'd deleted what he'd written when I entered, or hadn't written anything to begin with.

'What can I do for you . . . ?' Arthur asked, still smiling. Nevertheless, he hadn't used my name yet, and couldn't mask the uncertainty in his eyes.

'Gwinny,' I reminded him politely. 'The woman with the dogs.' I didn't mention Roy for fear of upsetting him.

'Yes, of course,' he said, relieved. 'Go on.'

I passed him the pages Birch had been reading. 'I wondered if this first draft of *Spitfire Behind the Wall* is based on a real mission. You told me before that some of the Jack Spitfire stories are inspired by real-life operations.'

'That's right. We all work out the stories together.'

'So was this one real? The mission to Berlin?'

I saw then what I'd failed to notice before, despite the clues being there all along. The slight worry in Arthur's expression, the internal calculations going on, and finally, a lie just plausible enough to pass muster:

'Remind me which one that is, would you? It's been a while since I saw the draft.'

I obliged, and recounted the scene. Spitfire arriving at the bar to meet his contact, Heidi; waiting in vain; returning to the street in case she went to a different bar; seeing a mysterious figure dash out of a courtyard entrance; finding Heidi in that courtyard, strangled to death. It seemed impossible that the parallels with my father's meeting with Gerber were merely a coincidence, and I said so.

'I didn't write that chapter,' Arthur said, though I suspected the truth was he'd never heard of it before. 'That must be one of Roy's.'

'But you said you plan the books together. Did Roy tell you he was going to write this?'

'We work out the story, then we write different

chapters, then we give it to Jane to edit. We've written a dozen books like that, you know.'

They'd actually written at least twenty, according to the editions on his shelf. Perhaps that was an indication of when Arthur's memory had begun to fail.

'So is it based on a real mission? A mission in Munich, perhaps? In 1988?'

A light came on in Arthur's eyes. 'Munich! That was a fiasco. Roy told me all about it after he came back. His man was supposed to deliver the asset to Roy, you see. Simple contact, "Come and meet my friend", boom. Target in the bag, bring him home on an RAF transport, Ivan would never even know we were there. But Roy's man fell for a fake contact sting and yapped. Stupid, really. Roy always had a code, he should have known that. So Ivan got to the target first and garrotted him, usual KGB method. Roy came back empty-handed and covered the whole thing up. He had a theory the fake contact was one of ours, a double agent, but he never did find out. Still bothers him . . .'

The light in his eyes faded along with his voice. Arthur fell silent while I sat back and assembled this surprisingly clear recollection into something that made sense. So Roy *had* been in Munich with my father, who was surely the 'man' in question. My father was to contact Gerber and persuade him to meet Roy, who would then spirit the German radio man back to England on a military aircraft. But someone – possibly a KGB agent – had tricked my father into talking about the mission, and before Roy could snatch him, Herr Gerber was killed.

Perhaps even on a courtyard bench. Roy and my father returned to England, where MI6 made up a story that Gerber had vanished, letting everyone assume he'd been taken across the Iron Curtain. That was the 'COVER-UP!' to which my father's notes had referred.

'Hang on, though,' I said. 'How did Roy get the Munich police to play along, if they had Gerber's body? Wouldn't they have insisted on recording that, rather than pretending he'd disappeared?'

Arthur shrugged. 'Everyone's playing the game. You're on one side of the Curtain or the other and nothing in between, that's what Roy always says. Keep the truth from Ivan at all costs.'

Including falsifying your own national security records in order to fool the enemy. What a sordid 'game' the Cold War had been. I still couldn't quite wrap my head around the idea that my father was somehow involved.

I left Arthur to his blank screen and stood outside in the hallway, looking up at the attic hatch. There was nothing else for it. It was time to take a proper look around up there.

Not wanting to disturb the dogs, I decided to return the manuscript pages to Birch after searching the attic. For now, I folded them and shoved them in my pocket. Then I took the hooked rod from the cupboard, opened the hatch, and watched the ladder descend with that familiar metallic scraping sound.

I didn't relish what I was about to do. The attic was dark and full of cobwebs, and I'd already found a dead body up there. Not exactly inviting. But Birch couldn't do it with his dodgy ankle, so I took a deep breath, told myself not to be a silly old scaredy-cat, and climbed the ladder.

Halfway up I remembered that I still had Paul's LED torch in my pocket, so fished it out and used that instead of my phone. It was much brighter, allowing me to see more of the attic, but also cast shadows dark and deep enough to make a German expressionist film proud. I hefted the weight of the solid LED torch in my hand. If Dr Caligari was lurking up here, I'd give him what for.

Thankfully, aside from the packing boxes and carpet offcuts I'd seen earlier, there was precious little to be seen. The mysterious tied-off bin bags turned out to contain old clothes or, in one case, unused plugs, wires and cables. I wondered if Birch kept a similar bag in his house. Chances were high, I felt.

Moving carefully beyond the boxes and bags, the only things I found lurking in the shadows were beams, joists and struts, and plenty of cobwebs, suggesting Arthur had been telling the truth; normally, nobody came up to the attic.

But someone had, to either dump Roy's body or murder him in situ.

I cast around the angled beams and struts, wondering if the shadows might serve to hide a killer. Not a power-mad German hypnotist, but a flesh and blood murderer patiently waiting for Roy in the attic, silently emerging to attack when he entered.

Except . . . how did they know he would come into

the attic? And how did they enter the house without triggering Zoe's CCTV cameras?

I weaved through the obstacle course of angled beams holding up the roof, hoping against hope to find something that might help. Arthur's ring had been found here, so perhaps there was more. A thread of fabric caught on a loose nail, or another personal belonging lying on the floor.

If there was, I couldn't see it. I raised the torch beam, looking back at the storage boxes and vanity dresser. I'd walked further than I realised—

Wait a moment. What vanity dresser?

I turned back, bumping my head on a beam. All these wooden joists and struts had disorientated me enough that I wasn't sure in which direction I faced any more. I swept the torch beam around and saw the storage boxes, cable bags and open hatch behind me. Then I turned ninety degrees to find a different set of storage boxes, a vanity dresser . . . and a second, closed hatch.

A second hatch? I pictured the layout of the quad below me and calculated that this must be Paul's attic. His mysterious phone calls came back to me as I crept further along, sweeping the light across the floor. Beyond this new hatch were more angled beams and struts, so I kept walking . . . and after another forest of corner joists turned again to find a third hatch, this time above Zoe and Willie Mac's place. Further on and another turn later I was above Jane's house, before finally completing a circuit back to where I began.

The attic space ran all the way around the quad.

CHAPTER THIRTY-THREE

Now I knew why Zoe's cameras hadn't recorded the killer going in or out of the door to Roy's house. Why risk being spotted when you could move about unseen using the attic?

In my mind, there was no longer any question that the scraping noise I'd heard in the middle of the night was the attic ladder opening. Had the killer used it to steal into Roy's bedroom, strangle him, then carry him up to the attic to hide the body? Or had they known he'd be up there at a certain time, and waited for him? But if so, how? And why was he going up there in the first place?

There was a possible answer to those last few questions which connected them all. That it hadn't been coincidence, or chance. That Roy and the killer had arranged to meet in the attic, away from the prying eyes of everyone else in the house. Roy would never have imagined he was walking to his doom.

If that was true, it still left several big questions. What had the meeting been about? With whom had it been? And why meet in secret?

Paul's torch suddenly felt heavy in my hand.

I pulled up the ladder from Roy's hallway and closed the hatch. Then I walked through the angled support struts towards Paul's house, where I opened the hatch and got down on my hands and knees, poking my head out to make sure there was nobody in the hallway below. Satisfied the coast was clear, I lowered the ladder and climbed down.

It made no sound. Did that mean the ladder was well used? Perhaps, although Roy's continued to scrape despite definitely having been used recently, so that didn't prove anything.

Paul was nowhere to be found upstairs so I descended to the ground floor, hearing voices grow louder with each step. He was in the kitchen, making tea and talking to Jane.

I knocked on the open door and said, 'Hello, you two.'

They whirled round in surprise. Paul almost dropped the teabag he'd been straining.

'Gwinny,' he gasped. 'You really must stop walking straight into people's houses, you know. Despite everything, you're still a guest.'

'I didn't come in by the door,' I said, without further explanation. 'Now, first things first: this is yours.'

He couldn't have looked more confused when I handed him the pocket torch. 'Where did you find this?

It went missing before you even arrived.'

'I know. Finish making your tea, you may need it.'

As he did, I told them about Arthur, his dementia and the box of stolen items. By the time I finished, Paul was sitting down at his small kitchen table, cradling his tea with a sad expression. Jane remained by the kitchen window, looking on in sympathy.

'It seems Roy was covering for him the whole time,' I concluded. 'We'll never know why for sure, but he evidently wanted to maintain the status quo for as long as possible.'

Paul nodded. 'This casts many things in a different light.' He sighed, though he seemed more annoyed than anything.

'Does it change what we were saying, though?' Jane said. 'I'm not sure it does.'

'Change anything about what?' I asked.

'When you came in we were exchanging theories,' Paul explained. 'I was pretty sure Arthur must have killed Roy. He's the only real, viable suspect. Now, though . . .'

'Being mentally unsound doesn't exonerate him,' Jane pointed out. 'He might have killed Roy in an inexplicable rage that he doesn't even remember.'

'I had the same thought,' I said. 'But I disagree that he's the only viable suspect. In fact, I think it could have been anyone.' I watched their faces carefully for any flicker of recognition. None came, but that didn't prove anything.

'Nobody left their house that night,' Paul said. 'Zoe

said there's nothing on her CCTV. Therefore, it must be Arthur.'

I had my doubts about Zoe's truthfulness on that score, but they weren't the most important thing right now.

'There didn't need to be anything on the CCTV,' I said. 'Remember I said I didn't come in by the door? Follow me.'

I turned on my heel and walked back up the stairs. After a moment's hesitation, Paul and Jane followed.

'Hang on, what do you mean by that?' Paul asked. 'What did you do, climb through an upstairs window?'

I waited for them at the top of the stairs, then gestured at the ladder. 'Nothing so crude.'

He seemed baffled. 'I don't understand. You've been hiding in my attic?'

'Really, Paul. Willie Mac already told me you have the house blueprints in that safe of yours, and you were the only person, besides Roy, living here when the extensions were built. Do you really expect me to believe you don't know the attic is one continuous space?'

He fixed me with a serious gaze. For the first time I saw a flash of the 'boss' that the other residents, and presumably many people in MI6, had dealt with.

'Roy worked with the architect and supervised the renovations,' he said calmly. 'I looked after the financial and logistical side of the work.'

'Why were you looking for your torch in the middle of the day?'

That threw him. 'I'm sorry?'

'As you pointed out, it was lost before Birch and I arrived. But when you came into Roy's lounge, the first thing you did was ask if anyone had seen your torch. Had you been looking for it because you knew you'd be going into the attic later?'

'I haven't been up there in more than a decade,' he protested. 'I wanted to know where it was simply because it was missing. Why wouldn't I?'

'Perhaps because the private areas of your house, as we saw yesterday, are a horrendous mess? I would have thought you'd assume it was lost in a pile of magazines or stuffed in an archive box.'

He bristled. 'That's not where I keep my torch. Everything has its place.'

'Yes, it does. Tell me, where's the place for a garrotte? Is that in your safe, too?'

Paul stared at me, dumbfounded. Then he laughed once, a loud and hollow sound.

'You can't seriously think I killed Roy, you stupid woman.'

Jane bristled. 'She has a point, Paul. You can't discount it just because you don't like it.'

He turned on her. 'This is absurd. It's obvious that Arthur did it. No messing around in the attic required. We even found his ring next to Roy's body.'

'That could have been planted,' I said.

Paul narrowed his eyes at me. 'Are you familiar with the principle of Occam's razor? Roy was found in Arthur's house, with Arthur's ring, and you have just told us that Arthur is a mentally unstable thief. Nobody else is remotely likely.'

'Nobody? Not even someone who said that "with Roy gone, there's nothing to stop me"? That you can now "stick to the plan", because "the others are completely unaware"? Come to that, I'd like to know what you meant by "Arthur will get what's coming to him". Because those don't sound like the words of an innocent man.'

Paul's expression turned to confusion. 'Have you been . . . *eavesdropping* on me?'

'It may not be as sophisticated as an electronic spy bug in your phone, but my ears work just fine. So what was the plan, Paul? You have several ex-wives and children, whom I presume have bled you dry of money. Does Roy's death clear the way for you to sell this presumably very valuable house and retire on the proceeds – all the while letting Arthur take the blame, thanks to the ring you planted on Roy's body?'

He reeled from my barrage of accusations. I had him on the ropes. He turned to Jane for help, but she folded her arms and waited for an explanation. Finally, Paul's shoulders slumped.

'Very well. Come with me.'

He limped past me, and the attic ladder, to his study.

CHAPTER THIRTY-FOUR

Once again I marvelled at the chaos that Paul kept tucked away privately, in stark contrast to the buttoned-up demeanour he presented elsewhere. I pitied whichever of his children would have to fly back from America to sort it all out when he was gone, knowing from personal experience what a daunting task lay before them.

He stood in the middle of the room, leaning on his stick. 'First of all, you should know – and Jane already does, perfectly well, despite her playing the innocent – that it is impossible for me to sell this house. In fact, thanks to Zoe's largesse, we all own it equally.'

'Zoe? I thought you and Roy bought this place together.'

'We did. Then, five years ago, Zoe made a lot of money. What's it called again?' He looked to Jane for help.

'Bitcoin,' she answered, explaining it to me. 'You know she's a tech wizard, of course. She makes investments online, trading and whatnot. One day, out of the blue, she announced she had something to tell us and assembled us all in Roy's lounge.'

Paul continued the story. 'She'd apparently made a small fortune, and had an offer to present. At the time, Roy and I held the mortgage, with each resident paying us rent. Zoe said she'd pay off the whole debt in one fell swoop, on the condition that we redistributed ownership equally among the six of us, and amended our wills so that anyone departing' – he emphasised the word's ambiguity – 'bequeathed their share to be split among the others.'

A puzzle piece slotted into place. 'Five years . . . Arthur seems to think that's how long you've been living here.'

Paul shook his head. 'No, we bought the quad fifteen years ago. Well, it wasn't a quad at that point, but you know what I mean. Arthur moved in with Roy about ten years ago, after we built the extension. The others joined soon after.'

'But his memory is shot, remember? And in the lounge, he thought Zoe had something important to tell you all . . . which she did, five years ago. I really should have spotted it sooner. *You* should have all spotted it sooner.'

Jane shuffled awkwardly. 'I did tell you that Roy was fibbing a bit when he presented us to you as a big happy community.'

'Nevertheless, with joint ownership of the quad, that means the last man standing gets the lot.'

She puffed out her cheeks. 'I hadn't thought of it like that. What a mind you have, Gwinny.'

I wasn't sure whether that was intended as a compliment or insult. It didn't matter.

'None of this explains why Roy "can't stop you" now he's dead,' I reminded Paul. 'Or why "Arthur will get what's coming to him".'

He sighed, then leant his stick against the desk and slowly crouched, wincing at his joints. The spilt stack of magazines Spiggy had knocked over still lay on the floor, leaving the safe visible. While Paul turned the dial, I sneaked a peek over his shoulder; as Willie had guessed, the combination was no simple date of birth, but something random and complicated. Finally, with a loud click, the lock released and Paul pulled open the door.

Still looking over his shoulder, I could see that the safe was full of folders, themselves stuffed full with papers. Despite the seeming disorder, Paul knew exactly where to find what he was looking for and retrieved several items. He stood up, placed them on the desk, then opened the topmost folder to produce a set of folded blueprints.

'First, you wanted to check these. I can't say I've looked at them since the work was done a dozen years ago.'

I unfolded the blueprints and examined them. I'm no architect and have never even had an extension built, so wasn't very confident that I knew what I was looking at, but I saw no indication of separating walls in the attic.

'Looks like it was part of the plan all along,' I said. 'But you claim you had no idea?'

'As I said, Roy supervised the work. I dealt with contracts and finances.' He took the blueprints from me and returned the folder to the desk, taking another in its place. 'As for what you think you overheard, this will explain everything.'

He opened the folder to reveal many pages of printed reports, letters, leaflets . . . and X-rays.

'Stage four,' he said quietly. 'Spread to my lungs and spine. The consultant tells me it won't be much longer before it reaches my brain. It's inoperable.'

'Oh, God,' Jane gasped. 'Is it . . . I mean, are you in pain . . . ?'

'Only spiritually,' he replied with a faint smile. 'That's how it reached this stage to begin with. Other than the old leg, up until a few months ago I felt fine.'

'But you weren't. For God's sake, Paul, why didn't you say anything?'

He merely shrugged. I'd only met him yesterday, but the answer was obvious; here was an intensely private and proudly self-sufficient man. There was nothing his friends could do to help him, so why distress them? I suddenly remembered how Spiggy had kept sniffing around him with such interest. Some people believe dogs can smell cancer.

'I did say something, actually,' Paul said. 'But only to Roy.'

'He knew?!' Jane seemed incensed that Roy should be privy to this while she wasn't. Understandable, given

270

how her own husband had succumbed to pancreatic cancer.

'Hold on, though,' I said. 'I still don't see how this explains what you said on the phone.'

Paul handed me a brochure. It was a glossy affair, depicting a modern but tasteful building in a green, wooded landscape under a bright blue sky. It reminded me of the advertisements for retirement villages I'd briefly perused when my father first became unable to care for himself. But then I saw the name, and realised this was a very different place.

The Arcadia Clinic, Lucerne, Switzerland.

'A clinic?' Jane said, looking over my shoulder. 'But you said it's inoperable.'

'It's . . . not that kind of clinic.' I showed her the welcome letter, complete with a photo of a close-up on two elderly hands wearing wedding rings and clasped affectionately. Below it was the clinic's slogan, '*Et in Arcadia ego*'.

'Roy and I argued about it. Rather a lot,' Paul explained. 'It may be my decision, but no assisted dying centre in the world will let you just walk in by yourself, and he refused to accompany me. I tried to make him understand it's for the best, but he wouldn't sanction it and I couldn't bear the thought of parting acrimoniously. With Roy gone, I can proceed at last . . . though I still need someone to accompany me.'

'What about your family? You have children, don't you?'

Paul balked. 'I wouldn't dream of putting them

through that. To tell the truth, I've been trying to persuade my solicitor. That's who you heard me talking to on the phone. He's understandably reluctant.'

Jane was fuming. 'You selfish bastard. What were you going to do, up and vanish one morning without telling us?'

'My plan was to inform you all the night before, along with my children, once arrangements were in place and the occasion was imminent. This reaction is precisely why I didn't tell everyone, by the way. It's my life, Jane. Mine to choose how to conduct it, and how to end it.'

I thought back to the calls I'd overheard. Everything Paul said made sense, apart from one thing. 'What will Arthur get that's coming to him?' I asked.

He sighed. 'Money. Apart from the house share, my current will leaves everything to Roy. With him gone, I earlier instructed my solicitor to amend it so that Arthur gets it all instead. But now I know he's not competent, and probably a killer, so I'll have to change it yet again. At this rate there'll be nothing left after the legal fees.'

No wonder he'd looked annoyed when I told him about Arthur.

'You've just admitted that having Roy out of the way eases your path to going through with this,' I said, 'and without wanting to sound indelicate, you quite literally have nothing to lose. Surely that's a motive for murder.'

He shrugged. 'Perhaps, but I promise you'll find

272

no evidence or proof that I killed my best friend. Not because I'm a criminal mastermind, but because I'm innocent.'

'If he was your best friend, how come you don't share his house?'

'Because the quickest way for friends to fall out is to live under the same roof, constantly under one another's feet.' Paul gathered up the brochure and papers into their folders, then replaced them in the safe. 'And before you ask, I have three failed marriages which will attest to the truth of that.'

'How long?' Jane asked.

Paul turned to her. 'To live? Six months to a year, they say. To visit the clinic? Eight weeks' notice, if I'm lucky.'

'Enough time to finally finish that jigsaw in the lounge,' I said with a sad smile. 'I'm truly sorry. I can't imagine what it must be like to make a decision like this.'

'I doubt anyone can, until they do. What was it Hemingway said about going bankrupt? *It happened gradually, then suddenly.*'

Much like my own father's death, in a way. For years, he and I both knew the end was drawing near – though we never discussed assisted dying, as he was much too stubborn and cantankerous for that – until one morning, sitting in the lounge and without warning, he 'suddenly' drew his last breath.

Jane and I left Paul in silence, going our separate ways in the cold garden as the winter night once again began to claim its territory. I barely noticed; my mind was racing, reorganising the puzzle of Roy's murder and trying to make sense of it. Was Paul truly innocent? Or simply confident that I couldn't prove anything? What *could* I prove about Roy's death, come to that? Not much.

By now the towels had finished washing, so I moved them into the tumble dryer before returning upstairs. Walking through Roy and Arthur's lounge, I saw Paul's jigsaw of the old London skyline. I recalled his words when I'd asked him about it: 'They can build all the bloody skyscrapers they like, but they can't escape the past.'

How true that seemed to be.

CHAPTER THIRTY-FIVE

Once again, the dogs treated me like a returning hero when I walked into the guest bedroom. Birch was back on his feet, holding on to the windowsill for support while he crouched up and down, rotating his foot.

'Feeling any better?'

'Swelling's gone down, which helps. How did you get on?'

I told him about the attic, Paul's cancer, and what Arthur had related about events in Munich.

'Blimey,' Birch said, sitting on the bed to massage his ankle. 'To think your father was right there in the middle of a botched mission.'

'Not just in the middle of it. If what Arthur said is true, it was my father's fault that it all went wrong.'

'Pardon, ma'am, but that's victim-blaming. The only person to blame is whoever killed Gerber. Without them, your father would have been fine and Gerber could have lived out his days in England.'

True or not, it didn't make me feel any better.

'This whole trip was a mistake, really, wasn't it?' I said. 'My father had a secret life I knew nothing about, the one person who could tell me about it is dead, plus you've injured yourself and missed your policeman's lunch to boot. Even Colin Bloody Prendergast doesn't remember me, so I doubt I'll be getting that part any time soon.'

'Would you want it anyway?' Birch asked. 'Director sounds like a nightmare. Calling you hysterical.'

'If only he was unique in that. Directors, producers, even other actors . . . every actress I know has been called "hormonal" and "hysterical" more times than we can count.'

'Doesn't make it right. Just like killing Gerber wasn't right, no matter what your father might have let slip.'

I took his hand, thankful that despite his occasional old-fashioned machismo, Birch was always on my side. Then I opened the photos on my phone again, looking through the pictures I'd sent Roy. If only I'd seen the file when my father was still alive, he could have told me about the mission himself, and explained what all these numbers meant . . .

'A code,' I whispered, as a puzzle piece slowly solidified in my mind's eye.

'Beg pardon?'

'Something Arthur said, when he recounted what went wrong in Munich. He said my father shouldn't have been fooled by the fake contact, because "Roy always had a code". And Roy told me that he'd deciphered my father's notes. It's what he wanted to talk to me about yesterday morning. So if those numbers are a code, it must have been something they both knew.'

Birch cleared his throat. 'Beg pardon, but neither Roy nor your father can decode it for us now.'

'Surely it can't be that complicated, though. OK, Roy was a spy. But no matter what he may have got himself mixed up in, my father wasn't. The code would have to be simple for him to use it.'

'Fair. Not like he had an Enigma machine in the attic.' He paused. 'Did he?'

I laughed. 'Thankfully, our attic was converted to another floor years ago. Probably for the best, otherwise after this week I'm not sure I could face going up there.' I returned to the numbers. 'So what could it be . . . ?'

C1972
20-31-3
319-23-4
359-14-6, 154-3-10 187-22-7, 404-3-4,
42-18-7 288-12-5 105-24-10
7-16-3 228-10-3?

'Perhaps each number stands in for a letter?' Birch suggested.

'One of the very first numbers is thirty-one. There are only twenty-six letters in the alphabet.'

'Thirty-six if you add zero to nine afterwards.'

'OK, how does that explain three hundred and nineteen?'

Birch didn't have an answer for that, but tried the code anyway, typing it out on his phone.

'T . . . E . . . C . . . either C-S, or E-I . . . W . . . D . . .'

'*Teccswd* or *Teceiwd*? I think you're barking up the wrong tree.'

He tried a few more times, shifting which number could represent A at the start of the sequence, but every attempt was gibberish.

'Well, it's obviously not that,' I said. 'The format doesn't look right for something that would form English words, anyway. Also, look: the final number of every trio is ten or lower. That seems unlikely to happen by chance.'

'Hmm, well spotted. You're right, it has to be something your father could do fairly easily and that Roy could decode here, without specialist equipment. He was long gone from Whitehall.'

'He hadn't seen my father in decades, either. They must have worked this code out years ago, yet Roy still recognised and decoded it when he saw the photos. Some kind of long-term shared knowledge . . .' I jerked upright, earning a grumble from Spiggy, who was asleep with his floppy-eared head on my lap.

Birch's moustache twitched. 'I know that look. What are you thinking?'

'Wait here. I have an idea.'

I gently slid Spiggy's head off my leg and stepped out of the room, turning down the hallway towards Roy's study.

As far as I could tell, nobody had been in here since

my last visit. The papers, printouts and reference books all remained in the same place. But I was interested in a different kind of book altogether. I ran my finger along the fiction shelf, beyond the Spitfire collection into the paperback thrillers. Le Carré, Cussler, Hassel, Smith . . . Forsyth.

My finger stopped on the cracked gold spine of *The Day of the Jackal*. I took it from the shelf, opened it to the indicia page, and nodded in recognition. I'd read the book myself when I was younger, intent on devouring my father's collection (much to my Regency-classic-reading mother's disapproval). Now, it might hold the key to everything.

Leaving Roy's study, I noticed Arthur's door was ajar. He wasn't in, so I slipped inside and walked to his desk.

Seeing Jane in Paul's house had reminded me of something I'd seen yesterday morning. I slid open Arthur's desk drawer and reached to the back, hoping it would still be there . . . it was. I'd been so preoccupied trying to find Roy, the incongruity hadn't stood out at the time. But none of the residents smoked, so why did Arthur own a metal Zippo flip-top lighter?

The answer was that he didn't. What I now held in my hand was Jane's lighter, stolen by Arthur along with Willie's gloves, Paul's torch and the other items I'd found. Why it was hidden here rather than in the utility room box with the other stolen pieces was a mystery, though. Did Arthur carry a torch, no pun intended, for Jane? Willie Mac obviously had for decades.

I gave the flint wheel an experimental flick, but it

barely sparked and didn't light, so I pocketed the lighter and made a mental note to return it when I next ran into Jane.

'It's not *circa*,' I said when I returned to the guest bedroom, closing the door behind me.

'Beg pardon?' Birch looked up from his phone, where he was still trying to decode the numbers.

I sat on the bed and brandished the golden *Jackal* paperback at him. 'I recognised this edition yesterday when I saw it on Roy's shelf, because I have the same one on my bookshelf at home.'

'Sorry, not following.'

'It's a book cipher, Birch. They're centuries old. Two people each have the same edition of a book, and the code numbers refer to words found in it. That's why the final number in every trio is so low; each line of text only contains so many words. And it's impossible to crack . . . unless you know *exactly* which book and edition is being used.'

'So how do you know this code uses that particular book?'

'When I first phoned Roy, he asked me questions to make sure I really was Henry's daughter. One was to name his favourite author. My father never expressed a singular favourite to me, but he'd apparently told Roy it was Frederick Forsyth, particularly *Day of the Jackal*. Add to that, this is the only matching book I've seen here so far. Finally, "C1972" doesn't stand for *circa 1972* like I thought. Look.' I opened the book and pointed to the indicia page:

Birch's eyebrows shot up. 'Blimey. Let's test it.'

'What's the first set of numbers again?'

He read from his phone. 'Twenty, thirty-one, three.'

I turned to page 20 and counted thirty-one lines down the page. Then I read the third word on that line: '*Munich.*'

Birch and I locked eyes. Sensing something in the air, Ronnie woofed quietly. Birch automatically reached out to stroke the Lab's ears and continued to read the numbers.

Later, as I rummaged around in my emergency dog bag, Birch asked, 'Are you sure about this?'

It was a simple question, to which I couldn't provide a simple answer. I was almost certain now that I knew who'd killed Roy, but I lacked definitive proof. Instead, I had to hope the murderer would reveal themselves. If I'd miscalculated, there was a good chance they'd go free.

'It's the only way,' I reassured Birch. 'Don't worry, it'll be fine. I hope.'

He clearly didn't think so. We'd discussed the plan for half an hour already, and I was confident it would work, but the lifelong policeman in him wanted more time to gather evidence, more interrogations to force a confession. I knew now that we'd never get enough.

I found what I was looking for in the bag and clipped Spiggy on-lead. He panted with excitement, ready and eager to venture out into the dark. Ronnie looked less enthused when I waggled his lead at him, probably because it was obvious Birch wasn't coming with us, but he let himself be clipped on all the same.

'I'll make the phone calls now,' I said, closing the door behind me.

Predictably, Arthur was downstairs in his favourite chair, reading his book of Soviet aircraft. I almost told him to stay put and not go anywhere, but where would he go? Come to that, when had he last had something to eat? Without Roy to arrange his days he might do nothing but sit there and waste away. I couldn't worry about that now. Other people would have to deal with him, once justice had been done.

In the hallway I slipped on my coat, my scarf and Roy's wellies (which I was becoming used to, despite my small feet), then turned to the phone table. The memo board above it listed each resident's phone line, all the same number except for the final digit. I picked up the phone and dialled.

'Paul Dixon.'

'It's Gwinny. I'm calling a house meeting.'

'Ms Tuffel, may I remind you again that you don't actually live here?'

'I know. But I also know who killed Roy, which I think qualifies as special circumstances, don't you? Be at Roy and Arthur's lounge in half an hour, please.'

He sniffed. 'Why not just tell me? What makes you think you've got it right this time, anyway?'

'Because now I'm sure, and everyone deserves to hear the truth. Besides, I need to take the dogs for a quick walk around the quad before I can finalise everything. See you then.'

Next I called Jane, then Zoe and Willie Mac, with the same brief message and invitation. Then I opened the garden door and walked out into the cold night air.

CHAPTER THIRTY-SIX

Despite Ronnie's initial reluctance, the dogs needed the walk. We'd barely stepped outside before they both crouched and toileted, leaving me bending over to pick up, a torch clenched between my teeth and a poo bag pulled inside-out over my hand. I hoped none of the residents decided to come early, not least so they wouldn't see me in this undignified position.

I tied off the bags, added them to the small but growing pile by the door, then proceeded into the quad garden's tall hedgerows, where the paths were still deep in snow. Soon they surrounded and enveloped me completely. Anyone looking out from their house would only know I was there by my torch beam, moving slowly through the high, sparse branches.

Somewhere, a door opened.

Ronnie walked ahead, peering into the hedges in case of wildlife. From time to time, he veered off to one side or another, but I pulled him back and kept him on track. Spiggy sniffed the ground intently, his nose and ears tucked low. I doubted anything had changed much since we were last here, but a dog's nose is orders of magnitude more sensitive than a human's, so perhaps he could detect something that would remain forever beyond my reach. For a moment, I enjoyed the quiet simplicity of being out here, alone, with the dogs.

Was I, though?

My footsteps crunched through the deep snow's semi-frozen crust, making it difficult to hear any other sound. I paused, straining my ears. Was that someone else's footsteps? Or the sound of my own, echoing off the close-knit shrubbery?

'Hello?' I called out. The sound hung in the stillness of the night, met by silence. Perhaps I was imagining things.

Spiggy cocked his leg up a nearby hedge then moved on, ears flapping, eager to fulfil his quest to sniff every square inch of the garden.

We turned a corner, and once again I could have sworn I heard footsteps. I stopped and turned in a circle, but saw nothing.

'Hello? Who's there?'

Perhaps this wasn't such a great idea. Suddenly, there was movement behind me, rapid footsteps approaching—

I gasped as someone threw a loop of cord over my head, then pulled it tight around my neck.

Immediately, I let go of the dog leads and torch to claw at my throat, gasping for air as I tried in vain to find purchase on the garrotte. My feet slipped in the snow, and I lurched sideways. The attacker held on, refusing to loosen their grip despite my sputtering and wheezing. My breath grew hoarser by the moment.

There was no doubt about it. They intended to kill me.

What was it Willie Mac had said about strangulation? That it was more about patience than strength. According to him, it took a minute or more to kill someone this way. How much time had passed already? Ten seconds? Twenty? Each tick became a lifetime as adrenaline flooded my body. I struggled against my attacker, the same person I was now sure had also killed Roy. I choked and coughed, falling to my knees as Spiggy and Ronnie took up the chorus. Surely someone inside the house must hear them barking?

My breath grew ragged. Somewhere in the distance, the Christmas lights around Roy's lounge window glowed dimly, their points blurred in my vision. More footsteps approached, but I couldn't tell from which direction. I ceased struggling, ready to drop to the ground . . .

'That's enough of that,' Birch said with characteristic understatement. The next thing I heard was a solid *crack*, and the pressure around my neck eased.

I fell to the ground, breathing heavily, then rolled onto my back and scrambled for the torch. My fingers closed around it and I shone the beam in Birch's direction. He stood leaning on a bench, with Paul's walking stick raised over his head. Below him on the ground lay a crumpled form, groaning in pain. Ronnie stood by his side, barking at the fallen attacker.

Jane pushed herself upright and snarled back. Ronnie whined and retreated behind Birch's legs.

More footsteps approached, then, and another powerful light beam – from a black aluminium LED torch, I'd wager – joined the fray.

'What the hell's going on?' Paul asked, taking in the scene.

'This oaf attacked me,' Jane pleaded. 'I don't know what's got into him.'

'You all right?' Birch asked me, ignoring Jane.

Spiggy trotted over to lick my face, showing concern. I ruffled his fur and got to my feet. Then, smiling at Birch, I unclipped the wide dog collar I'd been wearing under my scarf.

'Perfectly fine, thank you. I played a fairly convincing "woman being throttled", I thought.' I reached into the snow near Jane and retrieved the wire garrotte with which she'd tried to kill me. 'I know you lot are obsessed with your past lives, but this is an unusual souvenir to bring into retirement.'

'What are you talking about?' Another beam of light found us, this one carried by Willie Mac. 'Jane, what happened?'

'Let's go inside,' I said, picking up the dog leads. 'All will become clear.'

CHAPTER THIRTY-SEVEN

We sat in Roy and Arthur's lounge, with the fairy lights twinkling and the sparse tinsel shining. It wasn't quite a return to where things had started, as I now knew this series of events had kicked off long before Birch and I set foot in the quad. But, as the place where we'd first met Roy and the other residents, it seemed appropriate.

Birch took the sofa, with Ronnie curled up beside him. Arthur had his usual place by the fire; Paul the wing-backed chair with his jigsaw. Zoe positioned herself by the window, where Jane had stood on Tuesday afternoon. Jane herself had been guided to the second sofa by Willie Mac, where he sat beside her. No bare feet dangled over the sofa arm this evening. Instead, the Scot's back was straight and his expression stern, waiting to learn the truth.

I sat in Roy's chair, with Spiggy at my feet. He lay on a freshly dried towel, his chin on his paws, keeping a watchful eye on Jane.

'What the hell were you thinking?' Paul said to her, placing a piece of sky in his jigsaw. 'Explain yourself.'

Jane shrugged. 'I thought she was a burglar.'

'Aye, burglars always bring two dogs for company,' Willie said, dripping with sarcasm.

I rubbed my throat, still sore despite the collar's protection. 'Jane, I know you've managed to pull the wool over everyone's eyes for some time, but don't insult their intelligence.'

She regarded me coolly. 'Then why don't you explain, if you know so much?'

'Happily.' I waited for the others to give me their attention, then began. 'Let's start with what actually happened over the past couple of weeks. Last Monday I was sorting through my late father's documents when I found the Gerber file, apparently forgotten about after it had become lost inside a filing cabinet. On there I found Roy's name, calling him a liaison, and an old phone number. I called the modern equivalent of that number, which was picked up by a woman who first answered as "Central", then asked for my order as if they were a restaurant. I was very confused, and she ended the call. When I tried to call back only a minute later, the number had been completely disconnected.'

Paul nodded. 'That would have been the contact switchboard. She was waiting for you to speak a code phrase to prove you were genuine. Which, of course, you were not.'

'A phrase like "Soup of the day", perhaps?'

He mulled it over. 'Yes, that would fit. There are

many phrases, often unique to a particular mission or officer. When you failed to answer correctly, the number was marked as compromised and burnt – that is to say, immediately disconnected – to prevent exploitation.'

All this cloak and dagger business seemed exhausting. I continued, 'I thought I'd reached a dead end. But then Birch offered to find Roy and, incredibly, did so within just a couple of days.'

Birch looked very pleased with himself. 'Had some help from the boys in the Met. Simple enough when you know how.'

'That was last Wednesday, when I phoned here for the first time and spoke to Roy. I also heard Jane in the background. Perhaps they were together to talk about household bills . . . or edits on a Max Calibre novel. Either way, she overheard the discussion about the Gerber file, and my offer to send Roy a copy. I imagine that ignited her first spark of concern.'

'Is Roy joining us?' Arthur said suddenly. 'He should be here.'

Nobody quite knew what to say. The realisation that this was an ongoing problem they'd have to deal with was only now beginning to sink in.

'He's away at the moment,' Zoe said. 'But I'll let him know you were asking about him, OK?'

Satisfied, the big ex-MI5 man returned his gaze to the fire.

'How is this all linked to . . . Roy?' Paul asked, jigsaw piece in hand.

'We're coming to that. I assume he told you all that I'd called?'

Everyone nodded.

'He was delighted you'd found him,' Willie said. 'Roy really did like Henry.'

'Did he mention it again before this week? Or talk about the Gerber file?'

I looked directly at Jane, but she said nothing, and this time the others shook their heads.

'Then let's fast-forward to Tuesday, two days ago, when I found myself in Bath to audition for a play. I called Roy and arranged to visit. He gathered you all in this room, where you told me about the Gerber file and my father's work for Roy. Paul's torch had gone missing, as had Jane's lighter and Willie's gloves. You all made jokes about Max Calibre, and we agreed to stay for dinner.' A murmur of agreement rippled through the residents. 'But that evening several things occurred which, in hindsight, take on extra significance. Willie, you had an argument with Roy over dinner.'

The Scot shrugged. 'Sorry. I shouldn't have blown up like that.'

'I don't see why not. It was cruel of him to make light of your experience, one that obviously still affects you to an extent that I doubt the others fully understand. Not even Zoe.'

Willie looked at me with pleading eyes. Birch and I were the only people who knew about his macabre cadaver collection. I nodded at him, silently reassuring him we wouldn't tell.

'Nevertheless, Jane saw the hurt Roy inflicted on you. While it wasn't the sole reason she killed him, it undoubtedly didn't help. His fate was actually sealed when Roy later told me he'd lied, and that in truth he'd deciphered the notes my father made on the Gerber file. Roy said he'd tell me everything the next morning when we were all sober. At that moment, Jane passed us on the way back to her own house, apparently drunk. Earlier in the evening, I'd thought her a lightweight, as she seemed very unsteady despite not drinking much. Now I think Jane was faking it, and when she passed us in the corridor she overheard everything.'

She refused to look me in the eye, which was all the confirmation I needed.

'We then retired to bed, with Birch and me staying in the guest room. But I was awoken by noises in the night: someone moving around in Roy's study, followed by a sort of metallic scraping. The next morning we found Arthur in the kitchen. He said he'd seen Roy coming out of the bathroom and joked about how he was always late for breakfast. That's why we were so confused when Roy didn't appear, and asked if any of you had seen him. Notably, when I put the question to Jane she avoided giving a straight answer.

'Arthur unwittingly sent us on something of a wild goose chase. We assumed Roy had disappeared sometime after coming out of the bathroom. But how could he have? There were no tracks in the snow, and Zoe's CCTV cameras showed no sign of him leaving. In fact, they didn't show *anyone* leaving their house between dinner and the next morning. It seemed impossible.'

'Because it was,' Paul said, not looking up from his jigsaw. 'We now know that Roy had never left his house, and that Arthur's memory is unreliable.' Arthur looked offended. 'Sorry, but it's true.'

'Exactly. Arthur, you're so used to seeing Roy come out of the bathroom every morning that I think your mind simply filled in the blank with what you expected. But I don't think you did see him at all, meaning Roy could have been—' I stopped myself, not wanting to upset him. 'Meaning the incident could have taken place at any time between us going to bed and waking up the next morning. Suddenly, everyone's alibis were useless.'

Willie cast a sideways glance at Jane. 'Were they, though? You just said there's nothing on the CCTV. That's a pretty good alibi.'

'That's what I thought, but now I know better. When Roy oversaw the extension of the old farmhouse, he made a special request. It's not obvious at first glance, because you have to squeeze through a lot of structural beams, but the attic isn't divided like the houses. Instead, it's one continuous open space.' Willie and Zoe were the only people remaining to whom this was a revelation, and looked appropriately surprised. 'I did a full circuit up there myself earlier today.'

Zoe took this in. 'You're saying Jane entered the attic in her own house, walked through to Roy's attic, came down into the house, did for him, then carried him back up the ladder?'

'Not quite. I think they arranged to meet up there.

After dinner that night, Jane knew Birch and I were safely out of the way, walking the dogs in the quad. Standing near the fountain, we heard a phone ring. Was that you calling Roy to arrange a meeting, Jane?' She didn't reply. 'The attic was a perfect rendezvous. Nobody else knew they were there, and they wouldn't be seen on CCTV because they hadn't used their doors. So they met, and argued, and Jane finished it. I thought I'd heard Roy in his study that night, kept awake by Arthur's snoring. Now I believe it was actually Jane looking for something. It woke me, which made Spiggy bark, and that spooked her. So she fled back into the attic, pulling up the ladder behind her and making that metallic scraping sound.'

'But Arthur's ring was next to Roy's body,' Willie said, confused. 'How did that get there?'

I smiled. 'Everyone knows Arthur sleeps like a log. My guess is that before going in Roy's study, Jane crept into Arthur's room and stole his ring. She then planted it on her way back through the attic, knowing it would cast suspicion on him. There's a certain irony there, now that we know Arthur was the one responsible for stealing other people's possessions. But it was a successful bit of misdirection . . . as was her little one-act play with you, Willie, in the kitchen last night.'

Once again the Scot pleaded with me to keep his secret, but this time I couldn't. Jane didn't even have the grace to look embarrassed.

'I'm sorry to tell you all that Willie and Jane are having an affair. They have been for some time.'

Paul, Arthur and Zoe all gasped in surprise. But I was tired of all these lies.

'Zoe, don't overact. This morning I wondered if I should tell you about this. Then I discovered that you've already been covering for Willie by deleting CCTV recordings of him making . . . nocturnal excursions, shall we say. I find it hard to believe you haven't also worked out his relationship with Jane.'

Now she looked genuinely shocked. 'So that's why you were sneaking about in my room. I didn't think you'd know your way around a computer.'

'I don't, but Birch gives excellent instructions.' He smiled at this compliment.

Willie wasn't smiling. He looked like a man caught red-handed. 'Zoe, it's not— I mean—'

She sighed. 'Willie, don't. Losing my legs didn't suddenly make me blind and stupid. From the moment Jane moved in here, it was obvious you were still attracted to each other.' She came further into the room and caught Paul's eye. 'I won't pretend I like it, but with all Willie does for me . . . I've made my peace with it.'

The Scot looked crestfallen. 'Why didn't you say anything?'

Zoe wheeled towards him and took his hand. 'Because then it wouldn't have been exciting for you, would it? Do you really think I never crept around seeing men I shouldn't when I was younger?'

Paul held a puzzle piece in his hand, hovering over the jigsaw as he tried to find its home. 'Guinevere, what can this possibly have to do with Roy? And what did you mean about a "one-act play"?'

'It has everything to do with Roy,' I said. 'He threatened to end Jane's affair with Willie for ever, a prospect she couldn't bear now she'd finally got him. Their little display in the kitchen was for my benefit, intended by Jane to throw me off the scent. She crept across the quad, opened Zoe's door, whispered Willie's name, then kissed him in the kitchen.'

'But what makes you say it was deliberate?'

'Why call his name loudly enough for me to hear? Why say his name at all, rather than just walk into the house? Why risk an embrace in a brightly lit kitchen, in full view of the garden? Simple: Jane knew I was the sole audience member. She'd seen me coming out of your house, Paul, and knew everyone else was inside. She also guessed correctly that I'd watch to see what she was doing. You've all been keeping secrets, so Jane thought that if I "discovered" her affair with Willie, it would satisfy my curiosity enough to turn my attention elsewhere. It almost worked. But two things put me on the right track.'

'Ah. Finally,' Paul said.

Birch scowled at him. 'That's enough of that,' he said. 'If Gwinny hadn't been here, you'd all be none the wiser and Jane would have got away with it.'

'That may be true,' I said, 'but if I hadn't contacted Roy in the first place none of this would have happened.'

'Wasn't your fault. I said that before.'

'I know, but it's something I'll have to live with.'

'The two things . . . ?' Paul prompted impatiently.

I took a deep breath and sat up straight.

'First, let's finish the day's events. Birch and I went looking for Roy but couldn't find him. Zoe showed us the CCTV records, on which nobody had left the house, although I later discovered she'd deleted records of Willie going out to the shed during the night. I also learnt the truth about Max Calibre, and how almost everyone here played a role in that. We overheard Paul talking to what we now know was his solicitor. And in Jane's house we learnt that she wasn't just a secretary, as her nickname implies, but a fully fledged spy who'd been active during the Cold War. Then, finally, we found Roy in the attic.'

'You missed out my ankle,' Birch said.

I smiled. 'You're right, and that actually turned out to be quite important. Birch twisted his ankle, which prevented him investigating . . . or so we thought. Instead, he finished the new Jack Spitfire book, at which point I asked Arthur for permission to read the work-in-progress pages from the book he and Roy had been working on.'

'I don't see why not,' Arthur said from the fireplace. 'If Roy says it's OK.'

'The next morning, I discovered Arthur's problem. Two problems, actually, though I suspect they're connected. First, I found his toolbox with the stolen items, and when I confronted him I realised his . . . issues.' I glanced at Arthur to see how much of this he was taking in, but he'd already returned his gaze to the fire. 'The pages I'd found were all written by Roy. He was taking Arthur's raw, chaotic attempts, rewriting them into something coherent, then placing them on Arthur's desk to make it look as if he'd written them. Roy knew, you see. And I don't think he was the only one.' I looked pointedly at Jane.

'Hence Jane planting the ring on Roy's body,' Birch added. 'She'd worked out that Arthur was an unreliable witness to his own actions, so framing him would be easy. Sooner or later the police would also discover his issues, and from then on distrust anything he said.'

'But the police aren't here,' Willie pointed out. 'We haven't even called them.'

'Jane didn't expect the snow,' Birch explained. 'It took everyone by surprise.'

I continued, 'Reading the in-progress manuscript pages, Birch discovered that one scene was a dramatisation of what happened to my father, and Gerber, in Munich. I confirmed that with Arthur, who told me what had really happened over there. "A fiasco", as he described it.'

'How can you be sure his recollection is accurate?' Paul asked.

I shrugged. 'I can't, but it's well known that people like Arthur often have perfectly good recollection of their younger days.'

'That's probably why it slipped by everyone,' Birch said. 'If all you talk about is the old days anyway, you don't notice when someone tells the same stories over and over.'

'Exactly so. All the same, some people *did* notice. Roy, because he lived with Arthur; and Jane, because of her role editing their work. Which means two out of the other five people in this house knew full well that their friend needed professional care, yet neither sought it because it suited their own ends to keep it secret. Shame on you.'

Jane glared at me. 'It was Roy who asked me not to say anything.'

'It suited you very well, though, didn't it? Especially when you hoped to frame Arthur. Now, let's quickly finish. I returned Willie's gloves, and my conversation with him prompted me to search the attic, where I discovered it's all one space, and I used it to drop in on Paul unannounced. Jane was with him at the time, so now she knew I'd found the attic's secret. I imagine by that point she already had concerns I was getting too close to the truth, and she was right; it only took two more steps for me to confirm it. I then called you all to meet me here, being sure to tell you that I'd identified the killer, but I needed to walk the dogs in the quad first. That was a white lie. In fact, I was deliberately making myself a target, banking on the killer once again using a garrotte. One of my spare dog collars saw to that, and meanwhile Birch was also hiding out there, ready to intervene. As he carried no torch, he was all but invisible in the dark.' I turned to him. 'Ronnie could smell you, though. He kept wanting to veer off and find you.'

Jane glared at Birch. 'Weren't you supposed to be laid up with that ankle?'

He smiled. 'Thought I'd try a bit of acting myself. Still a bit sore, but not so much I can't walk.'

'I still don't understand *why*,' Willie Mac said plaintively. 'Jane, what did Roy do to you? If anyone had reason to want him dead, it was me, not you. Why?'

Jane returned his expression. She looked on the verge of tears herself, because she knew she was about to lose him for ever.

'Oh, Willie,' I said gently. 'Haven't you worked it out yet? Roy did, eventually . . . thanks to some help from my father.'

I could tell by their expressions that Paul and Zoe finally understood what I was implying, but the Scot remained confused. I explained:

'In 1988, Jane travelled to Munich and killed Dieter Gerber.'

CHAPTER THIRTY-EIGHT

Paul placed another puzzle piece in his jigsaw. He was close to finishing.

'Jane had no reason to kill Gerber,' he said without looking up. 'She wasn't even assigned to Munich at the time.'

'Really, Paul,' I said. 'You of all people should know how easily a spy can use a false passport to travel under a different identity. As for a reason, Jane had the oldest and simplest one around. She was following orders.'

I looked to Jane, giving her a chance to tell her side of things, but she glared at me with tear-filled eyes.

'In a way, Paul, your jigsaw helped me realise what had happened,' I said. 'You told me you like that image, with St Paul's still dominating the skyline, because it's how you remember London. "They can build all the bloody skyscrapers they like, but they can't escape the past," you said. Jane and Roy couldn't escape their past, either. I didn't truly understand that until I finally deciphered the message my father had written on his copy of the Gerber file.'

'What message?' Zoe asked.

'Arthur told me that Roy had long suspected Gerber's killer was a British agent. I think he shared that suspicion with my father, who made notes of what had happened when he returned home, using a code that he and Roy both knew. I assume he was planning to pass it to Roy, but Munich was the last time they worked together. A year later, the Berlin Wall came down and the end of the Cold War loomed, giving Roy much bigger concerns. The file was lost down the back of my father's filing cabinet, and once it was out of sight, it fell out of mind.'

'But what did it say, and how did you decode it?' Paul asked.

Birch pulled the paperback of *The Day of the Jackal* from his pocket and held it up for all to see.

'A book cipher,' I explained. 'Based on this edition, which Roy and my father both owned. Roy said it was Henry's favourite book, but now I wonder if he was simply hinting at their shared cipher, hoping I'd pick up on it. I wish I had sooner.'

'The message . . . ?' Zoe asked.

Birch read from his phone. '*Munich. Approached. Woman, British accent, beautiful, possible Soviet agent. Followed me?*'

'Hardly definitive,' Paul said.

'No, but I think it was the spark Roy needed to test his theory. First he wrote a new Jack Spitfire scene, in the books' fictional Berlin, that mirrored what really happened in Munich. Remember, the official line was that Gerber had simply vanished. Very few people knew the truth: that he was garrotted and left for dead in a Munich courtyard. Even many of you were surprised when Roy revealed that the other day.'

'Jane edits the books,' Arthur interjected. 'She reads everything.'

'Yes, she does. And Roy made quite sure she read that scene in particular, to provoke a reaction. When they met in the attic, it confirmed all his suspicions . . . and sealed his fate.'

Willie Mac shook his head. 'I still don't see *how*. OK, so your father's notes made Roy realise this double agent could have been a woman. But why Jane?'

'The final clue,' I said. 'In a way it was her only mistake. You see, I don't think I was the first to discover Arthur's toolbox. Isn't that right, Jane?'

Once again I waited to see if she'd come clean, but she said nothing.

'Very well,' I continued. 'Here's what I think happened. Roy knew about Arthur's toolbox, and in there he found Jane's missing lighter. At around the same time, I sent him pictures of my father's coded message, which he deciphered. The combination of those things convinced him, and so he wrote that scene into the new Spitfire book, taunting Jane. Then, after dinner on Tuesday, he told me he knew who'd killed Gerber. Jane overheard us, and called him upon returning to her house to arrange a meeting in the attic, away from prying eyes. While we all slept that night they met up there, and Roy revealed he'd found her lighter – but not that it was Arthur who'd taken it. That's why, after killing him, she looked for it in Roy's study but couldn't find it. He'd already hidden it in Arthur's desk, where Jane wouldn't think to look.'

Paul leant back from his puzzle, eyes raised to the heavens as he processed this information.

From my pocket, I retrieved Jane's metal Zippo lighter. She gasped.

'A gift, given forty years ago.' I looked directly at Jane. 'You were confident we wouldn't find this in your house because you knew Roy already had it. Not that it would have meant much to us at first glance, in any case.'

'It's just a lighter,' Zoe said. 'What does that prove?'

With one hand I gripped the Zippo's outer metal case. With the other I removed the internal refillable section, revealing words engraved in Cyrillic Russian underneath a love heart.

'A secret message, something hidden and special, that only the owner would see. I don't speak Russian, but my phone reliably informs me that this reads, "Remember Prague. Love, Valeria." One doesn't need a translation app to also recognise the universal heart symbol. So what was it, Jane? A honey trap, seduced by a Russian agent? Or did you simply fall in love with the wrong person?'

'Both,' she said quietly, knowing the game was up. 'Czechoslovakia, 1984. She was an artist, wild and bohemian. I was so stupid . . .' Her eyes filled with pain and regret. 'I didn't even consider that a beautiful young woman like that could be a spy. Ironic, isn't it?'

'In more ways than one,' I agreed. 'They threatened to ruin you unless you killed Gerber, I assume?'

She nodded. 'And more besides. But I couldn't bear to throw away the lighter she gave me to remember her . . . just as I couldn't bear to lose you, Willie.' She turned to the Scot, who trembled with shock and outrage. 'Don't you see? I knew that if you found out what I'd done . . . after what those bastards did to you in Minsk . . . and then Roy came to me with this ultimatum, saying if I didn't confess he'd tell everyone. I couldn't have that. I couldn't.'

A silence fell upon the room as everyone regarded her with a mixture of horror and pity. But I wouldn't have it.

'Let's not pretend this was an impulsive act, Jane. You can't expect us to believe there just happened to be an old KGB garrotte lying around in the attic. No, what you did was premeditated. You took the garrotte with you, knowing that to keep your secret safe you'd have to kill Roy. Just like you tried to kill me out there in the garden.'

'She killed Roy?!' Arthur leapt to his feet, shaking with rage. I winced at my own carelessness.

'Stand down, Harrison!' Paul barked, pushing himself upright with his stick. 'This is an internal matter. Leave it to the corruption unit.'

The big man wavered, and for a moment, I thought he might redirect his anger at Paul. But old habits and command structures both die hard, and he returned to his chair. I had no doubt that he would have liked to give Jane a taste of her own medicine with his bare hands. But time would pass, perhaps not much time at all, and he'd forget about it all over again. I wondered if Arthur would ever fully understand that his best friend was gone for ever.

'You know, it's rather pathetic,' Jane said, looking around the room. 'Here you all are, so-called men of experience, and none of you got it. It took a woman to uncover the truth, and not even a professional. An *amateur*.' She turned to me. 'Maybe there's more of your father in you than you realise.'

'I'll call the police,' Paul said. 'The forecast says this snow will start to melt come the morning, so they can take her away then. Roy, too.' He limped past Jane, shaking his head in disappointment.

Spiggy woofed quietly at the disturbance, and I looked over at Paul's table. The jigsaw was complete, a nostalgic vision of the past.

CHAPTER THIRTY-NINE

I stared at my phone, not wanting to answer.

My agent, Bostin Jim, had left several messages already, having tried to call me while I was stuck in the no-signal quad and then again as I drove home on Friday afternoon.

True to forecast, the snow had cleared up enough by that morning for the police to attend. The local inspector was not best pleased, to say the least, that we hadn't dialled 999 the moment we'd found Roy, particularly with a former policeman amongst our number. But the pathologist had given us a sideways compliment for preserving the body as well as we could in the circumstances, and the police certainly weren't complaining about the outcome. After confessing to everything, Jane was led away in handcuffs.

I'd apologised to Birch again several times for making him miss his policeman's Christmas lunch at the Dog & Duck. He milked my apology, for which I couldn't blame him, though eventually he admitted it had been worth it. Now he had a brand-new story to share with his old colleagues at their next get-together.

After dropping him and Ronnie off at his house, Spiggy and I returned home to Chelsea . . . where I saw the unopened Christmas card from the Dowager Lady Ragley on my mantelpiece and promptly ran back out again to the nearest card shop on the King's Road before it closed. Bostin Jim had tried to call me then, too, but I was too busy running home to quickly write the card and shove it through my neighbour's letterbox.

Now, though, I could put it off no longer. I left what I was doing and flopped onto the sofa, fussed Spiggy when he climbed up beside me, and answered my phone.

'Jim, darling,' I said brightly.

'At last! I've been trying to call you since Wednesday,' he boomed in his thick Brummie accent. 'Where've you been?'

'It's a rather long story, which I'll tell you next time we have coffee.'

I could almost see him roll his eyes. 'Gwinny . . . have you been playing Sherlock again?'

'More like Smiley, this time.'

'Who? Look, never mind. I'm calling about Colin Prendergast's play.'

'Ah. Yes. Well, the thing is, you told me it was a simple meeting. But when I arrived, he pressed me into a read-through right there on stage with the other actors. So you should probably apologise on my behalf for wasting his time, but you must understand—'

'He loved you, Gwinny. Said you were full of fire and energy, absolutely perfect for the role.'

I could hardly believe my ears. 'Come again?'

'You've booked it. Colin wants you in rehearsals first week of January.'

My hand froze on Spiggy's ear. He squirmed under my fingers, hoping for the fuss to resume, then gave up and hopped down to sniff around the lounge carpet instead.

Before I could stop myself, I said, 'Tell Colin Bloody Prendergast he can jolly well get stuffed.'

'You what?'

I reminded Jim of my history with the director, his disparaging remarks, his attitude, and finally his complete failure to remember me. I may be a woman of a certain age desperate for work, but I refuse to be disrespected like that.

'Something else will come along,' I concluded. 'That's what you always say, isn't it?'

Jim grumbled. 'Quoting a man's own words back at him rarely goes well. Are you sure about this? It's a good role with a veteran director. What you're talking about happened a long time ago.'

'Yet the *veteran director* doesn't appear to have changed one bit in the meantime. Yes, I'm quite sure.'

Jim sighed. We agreed to meet for coffee in the new year, and I returned to the task he'd interrupted: wrapping Birch's Christmas present.

Having failed to secure a gift earlier, I'd been wracking my brains ever since. What do you get a man who wants for nothing? I'd been on the verge of buying a big silk ribbon and wrapping myself in it for him as a joke, but just before we departed Nempnett Thrubwell inspiration had struck.

Now, I opened the cover of *A Man Called Spitfire*, the first book in the series, to its title page. Arthur had signed it:

To Larch,

You're nicked!

– Max Calibre

I'd been about to correct him when I saw a twinkle in his eye. 'Good days and bad days,' Arthur had said, closing the cover.

With the book wrapped, I located the familiar gold spine of a well-worn paperback on my bookshelves and pulled it out. Memories came unbidden of my father sitting here, in this lounge, turning these very pages. I placed it on my coffee table, next to the almost-completed jigsaw, and trooped upstairs to fetch the tree and ornaments.

Spiggy watched me, fascinated, as I built the tree and hung tinsel. I suddenly remembered my impulse purchase from Covent Garden and found the fake reindeer antlers still in their bag. The band was loosely elasticated, and slid over the Cocker Spaniel's head comfortably. He wouldn't win any reindeer lookalike contests, but he was cute enough to win any judge's heart.

As I strung lights around the tree and over the mantelpiece, I wondered what would become of the 'quad gang'. Roy and Jane were gone, Arthur couldn't live without help, and Paul didn't have long left. Only Willie Mac and Zoe had escaped relatively unscathed, though they'd have to deal with the fallout from Willie's affair. I wondered if they might agree to accompany Paul to Switzerland.

With the decorations finally done, I switched on the string lights and relaxed on the sofa, enjoying the quiet, cosy space I'd created. An hour later, with Spiggy snoozing by my side, I placed the last piece in my idyllic winter village puzzle. After the events of the past few days, I was no longer sure I'd like to live anywhere quite so remote. London suited me very well, thank you.

Fussing the Spaniel, I wondered what I should tell Yvonne when we next spoke. Perhaps I shouldn't mention Spiggy's proximity to a murder.

My phone rang again. This time it was my friend Tina, a fabulously successful actress with a country house in Hertfordshire. In a funny way, it was because of her that Birch and I had met, but that's another story.

'Merry Christmas,' I answered.

'We'll see about that,' she said. 'What are you doing over the holiday?'

'Spending most of it with Birch, I hope. Actually, there's a point. Do you know what he's bought me?'

Tina laughed. 'Even if I did, which I don't, I wouldn't tell you. Listen, I'm off to Guadeloupe to get away from this freezing bloody cold and see my cousins. Would

you look after Spera and Fede for me while I'm gone?
I'll just be a couple of weeks. I can bring your present
when I come round to drop them off, too.'

Spera and Fede were Tina's Salukis, expensive pure-
bred siblings who managed to somehow be both the
snootiest and laziest dogs you've ever met, though like
all hounds, they sprang into high-speed action when
there was food to be had.

I watched Spiggy's chest slowly rise and fall on the
sofa beside me, fake reindeer antlers slowly slipping
off his slumbering head, and basked in the glow of the
twinkling tree lights. I'd become used to quiet, peaceful
Christmases. In recent times, it had been only my father
and me, without even a dog for company in his final
years. Spiggy and I could do that. Just the two of us, for
a truly quiet and cosy holiday.

Or I could open the house and spend Christmas with
Spiggy, Ronnie and the Salukis all running around,
chasing one another and begging for food, making
Birch and me laugh while we tried in vain to eat turkey
in peace and watch James Bond on the telly.

I smiled and said, 'Darling, I'd love to look after
the hounds. But I warn you, my holiday rates are *very*
high . . .'

ACKNOWLEDGEMENTS

Given my background, with titles like *Atomic Blonde* and the Brigitte Sharp thrillers under my belt, it was perhaps inevitable that Gwinny's adventures would eventually bring her into contact with spies. If you go all the way back to *The Dog Sitter Detective*, you'll see I've been hinting at this from the start, and always intended to do a book centred around Henry's 'little favours'.

Aficionados will find many references to great works of espionage fiction within these pages. Fleming, le Carré, Deighton . . . *The Sandbaggers, Queen & Country, Callan*, even *The Man from U.N.C.L.E* . . . they're all in here somewhere. If you think you might have found one, the answer is yes. Then there's Forsyth, of course; rest assured *The Day of the Jackal* book cipher is real, based on my own copy of that golden-spined 1972 edition.

In the late 1990s I lived and worked in Bath, in

offices next door to the Theatre Royal, leaving me with many fond memories of the city and surrounding Somerset hills. If you've never been, I encourage a visit.

The quad and its grounds are inspired by two real places, though the house upon which I based the building isn't in Somerset, while the home with similar grounds is in Somerset but has no quad. Combining the two made for an interesting environment in which to stage a story, though I subsequently fictionalised almost everything about them for drama's sake. Yes, including the attic.

One of my favourite photos of my old dog Connor, a Saluki-cross Lurcher who died shortly before I wrote the first Dog Sitter Detective book, shows him in front of the Christmas tree wearing a pair of ridiculous, fake reindeer antlers. If you want to see it, just check my social media; I've posted it several times around Christmas, and no doubt will again.

Thanks to Penel Malby, who knows more about Spaniels than anyone I've met, for letting me pick her brains regarding Spiggy. Fellow author Jamie West put me straight on theatre protocol and lingo; German friends Eric and Sandra ensured *mein Deutsch* was on point; and a few very patient souls on the *Incomparable* Podcast Members' Discord walked me through Gwinny's stealthy peek at Zoe's computer. Any errors in these matters are mine alone.

As ever, my stalwart beta readers helped keep me to the path, checked my logic, and saved me from my own worst habits.

A hearty thanks to everyone at Allison & Busby for their ongoing support of Gwinny's adventures, not to mention their confidence in me and nimbleness upon seeing the potential for this book to be 'the Christmas one'.

My longstanding agent, Sarah Such, of the Sarah Such Literary Agency, is one in a million.

My partner, Marcia, is even more precious, and I really couldn't do any of this without her support. Onward we go.